Titles by Laurie Cass

A Troubling Tail

A BOOKMOBILE CAT MYSTERY

Laurie Cass

BERKLEY PRIME CRIME
New York

BERKLEY PRIME CRIME
Published by Berkley
An imprint of Penguin Random House LLC
penguinrandomhouse.com

ISBN: 9780593547427

First Edition: August 2023

Printed in the United States of America
1 3 5 7 9 10 8 6 4 2

Chapter 1

It was the perfect spring day. After an interminable series of dark and dreary weeks that had brought a staggering amount of slushy rain, instilling thoughts of emigration in the hearts of many northwest lower Michigan residents, the thick cloud cover had blown off to reveal that the sun was indeed still part of our solar system.

I peered over the bookmobile's steering wheel, looking through the windshield, drinking in the deep blue sky and smiling contentedly.

It was May. The month when the trees would leaf out in full, transforming the world. When the hillsides would be covered in wildflowers. When I'd be able to take the thick mittens out of my coat pockets and push my boots to the back of the hall closet. When I could consider moving the ice scraper from the floor of my car's back seat to the trunk. When—

"Phoenix," my companion said.

I glanced over at Julia Beaton, currently a part-time bookmobile clerk but a former full-time actor.

Julia had zoomed off to the bright lights of New York City immediately after high school. Though her modeling career hadn't taken off as she'd hoped, her fallback career of acting had. She, with her husband in tow, had returned to Chilson with a suitcase full of Tony Awards when the roles dried up. Now in her mid-sixties, Julia helped out on the bookmobile a couple of times a week, clerking and telling stories like no one else I'd ever heard.

"What about Phoenix?" I asked.

"Last week," she said, rearranging her long strawberry blond hair from a single braid into a twisty sort of bun, "it was the only place in the continental United States that had any sunshine."

"Huh." Maybe that explained the sudden vacation of Deputy Ash Wolverson and his fiancée, Chelsea Stille. I'd heard they'd gone to Southern Arizona. "Why do you know that fun fact?"

Julia smiled. It was a sly smile, and I knew she was about to slip into a self-imposed role.

"I know all sorts of things, my dear," she said in a raspy voice that conjured up crystal balls, tea leaves, and tarot cards. "But mainly," she said, returning to her normal voice, "after the last couple of weeks, I was in desperate need of sun-induced vitamin D. I was booking flights when the husband looked at the long-range forecast and saw we were going to get our own sunshine, right here in Chilson, at no extra expense."

"Mrr?" our other companion asked.

"Of course I would have taken you." Julia leaned down and stuck her fingers through the wire door of the cat carrier strapped to the floor near her feet. "Nothing like sunshine on a furry tummy, yes?"

Even over the hum of the engine, I could hear my cat's contented purrs. Eddie, my black-and-white tabby with a penchant for making friends wherever he went, had been on the bookmobile's maiden voyage just over three years ago. Though he'd been a stowaway, it had quickly become obvious that the patrons liked him better than they liked the human staff, and he'd been a fixture on the bookmobile ever since.

"Mrr," Eddie said sleepily, and I cast him a fond look. Eddie and I had seen each other through thick and thin, and at the beginning, he had been very thin.

A little more than three years ago, I'd taken a walk on a fine April morning in lieu of cleaning chores and wandered through the local cemetery, soaking in the blue views of the twenty-mile-long Janay Lake and the thin line of Lake Michigan over the hills to the west.

The quiet calm of my walk had been interrupted by the "Mrr!" of a black-and-gray tabby cat, who had blinked up at me from the gravesite of Alonzo Tillotson, born 1847, died 1926.

At the time, I knew nothing about cats due to my father's allergies and tried to shoo him away home. That, of course, hadn't worked. He'd followed me back to town, much to the amusement of passersby. I'd taken him in, cleaned him up, realized that under the grime he was a black-and-white tabby, and contacted the local veterinarian. "About two years old," Dr. Joe had said, so I'd dutifully run a FOUND CAT notice in the newspaper. Happily, the ad had gone unanswered, and the two of us were now bound to each other forever.

"In more ways than one," I muttered, batting away an airborne Eddie hair.

"What's that?" Julia asked.

"I wonder how Eddie would like flying." I flapped my elbows.

"Bet he'd like it fine if he could be up front in the cockpit."

"Mrr!"

Julia and I laughed, but there was a lot of truth in what she'd said. Eddie, like most cats, was a control freak, and if he could tell the pilot where to go, he'd probably choose flying over driving.

I thought about a world run by Eddie choices. No sudden loud noises. No rain, no wind. Plenty of sunny spots. Lots of nap time, and plenty of on-demand petting. Didn't sound all bad, except he'd probably ban all dogs, too.

Julia tapped the top of Eddie's carrier with her toes. "What's the plan for him? In or out?"

For the first time ever, we were stopping at Dooley Elementary School, roughly in the middle of Tonedagana County. Over the years, the population of the Village of Dooley had dwindled to the point that, until recently, the school board had considered shuttering the building. A recent surge in remote work, however, had created an influx of families with young children, and the school's head count was higher than it had been in decades.

The morning's plan included a visit to the bookmobile by each classroom, then a Julia-led story time for all in the gymnasium. If everything went well, we'd do it again in three weeks and hope like crazy the kids would remember to return the books they'd borrowed, because we wouldn't be back until September.

Julia's question of "in or out" referred to Eddie staying in the carrier or letting him out.

Though he enjoyed the company of people in general, he was still a cat in possession of all his claws, and I was constantly mindful that a small child could be a little too enthusiastic in showering Eddie with affection. Not that anything horrible had ever happened, or even come close to happening, but I was determined that it should ever be so.

"In," I said. "Especially with the youngest kids. With the fourth and fifth graders, I'll open the carrier door. If he wants out, we'll keep an eye on him. If he wants to stay in, that's fine, too."

It wasn't fine, not completely, because there would be some very disappointed children—and a couple of disappointed teachers—if the bookmobile cat chose to stay in the carrier the entire time. Leah Wasson, the fifth-grade teacher who'd requested the visit, had confessed that Eddie was the main draw.

In addition to a fuzzy feline, the thirty-one-foot-long vehicle, twenty-three thousand pounds when loaded, had lots of books—more than three thousand of them. It also had print magazines, jigsaw puzzles, CDs, DVDs, video games, e-readers, and electronic tablets. And in the last year, thanks to some odd donations, we'd also started lending fishing poles, small power tools, ukuleles, snowshoes, and a croquet set.

The library staff had had a number of long discussions about the appropriateness of the sports equipment, and since the vote had been split, we'd trooped upstairs and asked our boss to make the final decision.

Graydon Cain, the best library director ever, had looked at us, his expression one of mild exasperation tinged with a hefty dollop of amusement. "You're making this more complicated than it needs to be," he'd said. "What's the library's mission?"

The others had looked at me, and I'd quoted what was literally etched into the wall at the library's entrance. "The Chilson District Library," I said, "provides materials and services to help community residents obtain information meeting their personal, educational, and cultural needs. The library serves as a learning center for all residents of the community."

Holly Terpening had frowned but nodded. "Learning center. Okay, I guess lending snowshoes so you can learn how to snowshoe fits."

"Same with fishing gear," Josh Hadden, the library's IT guy, had said. "Every time I go out fishing, it's educational."

"Well, there you go." Graydon had made the brushing-hands-together gesture and shooed us away, even though I questioned what, exactly, Josh learned every time he fished, other than the ideal amount of ice to put in the cooler at any given temperature.

The nontraditional lending had quickly turned into a huge success. There was a waiting list for all of it except the ukulele, and we'd ended up with a number of new patrons who'd come for the sports stuff and stayed for the books. Truly, I had the best job in the world.

Now Julia looked at me. "What if Eddie sleeps the entire time? He's done it before. And what if he . . . you know?"

I winced. My furry friend, when in deep sleep, had a snore that rattled windows. If he really got going, it could scare children and startle adults. Spinning it out into the worst-case scenario, Eddie in Full Snore Mode contained the slight but real possibility of frightening kids away from the bookmobile—and even books—forever. But I'd anticipated the situation.

"Won't happen," I said confidently. "He'll be wide-awake all morning."

That little trick had been accomplished through the combined efforts of my fiancé and myself. Last night we'd had Eddie chase wadded-up balls of paper, leap after feathers at the end of a string, dart after a laser beam, and run up and down the stairs chasing a catnip mouse. He'd crashed at nine o'clock and hadn't moved a muscle for more than twelve hours. He was now set to stay perky all day.

I also planned to put Eddie's carrier on the console between the front seats so everyone could see him. This was critical because as teacher Leah Wasson had said, smiling over the cup of coffee I'd handed her in my office when we were discussing logistics, "Sorry, but it's the bookmobile cat they most want to see, not the books."

So I had to make sure they would see the bookmobile cat, one way or another, and I was pretty sure I'd covered all the bases.

Julia flung out one long arm. "The way is before you," she croaked out, back in fortune teller voice. Or at least her version of a fortune teller voice.

But she was right. Straight ahead of us was the 1960s-era school, in all its single-story, flat-roofed, blond-bricked glory. The original wide plate-glass window spans in each classroom had long ago been filled in with stucco siding and plain double-hung windows, but that looked like the only thing that had changed in its many decades of life.

"Well, except maybe a new flagpole," I said, eyeing the metal, shiny in the sunlight.

Julia blinked at my non sequitur. Her mouth opened and closed a couple of times, clearly not coming up with a reasonable response, and she eventually looked at her feet. "Mr. Edward, I think your Minnie has loosened her last screw. You might want to take care of that."

"Mrr!"

His response might have meant "You bet, I'll get right on that soon as possible because I want Minnie to be healthy and hearty," but I was willing to bet it was more like "What? Were you talking to me?"

Smiling, I flicked on the turn signal, and we eased into the school's parking lot. By prior arrangement, the nonhandicapped parking slots closest to the entrance were empty, and I eased the bookmobile into our temporary home.

A few minutes later, we'd flipped the driver's seat around, lowered the counter that created the front end checkout, started both the front and the back computers, detached the bungee cord that held the rear checkout chair in place, and done a quick straightening of any and all materials that had jostled loose during the drive.

If pushed, Julia and I could do the whole routine

in less than five minutes. Our other bookmobile driver, Hunter Morales, said there was no way that was humanly possible, but he had the sense to keep his opinion to himself when Julia was around.

"Hark!" Julia cupped her hand around her ear and struck a listening pose. "Methinks I hear the sound of small feet stampeding in our general direction."

Grinning, because what could be more fun than introducing a horde of youngsters to books in general and the bookmobile in particular, I unlocked the door and pushed it wide open, letting in sunshine and fresh air and what seemed like a thousand small human beings. "Welcome!" I sang out, and was almost trampled.

"Sorry about the high energy level," the kindergarten teacher said as she climbed the steps. "They're just so excited. You don't mind, do you?"

I laughed. "I can think of worse problems to have."

For the next couple of hours, Julia and I gave multiple classrooms the basic bookmobile tour, starting with the checkout desk at the back, moving through the grown-up books, then through the children's section, and ending with the tour's high point, the bookmobile cat.

Eddie, who'd eventually chosen to leave the carrier and draped himself across the dashboard, bore all the oohs and aahs with great patience and even doled out the occasional "Mrr."

We also answered questions that ranged from "Where do you eat?" (Answer: From brown bags.) to "What happens if you hit a really big bump and the books fall off the shelves?" (Answer: We spend hours and hours putting them back.) to "Do you have a radio?"

I looked at the child who'd asked the radio question. He was with Leah Wasson's fifth grade class, the final group to take the tour before we went into the gym.

"Eli," Leah said, giving me an apologetic look, "we're supposed be asking questions about books and the bookmobile, not radios." Leah was a few years older than my thirty-five and was a few inches taller than my five foot nothing, with straight shiny light brown hair that I tried not to envy. She was also one of those people who was so permanently cheerful that, during the gray days of winter, you wanted to take her home with you.

"No worries," I said, smiling. "He's fine. And I suppose there is a radio. I just don't think we've ever turned it on." Maybe I'd tried it when the vehicle had first been delivered, but I couldn't summon any memory of doing so.

Eli gave me a blank look. "Doesn't it work?"

I glanced around. The kids who weren't petting the very relaxed Eddie had selected books and moved to sit on the carpeted step that ran the length of the bookmobile, which served both as seating and as a step stool for youth and the vertically efficient such as myself. "Let's find out," I said, and edged around the backward-facing driver's seat and reached forward to poke at buttons.

"You don't know how to turn it on," the kid said.

This ten-year-old would not be allowed to assume things about me. "Of course I do," I said smoothly. "However, a certain upload sequence is required; otherwise, it would create a feedback loop that would interfere with the computer's Wi-Fi hotspot."

"Oh," Eli said. "Sure."

My techno-babble-speak had worked! I felt a flash of victory, which was quickly replaced with a swelling flush of shame that I'd let myself be pushed into a competition with an elementary school student. What kind of person was I? A horrible one.

Then, out of the corner of my eye, I saw Leah giving me a surreptitious thumbs-up, and the shame faded a bit.

Turning my full attention to the dashboard controls, I realized that all I needed to do was turn the thing on, push the FM button, and adjust the volume. "And here we go," I said, pushing a couple of buttons unnecessarily, twirling the passenger's side air flow for no reason, and with a flourish, finally hitting On and FM.

Out of the speakers came a loud burst of static. I hunched my shoulders up around my ears and turned the volume down to a tolerable level. "Now," I said, "let's see what we can get, receptionwise."

Down here in the valley, it was possible that we wouldn't get anything at all, but nothing ventured, nothing gained, so I tapped the Search button and was mildly surprised to see it settle on a station out of Traverse City. I heard a quiet voice coming through the speaker and turned up the volume.

"—local law enforcement is on the scene in Chilson," the radio announcer said.

Her somber tone made everything in me go still. Something had happened. Something bad. The school? Was Rafe okay? Had something happened at the library? To any of my friends? To anyone I knew? To anyone at all?

I turned up the volume and ignored Eli's plea to switch the radio to music.

"The presence of law enforcement," the announcer went on, "is adding another piece to the evolving story at the popular Henika's Candy Emporium. Has there been foul play? We'll just have to wait and see if it was an accident or something else that killed the store's owner, William 'Whippy' Henika."

"Oh no," I whispered. Not Whippy. Not the friendly guy who had a new horrible dad joke every time you walked into the store. Not the guy who winked at you while filling small white paper bags with candy from glass jars and added "just a little extra to sweeten your day." Not the guy who dressed up as Santa Claus every year.

A small hand clutched at my sleeve. "Ms. Minnie?" Eli asked urgently. "Ms. Minnie?"

I pulled my brain back to the here and now. "What's the matter?"

He was pointing at his teacher, who was white-faced and swaying.

"Sorry . . ." Leah said vaguely. "I think . . ."

Then her eyes rolled impossibly high, and she crumpled to the floor.

Chapter 2

Leah Wasson, you mean?" Rafe asked. "Is she okay?"

I didn't answer at first, as I was twirling spaghetti around my fork. With time, I could do it without splattering marinara sauce onto my shirt, but it took a certain amount of concentration. "She's fine," I said.

Two minutes after she'd dropped like a rock, she'd given every appearance of that being true.

"So sorry," she'd said, over and over again, mostly to reassure Eli, who'd gone from precociously inquisitive preadolescent to frightened child in the time it had taken his teacher to fall down. She was conscious and sitting up before the other kids even noticed anything was wrong. "I was silly this morning," she'd said, eking out a weak smile. "I overslept because I got home late last night from a trip and didn't have any breakfast."

Eli had half nodded, half not. "My mom says breakfast is the most important meal of the day," he'd said uncertainly.

"And she's right." Leah's smile was stronger the second time around.

She'd started to stand, but I'd put a hand on her shoulder. "You look comfortable down there. Let me get you some water and a protein bar. We keep a stash onboard in case of emergency."

Now, with one bite of spaghetti inside me, I began planning the next. "But it was the timing of Leah's faint that made me start to wonder."

"What do you mean?" Rafe, who never had any problems with pasta, looked up at me while rotating his fork.

Rafe Niswander and I had been engaged since last August, and we were getting married in late September on the third weekend. Or maybe the fourth. I could never remember for sure which one without using my phone's calendar. Dates were not my thing.

Luckily, Rafe had known me for more than twenty years, and he didn't take it personally. Back in the day, Rafe, my best friend Kristen Jurek, and I had met on the city beach during the summers my parents had sent me north to stay with my aunt Frances at her boardinghouse. Though Kristen and I had stayed in touch over the years, our friendship reached a new level six years ago when I'd happily taken the assistant director position at the Chilson District Library and moved north permanently.

The relationship between Rafe and me had taken longer to develop—at least on my end—but everything had turned out right in the end. We were now living in the hundred-year-old house he'd been renovating bit by bit for years, and there were days I felt so happy that it wouldn't have taken much to convince me that I was living in the happily-ever-after segment of a romantic comedy.

Rafe looked over the edge of the dining table, back at me, then elbowed a crumbled piece of garlic bread to the floor, saying, "Hey, Minnie, what's that out the window?"

Then again, there were days when I knew full well I was living in reality.

"Didn't we make a pact not to feed Eddie from the table?" I asked. "Didn't we agree it would only encourage bad behavior?"

"Yeah, but this wasn't feeding." Rafe grinned, his teeth showing white against skin that was an inheritance of distant Native American ancestors. "I was giving him a toy."

True enough. We both listened to Eddie bat the bread chunk from one end of the bookcase-filled room to the other. He galloped after it, misjudged the distance, then in a home-plate slide, banged into one of the bookcases.

Early on in Life with Eddie, I would have winced and rushed to make sure he was okay. Now, I knew he'd misjudged the distance on purpose for the pure pleasure of crashing into something.

"Anyway," I said, watching my cat gallop away with the bread in his mouth, the victor rushing off to the kitchen with his spoils, "Leah hadn't seemed light-headed until I turned on the radio and we heard about Whippy's death. But afterward, I asked about it. She said she hardly knew him."

"So you heard." Rafe put his fork down. "I was going to ask."

"All I know was what they said on the radio. Did you hear anything else?"

Rafe's job as middle school principal connected him with hundreds of people in ways that I was still learning about. And the fact that he'd been born and raised in Chilson gave him easy access to all sorts of information. For instance, he'd gone to high school with half the law enforcement in the city and county, including detective-in-training Deputy Ash Wolverson.

Rafe pulled in a deep breath, then let it out. "When I came home, I saw Ash in front of the candy store."

I didn't like what that meant. At all. "I figured it was a heart attack, that what the radio was saying about law enforcement on-site was just protocol. But if Ash was there hours and hours after they found Whippy, it was . . . probably . . . has to be . . . murder."

"Afraid so," Rafe said. "I stopped and talked to Ash. He said the sheriff's office will release a statement soon."

We sat there staring at each other, not wanting to think about the unthinkable. Murder. Whippy? It couldn't be. Not possible. How could anyone have killed that kind, cheerful man?

"This is going to be so hard for his wife," I murmured.

"Ash said she was downstate," Rafe said. "Visiting their son and his family. They got a second grandchild just before Christmas."

My heart ached for Colleen Henika. For the Henika children and grandchildren who'd had so many future memories stolen from them. A sudden death from something like a heart attack or a car accident was tragic enough; a murder was pain on a completely different level.

"There is one thing," Rafe said. "At least this time there's no reason for you to get involved."

I nodded. "No reason at—"

"*MRR!!*"

Eddie ran pell-mell from the kitchen through the dining room, into the living room, and pounded up the stairs.

Rafe and I exchanged a bemused glance.

"If he's trying to tell us something," I said, "he needs to work on his diction, because I didn't understand a word."

"Mrr!" came a distant cat voice.

"Timmy fell down the well," Rafe said, nodding.

"We should probably check on him."

"After dinner."

"Excellent plan." I smiled, but my thoughts were with the Henika family.

The next day was a library day. The sunshine seemed to be sticking around for the time being, so it was an easy decision to walk to work. In my head, blue skies and sunshine went along with the month of May, and it was nice that reality was, for once, matching my imagination.

"Lambs are coming," I announced to the downtown sidewalk, because maybe it could use a reminder that no one would throw salt on it for at least five months. "And baby cows. Plus tulips and lilacs."

I smiled in anticipation. We had an ancient lilac bush at the house, underneath the bedroom window, which meant I was only two or three weeks away from keeping the window open at night and falling asleep to the scent of lilac blossoms. That is, if Eddie didn't get too carried away.

Last year, back at the boardinghouse, at two in the morning, he'd clawed a cat-size rip in my bedroom screen, squeezed himself through, and trotted out onto the steep roof. I'd lunged after him, but he was out and free, and only the dulcet tones of treats rattling in the can had lured him back inside.

"Rotten cat," I muttered, remembering.

"You're not talking about that Eddie, are you?"

I blinked and looked up. By this time I was downtown, walking past the bakery where the baker himself, known to young and old as Cookie Tom, was out in front of his store, sweeping the sidewalk.

Tom Abinaw was a top candidate for the skinniest baker ever, which you wouldn't think would be a good advertisement for his business. Maybe it was genetics, or maybe he wore off all the calories by working so hard, because it certainly wasn't the quality of his cookies. Even better for one Minnie Hamilton, Cookie Tom loved the bookmobile. Not only did he give me a discount on cookies headed in that direction, but he also let me sneak in the back to pick up a bag on summer mornings and avoid the long lines.

"Morning," I said, slowing to a stop. "Yes, I was talking about Eddie, but with great fondness. Truly." Tom had been one of the first Eddie spotters, back on the day my fuzzy friend had followed me home from the cemetery.

"Tell him I said hello." Tom's smile faded quickly. "You heard about Whippy?"

I nodded. "So sad. Have you heard anything new?"

"Only what they're saying at the Round Table."

The local diner, just down the street, had a regular group of retired men who gathered together every morning and who had all the answers to everything. Because the pronouncements were typically based purely on rumor and conjecture, I rarely paid any attention, but every so often they did have some insider knowledge.

"And what's that?"

Tom gave the sidewalk one last sweep. "That he was in the store late because it was the beginning of the month, and that's when he always does inventory. And he had to have been killed by a thief looking to score some cash, because everyone knew Whippy kept a lot of cash in his register."

I glanced at the empty streets. "A lot of cash? This time of year?"

"You know how those guys talk." He smiled, and I smiled back. Even though the Round Table curmudgeons could be high-handed, narrow-minded, and biased, they were our curmudgeons.

I sketched a wave and continued my walk through downtown. As always, I enjoyed the mix of architecture. Hundred-year-old structures and buildings new last year. Most stores sided in clapboard, some in brick, a couple in fieldstone. The blend combined to make a whole that fit together in a completely satisfying way.

Satisfying, that is, except for one thing: the bright yellow police tape across the front door to Henika's Candy Emporium.

There was no law enforcement in sight, so without anyone to ask about the investigation—and I assumed it was a murder investigation, because why else would that disconcerting yellow tape still be up there?—I kept walking up to the library, trying to shake away the dark thoughts of murder. But I didn't come anywhere close to succeeding until I was in front of the library itself.

I slowed and, as I did almost every time I came to work, admired the building and what the citizens of Chilson had done. Just a few years ago, the Chilson District Library had been housed in a sixties-era building with zero charm and less soul. Though it had been efficient, back in the day, the area's steady growth and the seismic change in technological needs had pushed the city movers and shakers to propose a short-term millage.

The voters overwhelmingly approved the plan to convert an empty school into the new library, and now I had the great good fortune to work in a lovingly restored building with the Craftsman features of exposed oak beams, floors and foyers with metallic tiles, and best of all, a reading room with window seats and a functional fireplace.

I smiled at it all with fondness as I shut the door, making sure it locked behind me, because the library wouldn't open to the public for another hour and a half.

And since I was almost certainly the first one in the building, I headed straight for the break room. First in, according to the staff's unwritten rules, meant you could make the coffee the way you wanted, and in my backpack was a new blend I wanted to try.

Humming a bit at the happy prospect, I hurried through the main lobby, past the front desk, down the hall, and into the break room. I slapped on the overhead light . . . and came to a sudden stop.

"What the . . ."

I stared at the large object in front of me. The large two-wheeled object. The large and extremely yellow two-wheeled object that sported a massive box, also yellow, behind the seat.

"It's a book bike," I said out loud. As an upstanding member of the Association of Bookmobile and Outreach Services, I knew what the object was. It was a bicycle used as a mini mobile library. But where had it come from? And why was it in our break room?

"You found our new acquisition, I see."

I turned around at the amused voice. Graydon Cain, library director and my boss, was walking in the door, coffee mug in hand.

"Hard to miss," I said, still bemused. I repeated my internal questions, only this time out loud.

"It came," Graydon said, filling his mug from an already brewed coffeepot, "from Trent's basement workshop. He's been working on it for months. As a surprise."

There were a number of curious things about those statements. That the urbane retired attorney and current library board president Trent Ross even had a workshop. That he was adept enough to retrofit a bicycle as a book bike. That he'd created it as a surprise. And most especially, that he'd done it in the first place. Trent, while a fine leader of the board, just did not seem like a tool guy. Which, I suppose, just goes to show that you never know about people.

"Um . . ." I said.

"I know." Graydon sipped from his mug. "It's a one-speed bike. It's made over from a vintage who knows what. It weighs about a thousand pounds, and that's without any books in it."

"Maybe it's not as heavy as it looks." I said it as a sort of question.

Graydon laughed. "I like your optimism, but I helped Trent offload it from his SUV. It's built like a tank."

Just then, Josh walked in and did a double take when he saw the yellow bike. "Oh, geez, the bookmobile broke down, didn't it? Going to take you a while to get to the east side of the county on that thing, Minnie."

As if. Riding that thing over the huge hills between here and, well, anywhere, was not going to happen. If I had anything to do with it anyway.

Holly Terpening, one of the library clerks, came into the room. "Oooh, a book bike!" she said, clapping her hands. "It's adorable! Huge but adorable. Where did it come from?"

"Um . . ." I said.

Graydon smiled, but I thought I detected a hint of evil gleaming in his kindly face. "It's a gift from Trent Ross," he said.

All the extra air in the room seemed to vanish. Josh stuck his hands in the pockets of his cargo pants and scowled. Holly's perky face went flat. They'd both been library employees for years and knew what was coming.

Graydon continued to smile. "This was a pet project of our board president from start to finish, and we're going to come up with a way to incorporate it into the library outreach services, aren't we?" There was a short pause when none of us said anything. "And by 'we,' I mean not me," he added, looking directly at the assistant librarian.

"Um . . ." I said.

"You'll figure it out." He cheerfully patted me on the shoulder and headed for the door. "Trent will want a report at the next board meeting," he said over his shoulder.

I closed my eyes and took a couple of calming breaths. This would be okay. Things would work out. When I opened my eyes, either the book bike would have vanished, or my friends would help me with viable options.

But when I opened my eyes, the yellow behemoth was still there.

And both Josh and Holly had fled.

That evening, I hadn't come up with any brilliant ideas for the bike, and I was telling the story to Rafe, my aunt Frances, and her husband, Otto. Who, I'd belatedly realized, I should be calling Uncle Otto, but since I'd known him before the marriage, I was having a hard time with the switch.

"Trent Ross made a what?"

Aunt Frances frowned at me over the hood of their SUV. She and Otto were about to embark on a 1,200-mile drive around Lake Superior, and Rafe and I had stopped by to wave them off. They planned to stay in hotels and the occasional campground if the weather was warm enough. Accordingly, there was a plethora of camping gear spread across the driveway, and of the four of us, only Otto was sure it was all going to fit.

"A book bike," I repeated.

"Didn't know the man had it in him." My aunt made a noise that, if she'd caught a student making it, she would have reprimanded said student. The previous week, however, she'd retired from teaching woodworking at a nearby community college. According to her, her last words as she left the building were "Never forget: do as I say, not as I do," but I was sure that wasn't true. Pretty sure anyway.

My aunt was tall and rangy and attractive in a Katharine Hepburn sort of way, which matched well with Otto, who was tall and lean and attractive in a Paul Newman sort of way. For a number of years, I'd lived with my aunt during the cold months of October through April and moved to the cutest-ever little houseboat May through September while my aunt ran a boardinghouse. She'd sold the boardinghouse to our cousin Celeste when she married Otto, and I was now with Rafe. Lots of changes, all for the better, but a tiny part of me missed the winter nights when my aunt and I ensconced ourselves in front of a roaring fireplace to watch movies and throw Eddie the odd piece of popcorn.

Rafe handed Otto a cooler. "What do you have against Trent Ross?" he asked.

"Nothing. I just didn't peg him for being handy, that's all," my aunt said, echoing my earlier thought. "He's an attorney."

"Retired," I murmured, but that just made Aunt Frances roll her eyes. "Anyway, if anyone has any bright ideas about how to deal with this, I'd love to hear them."

"Check the brakes before you take it anywhere," Aunt Frances said darkly.

I was fairly sure that all the bike had was coaster brakes, but I supposed even those could fail. Couldn't they? "I'll have Cody at the bike shop take a look."

My aunt made a grunting noise that could have

been interpreted as an acknowledgment that I'd said the right thing.

"What color did you say it was?" Otto asked.

"Yellow."

Rafe grinned. "Like a warning sign? Danger, Will Robinson. Watch out, everyone, the big bad book bike is headed your way!"

Now that the bike's existence was being maligned by my nearest and dearest, I felt a sudden surge of defensiveness for the thing. "It may be big and yellow and . . . and . . ."

"Ugly?" my aunt supplied.

"Ridiculous?" Rafe said, laughing.

"Inappropriate?" Otto asked gently.

"And heavy," I said, ignoring their suggestions, even Otto's conciliatory one, "but Trent's heart is in the right place. He spent hours working on it, and I'm going to figure out a way to make it part of the library. Don't forget, not that long ago, people made fun of the bookmobile, and now we lend more materials per patron than the library does, and our patron count goes up every year. Or do you think I'm not up to the challenge, is that it?" I asked, my voice rising.

By the end of my impromptu speech, Otto was smiling, and Aunt Frances and Rafe were looking abashed.

"You can do anything you put your mind to," my aunt said. "As long as you're sure Trent didn't do this as some sort of test."

The idea was ridiculous. I said so and turned to my beloved.

"Sorry," he said. "It was the image of little you

versus a great big bike and"—he noted my narrowed glare—"and of course I think you can make it a success. If anyone can, it's you."

"Okay, then." I gave him a sharp nod. "The wedding is still on."

"Speaking of which." Aunt Frances rubbed her hands together. "We need to talk."

Without thought or conversation, Rafe and I drew closer, presenting a united front. The previous year, Aunt Frances had decided to embark on a postretirement career of wedding planning for couples like us who didn't want the expense and fuss of a big traditional event. Months ago, soon after we'd set our wedding date, Rafe and I had spent an entertaining evening making a list of wedding and reception venues. We'd sent the names to my aunt, asked her to pick whichever worked out best, and told her we'd host a reveal party when the time was right. My aunt had been nagging us to set a party date for weeks, but our schedules had been so full that we hadn't sat down to figure it out.

"Not sure you have time, Frances," Rafe said, looking at his watch. "Don't you need to get on the road now if you're going to make it across the bridge in time for a nice leisurely dinner in St. Ignace?"

"That's right." I nodded eagerly. "You plan to eat at the Village Inn, right? Better get going. Don't want to risk them running out of the planked whitefish."

"Stop it," my aunt commanded, and Rafe and I hung our heads. "Otto and I will be back no later than Memorial Day, by which time you will have decided on a date for your reveal party."

She gave us a penetrating stare, muttered something along the lines of "Should never have let you do it this way in the first place," and gave us both good-bye hugs. Otto hugged me and shook Rafe's hand.

They got in the vehicle, and we waited side by side on the driveway, standing tall and giving a crisp salute as they drove off.

We watched the SUV turn the corner and disappear. "Do you want to sit down and coordinate our schedules, the schedules of our wedding party, and the schedules of our families?" I asked Rafe, wrinkling my nose. It was a lovely spring evening, made for a walk around town and serendipitous meetings with people we hadn't seen all winter, and the last thing I wanted to do was talk about wedding minutiae.

"Nope. Do you?"

"As if."

"Your aunt won't be happy."

"She will not," I said, then smiled. "But we have time to procrastinate, so I say let's make the most of it."

And so we did.

Saturday morning I sat at the kitchen island in my fleece bathrobe and fuzzy slippers, watching Rafe cook breakfast. "You're getting good at this," I said, watching him flip a blueberry sour cream pancake with surprising expertise. "How did that happen? Do you get up in the middle of the night to practice?"

"Skill transference," he said. "All those years of playing pool and darts are coming in handy. Wrist action, see?" He flipped a pancake high into the air, and it came down half on the griddle and half not.

"I do see." I wrapped my hands around a mug of

hot coffee. Though I was normally up at the same time as Rafe on weekends, the night before I'd stayed up way too late reading *Once Upon a River* by Diane Setterfield and hadn't surfaced until the smell of breakfast wafted up the stairs. "The big question is, who's going to get the pancake that you mangled due to show-off-ery?"

"Mrr."

Rafe made a quality flip. "Eddie thinks you're being unkind and that the pancake you so quickly dismissed as mangled is actually the best kind of pancake, broken open to allow the intake of more maple syrup."

More like Eddie wanted fresh water in his bowl. I looked over at my cat, who was ensconced on the stool adjacent to mine. He was usually very attentive to cooking efforts, especially those involving meat—Rafe also had bacon in the oven—but this morning his furry attention was focused on the small glass bowl in the middle of the kitchen island.

The bowl had evolved to become our snack center and varied widely in content, depending on who was filling it and when. We'd had apples, oranges, candy, protein bars, and one magical time after my best friend and restauranteur Kristen had stopped by, cookies decorated to look like Eddie. She'd prefaced the gift by saying she was no Cookie Tom, but her infant twins had both been sleeping at the same time, so she'd taken advantage and done some baking.

"Sorry, Eddie," I said, pushing the bowl out of his theoretical reach. "Cat treats are in the cupboard."

He gave me a dirty look, turned to present his hind end to me, and loudly jumped to the floor.

"What did you do to deserve that?" Rafe asked, piling a plate with pancakes and bacon and sliding it over to me.

"Breathed, I guess." I accepted the jug of buttered and pecaned maple syrup and poured liberally. "Thanks for cooking. This looks great." I also needed to thank Aunt Frances for sharing her boardinghouse breakfast recipes.

"Long as you do the dishes, I'm okay with cooking."

It was a deal we'd come to over the last few months, and so far, it was working. I was no cook, by inclination or ability, but even the worst cook in the world can scrub a pot.

We ate and drank coffee, and when the plates were polished off, we pulled out our cell phones and did what people do: checked the phone weather in lieu of looking outside.

"Not what they were saying yesterday." Rafe frowned.

I frowned, too. "Not even close."

We exchanged a glance and then looked out through the windows at our backyard, and beyond that, Uncle Chip's Marina, and beyond that, the waters of Janay Lake.

Instead of the blue sky we'd anticipated, we saw a solid line of approaching clouds. Low and dark, they were menacing, and worst of all, they were coming from the east, which almost always heralded a stretch of crappy weather.

I sighed. The day before, this weather had been predicted to show up late on Sunday. "Doesn't matter. We still have to go."

"You could take a really long time doing the dishes," my beloved said. "All day, even."

"It's Chilson's first-ever Trout Lily Festival." I said this as severely as I could. "We have to at least make an appearance." He didn't respond, so I elbowed him. "Come on, it'll be fun."

"What part? Walking around in the rain? Or, let me see, walking around in the rain?"

I eyed him. "Are you feeling okay? Normally you're fine with any weather. What is it you say— there's no bad weather, just bad clothing choices?"

After a few more penetrating questions, the true reason for his reluctance was revealed. "Seriously?" I asked. "You'd rather drive down to Traverse City with your buddy to check out new golf clubs than support a community event?"

The love of my life shrugged. "What can I say? I'm a guy."

"And all guys would do the same thing?"

He grinned, his teeth flashing white. "All the guys I know."

Which was probably the absolute truth. "How about a compromise?" I asked.

"Listening," he said.

And so, without too much trouble, we arrived at a workable solution. Rafe would come to the festival and stay at least until noon, at which time I wouldn't object if he bailed on me.

"'Bail' is a strong term," he murmured as we walked to the waterfront.

"What would you call it?" I swung his hand back and forth, higher and higher, to prove that I wasn't upset. And I wasn't. I hadn't expected him to stay any longer than noon in the first place, something he didn't know and I didn't anticipate ever telling him. Some things are best kept to oneself.

"Appropriate time allocation."

"Sounds like it should be an acronym," I said.

He tried it out loud. "ATA. Not bad. It might even stick."

By this time we were downtown. Mitchell Koyne, former perennial slacker, now successful manager of Chilson's toy store, was standing in front of his store, arms crossed, his face creased into a frown.

It was an unusual expression for him. I looked around to see what was going on, but all I saw was what I'd expected to see. Cars on the street, people on the sidewalk, people crossing the street. It was busy, but not overly so, a mild harbinger of what the summer would be like.

Rafe and Mitchell did the fist-bump thing. Easy for Rafe, as he was only a few inches shorter than the extremely tall Mitchell. I just nodded.

"What's up?" Rafe asked. "You look like someone knocked your ice cream into the dirt."

"That new chamber director," Mitchell said, and it sounded almost like swearing. "It'll be great, he kept telling us. I've done events before, he kept saying. I have it under control, he said over and over."

"Um . . ." I still couldn't see a problem.

Mitchell raised a long arm and pointed at a city parking lot.

I shrugged. "Looks like a lot of trucks towing fishing boats."

"Exactly!" Mitchell thundered. "They thought it was a fishing contest. Trout Lily Festival. Heard the trout part, didn't pay attention to the lily part. Dozens of people here to fish, and there's no contest. They're going to go away mad, telling everyone they know that Chilson is full of morons, and whose fault is it?"

"Um . . ."

"The new chamber director! The messaging was completely off! The guy has to be tone-deaf for marketing. How could he not have anticipated this and got out in front of it? And don't get me going on all the skateboards, and now there's all these scooters downtown. Someone's going to get hurt. Scooters are way different from cars and bikes. It's hard to find a place for them to belong, you know?"

Rafe and I briefly commiserated, then I tugged at Rafe's hand and we moved off before I started laughing out loud.

"I don't know what's funnier," I was finally able to say. "The trout thing or the fact that Mitchell has an opinion about the chamber of commerce."

Rafe shook his head. "Two years ago, Mitchell didn't have a clue where the chamber office was. Now he wants to be on the marketing committee."

"What's so funny?" Pam Fazio asked.

Pam, friend and owner of the eclectic retail store Older Than Dirt, was standing with Dan Calhoun, another store owner. Both were in their fifties but looked a decade apart. Pam was a little taller than me, with short black hair and a permanent smile. Dan was a foot taller than me, had almost no hair—what there was of it was gray—and if the man ever laughed out loud, it would have been news fit to report in the *Chilson Gazette*. I reminded myself that his wife's death from cancer a couple of years earlier had been a hard blow, but he hadn't laughed much before she got sick, so . . .

"Everything's funny at the Trout Lily Festival," Rafe said. "Thought you knew."

Dan snorted. "Fine. Don't tell us." He spun around and marched off toward his store but soon slowed to talk to someone I didn't recognize. Mr. Unknown was about Dan's height and maybe thirty years younger than Dan. I assumed he was an employee, and I turned back to Pam.

"Don't mind Mr. Sourpuss," she said. "He's just mad because having all the law enforcement around is cutting into his sales. Or so he says. Seems to me the visibility would be good, but what do I know?" She rolled her eyes.

"That's right. Dan's place is next to Henika's, isn't it?" I paused, then asked, "Have you heard anything new about Whippy's death?"

"Wait, you're the one asking me?" Pam's eyebrows went up. "Usually it's the other way around. But no, I don't know a thing. Everyone's assuming Whippy was murdered, but all I know for sure is the police are taking their time in there."

The three of us glanced up the street toward Whippy's candy store and Dan's T-shirt and Up North memorabilia shop. Even from here, we could see the crime scene tape swaying back and forth in the light breeze.

"Hi, Mr. Niswander."

I was startled by the formal manner of address and blinked at the young man who'd slouched past in jeans and an oversized sweatshirt, the guy who'd just been talking to Dan. "Who's that?" I asked after he'd passed.

"Toby Guinn."

I blinked again; Rafe and Pam had said the name simultaneously.

Pam went first. "Last summer, he applied for retail jobs all over town, but he didn't have any retail experience, and who has time to train anyone in July? I told him to come back in the spring. Maybe that's what he's doing now."

We watched, but Toby's route was straight down the sidewalk. No detours into any stores.

Rafe shook his head. "Toby was one of my kids when I was a student teacher. He . . . Well, let's just say he never grasped the concept that sometimes life is hard work."

"It is?" Pam made a face. "Well, dang. Here I thought I could start taking things easy."

I smiled at her fondly. Pam was an Ohio transplant, a former very successful corporate graphic designer. She'd made a place for herself in Chilson through hard work, grit, and vast quantities of caffeine. "As if you'd know how to do that," I said.

She lifted her chin. "I'll have you know that, in November, I'm planning to take a vacation. A real one. Not a trip to Ohio to visit the family."

Rafe and I congratulated her and moved on. There was a big tent set up on the waterfront park with booths to visit, and time was ticking away toward noon.

As we made our wandering way toward the fun, I caught another glimpse of Toby Guinn, still slouching, but this time standing at the window of the jewelry store, looking at the sparkling goods with a startling hunger.

Chapter 3

I t was weird, that's all," I said to Kristen. "What guy spends time looking at pendant necklaces?" Because that's all there'd been in the window; I'd checked.

My best friend shrugged. "Well, Toby *is* weird, so it follows," she said, tucking a fleece blanket around her sleeping infant boy with one hand and wiping a bit of drool from the mouth of the infant girl she was holding.

The twins were two weeks old today, and I felt honored that my house was the first place, outside of the doctor's office, that they'd visited. I was inexperienced in the ways of babies and was finding everything about them simultaneously fascinating and frightening.

I watched Kristen deftly multitask: jiggling Eloise Minerva, adjusting the covers of Lloyd "Cooper" Oliver, talking to me, and still managing to stay upright and coherent. Maybe her profession as owner and manager of Three Seasons, a top-notch destination restaurant, had helped prepare her for twin motherhood.

Sure, the last year or so she'd stepped away a bit from hands-on management, as she'd married and started working more with her husband, producer of a nationally syndicated cooking television show, but the long hours and painstaking attention to detail were surely valuable now.

"How's Dad doing?" I asked. Scruffy (not his real name) Gronkowski had met Kristen when the show hosted by his father, *Trock's Troubles*, did a segment on Three Seasons. Scruffy was always impeccably dressed, hence the ironic nickname, and I was curious how he was dealing with the inevitable products that babies bestowed.

"Like a duck to water." Kristen smiled. I examined her for any hint of the sharklike smile she'd been known to use on occasion, but all I saw was happiness. "When he dropped us off here, I noticed he had a spot of spit-up on his shirt. Silly me, I said something, but"—she jiggled Eloise again—"you know what? He didn't care. What are the odds?"

Two weeks ago, I would have guessed a quinzillion to one.

She jiggled Eloise again and laid her gently in the infant carrier. "There. With any luck she'll sleep for a least half an hour."

Kristen kissed her daughter's forehead, whispering, "Sleep tight, my darling," and I felt my eyes mist.

"What's the matter with you?" Kristen asked, plopping down on the living room couch, an arm's length away from the twins, who were on the coffee table.

"Sun in my eyes," I said, wiping away the moisture. Which made no sense, given that the cloud cover was thick and that we were inside, but I circled back to the earlier topic. "You know Toby Guinn?"

"Like what Pam said. He made the rounds last summer looking for work. I'm always looking for good staff, so I talked to him."

"And?" I prompted.

She shook her head, tossing her long blond pony-tail back and forth. "And nothing. I was looking for low-level work—bussing tables and washing dishes—stuff you can teach in half an hour, but something about him just wasn't . . . wasn't right."

And it wasn't like Kristen to be inarticulate. Either the babies were distracting her, or something was really off about Toby. I felt a pang of sympathy for him. Maybe he was wired in an unusual way, and so he didn't fit in with the way the world worked. I knew how that felt, at least in a small way.

Eddie materialized on the couch between us. "Mrr."

"Hey there, buddy." Kristen patted the top of his fuzzy head. "Thought you were upstairs sleeping. Do you want to meet my offspring?"

"Mrr."

I glanced from cat to kids. "Not sure he's ever interacted with humans this small."

"Oh, it'll be fine." Kristen gave him a long pet. "He's good with littles on the bookmobile, isn't he? Why should this be any different?"

I could think of a lot of reasons but decided not to worry her. After all, if something went south, I was right there and could rescue kids from a cat.

Eddie flicked his tail, sending a few loose cat hairs into the air, and jumped to the coffee table.

"Um . . ." I slid forward on the couch, hands out-stretched and ready to pull my cat away from . . . from whatever.

"Stop worrying." Kristen laughed. "They're both sound asleep. What's going to happen?"

Eddie walked around the perimeter of Eloise's carrier, sniffing all the way. She slept on, her tiny chest going up and down and up and down. There was one final cat sniff of her blanket, then Eddie moved on to Cooper.

Silent cat feet circled carrier number two. Eddie took a sniff of the blanket and sat, statue-like, be-tween them.

"And there you go," Kristen said. "The Eddie stamp of approval. The kids will undoubtedly grow up to be huge successes in life."

Suddenly, Eddie sneezed. The biggest, loudest cat sneeze I'd ever heard.

Eloise and Cooper's eyes shot wide open. Their arms and legs started waving, their faces screwed up, and their tiny mouths opened.

"Uh-oh," Kristen murmured.

"Waaahhhh!!"

The double howls were deafening. I winced, Kris-ten sighed, and Eddie freaked.

"Mrrr!!!" he howled, making it a triple. "Mrr!!" His fur expanded to make him look twice his nor-mal size, and he looked from one baby to the other, giving every appearance of being trapped by the noise.

"Waahh!!"

He flattened himself on the table, and when that didn't reduce the assault on his eardrums, he did a quick ooze to the floor, then hurtled toward the stairs. He stopped halfway up, howled one more time, followed it up with a growling hiss, and ran off.

Over the noise of her crying babies, Kristen said, "And that's that." She stood, all six feet of her, and bent over both infants, cooing soothing sounds.

"Sorry," I said, feeling helpless.

"Text Scruffy to come get us, will you?" Kristen asked. "Sounds like they're going to go on for hours."

In short order, their car was in front of the house, and I was waving good-bye. None of them paid any attention to me, of course. Scruffy was driving, and Kristen was half turned in the front seat, focused on the babies, who were still wailing at the top of their lungs.

I climbed the stairs and eventually found Eddie. "Nice new hiding place," I said, flat on my stomach and peering at him. "I wouldn't have thought you'd fit underneath the laundry hamper."

Yellow eyes blinked at me.

"This wasn't anyone's fault." At least I was pretty sure it wasn't. "If anyone's to blame, it's me for not making sure you stayed upstairs the whole time." Introducing the twins to Eddie, and vice versa, had not been the point of the visit. Kristen had mostly wanted to get out of the house, and I'd been handy.

"Mrr," Eddie said, but didn't move.

To calm him, I kept talking, and as per usual, when I talked for a long time, I started to babble.

"If you'd been there to see Toby, you would have thought it was weird, too. Although, come to think of it, Dan Calhoun was also acting kind of weird. Then again, Dan isn't exactly known for his kindly demeanor. Can't be easy, though, to have a store next door to a crime scene. Poor Whippy. Has to be hard for his wife and kids . . ."

"Mrr?"

"Sorry. Didn't mean to stop. I was thinking about Leah's reaction, that's all. Remember, on the bookmobile? She fainted when she heard about Whippy's death, then said it was because she hadn't eaten anything that morning. It seemed obvious to me she was lying, just saying that to keep Eli from being scared. And afterward, she said she barely knew Whippy, but—"

A white paw snaked out from under the hamper and paused in midair.

I had no idea what he was doing, so I kept talking. "But that didn't feel true, either. So why did she have such a dramatic reaction? What kind of tie could she have to Whippy? What wouldn't she want to talk about?"

There was, of course, a stock answer. Which was absurd in this case, but it had to be discussed. "What do you think? Could Leah and Whippy have been having an affair?"

"Mrr!" The white paw smacked me on the nose.

Eddie squirmed out from under the hamper, shot out of the room, and thundered down the stairs.

"Does that mean no?" I called after him, but he didn't answer.

Cats.

Early the next afternoon, I sat down in a booth at Corner Coffee with Carolyn Mathews, the newest member of the library's board of directors.

"Thank you for agreeing to meet me on a Sunday," Carolyn said. "I'm sure you must be busy with wedding plans."

On the inside, I was laughing hysterically at her assumption, but it was usually a bad idea to contradict someone who had the power of hiring and firing you and your boss, so I said, "Thanks for the invitation. I can't imagine how busy your schedule must be."

Carolyn, in her mid-fifties, was administrator of the region's largest hospital, and had been for about two years. Before that, she'd been a successful and popular doctor in Chilson. I didn't know her husband, who'd been elected circuit court judge the previous fall and was the latest in a long line of attorney ancestors, but Carolyn had been semi-active with the Friends of the Library for a number of years.

The library staff had been thrilled that she'd been voted in as a board member and that she was taking time to meet with me outside of the library. "Just to get to know each other better," she'd said on the phone, which, to me, spoke volumes about her management style.

I knew only the bare bones of her personal life. She was from downstate, she'd met her husband at a legal conference where she'd given a session on health in the workplace, and they had two kids in the Chilson school system. She seemed kind, funny, and intelligent, and I was looking forward to deepening our relationship.

Now Carolyn smiled. "Better to be busy than bored, right?" Her short brown hair dropped into her eyes, and she pushed it away. "And one of these days, I'll be unbusy enough to get a haircut."

"Let it grow long," I suggested, tugging at my

too-curly locks. "I get a cut maybe once every six months."

She nodded as if she were taking my silly suggestion seriously. "Not a bad idea. Speaking of ideas, how are you and the book bike getting along?"

"Right. The book bike." I tried not to heave a huge sigh. I must have failed, because Carolyn laughed out loud.

"The day Trent dropped it off at the library, he texted photos to all the board members. The responses were . . . interesting." Her eyes danced, and I was tempted to ask about specifics but figured I was better off not knowing.

"I'm working on possibilities." Or I would be soon. "Graydon asked me to present a plan at the next board meeting." Which, happily, wasn't until the first week of June.

Carolyn toasted me with her coffee mug. "Looking forward to that already. That thing is a behemoth. The Sherman tank of bikes."

"If you or the rest of the board have ideas," I said, "I'd love to hear them."

"Any ideas?" She was laughing again. "My favorite was to set it in concrete in front of the library, make it a statue. Turn the box part into a flowerpot. Added value, see?" She laughed so hard she started clutching her stomach. "Oh, it hurts," she gasped, still laughing. "Just too funny."

I laughed along with her and wondered how many of the hundreds of hospital employees ever saw their administrator doubled over with laughter. All of them, I hoped.

When her laughter subsided, I asked, "Any chance of a workable idea?"

"None whatsoever," she said, wiping her eyes with her fingertips. "And—" Her gaze suddenly fastened on something behind me. I started to turn, but she refocused on me. "And if I hear anything remotely possible about the book tank, you'll be the first to know."

Our conversation became more general after that, and fifteen minutes later, her phone dinged with an incoming text. She took one look, stood, and apologized, saying she had to deal with a hospital issue.

I thanked her again for her time and the coffee and, after she'd left, slipped around to the other side of the booth, curiosity pecking at me to find out what had caught her attention. No one had been sitting in that section of the coffee shop, and if someone had been walking past on the sidewalk, I'd never know.

But there was one thing that was glaringly wrong and horribly out of place: the flutter of police tape at Henika's Candy Emporium.

An hour later, I stood on the marina dock that led to my houseboat and tried to figure out exactly how I felt.

For years, my summer living quarters had been tied up to a slip in Uncle Chip's Marina, the marina used by people without venture capitalists on their cell phone's favorites list. The pricey marina out by the point had emerald green lawns, a bar, restaurant, and beach cabanas, but Uncle Chip's had a gas grill we could reserve and Friday-night parties all summer long. Parties that I wouldn't be invited to because I didn't live there any longer.

"No change is one hundred percent positive," I said.

"What's that?" Rafe gently bumped my back with the corner of a moving box.

Since I wasn't about to hurt his feelings by repeating my melancholy statement, and since getting engaged and moving into the house was very close to completely positive, I said, "Anyone who lives on a houseboat is one hundred percent sensible."

"If by 'sensible,' you mean a little looney tunes, then sure."

I moved aside as Rafe stepped around me and got the feeling this was going to be one of the days he pretended to be way dumber than he was, when he played the role of Up North hick. In the past, I'd accused him of doing this to get out of additional work, but today that didn't make sense, because we were helping my first-ever houseboat renters move in.

"Why are you such a pain?" I said, following him down the dock, carrying an armful of hanging clothes and dodging a mountain bike and a white scooter.

"Who, me?" Rafe paused, one foot still on the dock, the other on the houseboat, and looked at me blankly.

"Keep moving." I nudged him. "You're an impediment to progress."

"Big college word," he said, shaking his head. "Thought we weren't using those today."

"And lose half my lexicon? I don't think so."

"Might do you good."

Or not. One of those. I gave him a firmer nudge and he stepped onto the front deck. "Where should I put this?" he asked.

Isabella Moncada, who was Kristen's newest sous-chef and wife of Corey, looked at him through the open door. "What is it? Oh, the box of pots and pans. Um, how about here?" She pointed at the dining table, which could be lowered to the level of the banquette seats and become a sleeping platform.

"On it," Rafe said, although the table was already piled high with other kitchen items. "Corey's waiting for me to help him with the cooler. We'll be right back."

"Sure," Isabella said distractedly.

I smiled at her. "I know how you feel. Happened to me every spring when I moved in here."

"Really?" She turned to me, her long silky dark hair slung over one shoulder in a loose ponytail. "Every year you thought all your possessions had expanded to twice their size and there was no way everything was ever, ever going to fit, and you had no idea what you were going to do, but at least you were finally going to be able to throw away your husband's ancient ratty sweatshirt?"

"Everything except the sweatshirt, yes."

We laughed, and once again I was pleased that this was all working out. I'd dithered for months about the houseboat's future. Keep it in storage? Sell it? I'd waffled back and forth, then at last lit upon the perfect (and in retrospect obvious) solution: rent it out.

Chilson, and all of northwest lower Michigan, was in dire need of additional housing, especially in the summer, when the area's population tripled. The last couple of years, it wasn't uncommon for businesses to be closed one or two days a week due to staffing shortages, and a lack of affordable housing was one of the reasons staff weren't available. I didn't have the financial wherewithal to do much, but I could help in a very small way.

I'd originally thought that my part-time bookmobile driver, Hunter, and his wife, Abigail, might be interested, as they were living with his parents, but he was trying to get a welding business started, which meant lots of tools with all sorts of electricity and space requirements. Helping a twenty-something couple brand-new to the area was working out better anyway. This way Rafe and I could indoctrinate them properly in the ways of Up North.

"Don't forget there's storage in here." I toed one of the banquette benches. "And you can slide some stuff above the kitchen cabinets." Gesturing with my chin at the clothes I was still holding, I asked, "Tiny little closet?"

Isabella nodded, and I went down the short flight of stairs that led to the rear of the boat, the stairs that Eddie had typically jumped over in one leap. As I squeezed the clothes into the closet shoehorned between the bedroom and bathroom, I wondered if Eddie would miss the houseboat and, if so, how we'd know. Mournful glances toward the marina? Howls of anguish? Okay, but how would those differ from the howls he gave when he wasn't getting enough treats?

By the time I returned to the main cabin, Rafe and Corey, the new daytime manager of Shomin's Deli, were wrestling a huge cooler in through the door.

"Never going to fit," I said. "Not the contents and not the cooler."

Isabella gave her husband a look. "I told you we were going to have to get rid of it."

"No worries, we got a plan." Rafe grinned, and what I got was a sneaking suspicion about what the plan involved.

The cooler thunked to the floor. I flipped up the lid, and just as I'd thought, two-thirds of it was full of beer. "Going to share your plan?" I asked.

"Sharing, like you said." Rafe took advantage of the open cooler and withdrew two cans of beer. He handed one to Corey and one to Isabella, then got one for himself. "You want one? Okay, maybe later. See, this is investment beer. I'll pop over to the office, tell Chris that the Moncadas are having a houseboat warming, and there will be people here in five minutes."

"That's an investment, how?"

"Because," Corey said, popping the top of his can, "that way we'll meet people, make friends, and with any luck, end up with a place to store the cooler that's handier than the storage shed."

The whole thing sounded like a Rafe-inspired plan from start to finish, but Isabella was smiling, so I mentally shrugged and rooted around in the cooler for a bottle of water. "Corey, you're, what, six feet tall? Watch your head going down the cabin stairs. You could give yourself a good knot on the head." I felt a little like my mother, but I'd felt compelled to warn him.

"Will do," Corey said. "But Isabella and I . . ." He looked at his wife and she gave him an encouraging nod. "Well, we have a question about Chilson. I thought this was a place where no one ever locks their doors, but now we hear there's been a murder."

My mood sank. I did not want to talk about Whippy's death. "Ah," I said vaguely, casting about for a new topic.

"Didn't you hear?" Isabella asked. "The owner of that cool candy store is dead. The police say he was murdered."

"Makes you wonder," Corey said. "I thought small towns were safe."

"Are the local police any good at investigating?" Isabella asked. "Or do you think they'll bring in the state police?"

Corey put his arm around his wife. "It worries me to have a killer running around free, you know?"

I did. And I also knew that if the killer wasn't found soon, the worry would spread through Chilson like a toxic ooze, damaging everything it touched.

The next day was a bookmobile day, and Eddie was up bright and early.

"Mrr," he said to my face, which up until that point had been sound asleep.

"And a good morning to you, too," I said, rolling over and sliding him off my chest. "Or did you say something else?"

"Mrr!" he said, running downstairs.

"No idea what you said," I called after him.

"Mrr!!"

When I got down to the kitchen, showered, dressed, and mostly awake, he was in his carrier. Rafe was already gone due to an early staff meeting, and I happily ate the oatmeal he'd prepped and put in the refrigerator for me.

"Odds are good," I told Eddie as I buckled his carrier into the front seat of my car, "that I'm the luckiest person in the whole wide world. Not quite as lucky as you, of course, because you don't have to clean up your stray cat hairs or your litter box, but peoplewise, I'm right up there."

No response from my fuzzy friend. "What's that?" I asked. "Cat got your tongue?" I laughed harder than a fourth grader watching the Three Stooges. But truly, that joke never got old. "Get it? Cat, tongue, and you're a cat?"

Nothing. And still nothing when I lifted him out of the car and into the bookmobile.

"He's in a mood today," I said, handing the carrier to Hunter. "Mr. Vocal first thing, even before I got out of bed, and now he's giving me the silent treatment. He could be planning an escape, so make sure the carrier door is tight." Every once in a while, the bookmobile hit a big bump and jiggled the door loose. I kept meaning to figure out a way to make it more secure, and someday I actually would.

"Mrr."

I looked at Eddie, who was looking at my co-worker. "Okay, he's giving *me* the silent treatment," I said. "You must be on his Good List."

Hunter strapped the carrier to the floor in front of the passenger's seat. "That's because we're guys. We have a bond."

"As long as the bond doesn't involve knock-knock jokes, I'm good. Who's driving today? I don't remember."

Not that long ago, I'd been the only driver the bookmobile had ever known. Its success, however, had led the library board and Graydon to push for expanded hours on the road. This had, in turn, created the need for an additional driver, and Hunter was our happy choice.

At first, when Hunter and I ended up on the bookmobile on the same day, I'd focused on getting him comfortable with driving the long vehicle, but he could now back it into the tiniest of parking lots without an increased heart rate, so these days we tended to switch drivers.

"I don't remember, either." Hunter gave the carrier a pat and stood.

His lean frame looked thinner than ever. He was working too hard, attending college classes and working for the library and building his business, and I hoped he didn't wear himself out. Then again, he was young and healthy, and what were your midtwenties for if not to test your limits?

"Rock, paper, scissors," I said, holding my hands in the ready position. Hunter did the same, and on the count of three, since paper covers rock, I became driver for the day.

"If you're good," I said, sliding into the driver's seat after the preflight check, "I'll let you drive this afternoon."

"Mrr!"

"Sorry, bud. You don't get to drive. No thumbs."

Hunter fastened his seat belt and leaned forward. "Work on the thumb thing," he whispered loudly. "Soon as they come in, I'll start training you."

"Mrr."

"Nice move," I said. "Making me out to be the bad guy."

"And that could be our question of the day." Hunter grinned. "Favorite bad guys. Books only."

"Excellent."

And so we spent the rest of the morning discussing Hannibal Lecter, Professor Moriarty, the White Witch, Dracula, Lord Voldemort, and Iago.

"True confession," I said as I flicked on the turn signal. "The bad guy that scared me the most was Bill Sikes, out of *Oliver Twist*. He frightened the daylights out of me." I shuddered, recalling Nancy's murder all too well.

"Mine was the Wicked Witch of the West." He squinted as I parked in the elementary school parking lot. "Or was that because of the movie? Were the flying monkeys even in the books?"

"Not sure. And now I'm going to have to do some rereading. Thanks so much."

Hunter laughed. "Glad I could help." He nodded at the school. "Just wondering why we're here. You and Julia stopped here last week, didn't you?"

I nodded, pleased that he knew the bookmobile's schedule so well. "Yup. One of the teachers e-mailed and asked me to drop off some STEM books when we were next in the area. You stay here, I'll be right back."

Before he could make any objections, I jumped up, grabbed the pertinent crate of science books from the back of the bus, and hurried out.

Inside the school's main office, I said I had a book delivery for Leah Wasson's classroom and was directed to a door at the end of a wide hallway. I knocked on the door's tall skinny window and waited.

"Minnie," she said. "You brought the books already? Thanks!"

I nodded at the crate. "We were close by. Say, do you have a minute to talk?"

She glanced into her classroom. "Sure. The kids are working on team projects until half past. What's up?" She stepped into the hallway but left the door open.

"We've never had anyone faint on the bookmobile before." I smiled. "I just wanted to make sure you were okay."

"Oh. That." Leah took another look inside her classroom and pushed the door mostly shut. "No, I'm fine. Like I said, it was just . . ." She frowned. "I mean . . . um . . ."

"You said you hadn't had anything to eat."

"That's right," she said, nodding. "Nothing to eat. That's what happened."

Right. And I was the tooth fairy. "Okay. But are you sure that's all? You looked upset when we heard about Whippy's death. Sad, like you were really going to miss him."

She shook her head. "I hardly knew him. Honest, I didn't, hardly at all."

Something wasn't being said. I could just feel it, not only from her uncharacteristic vagueness, but also because she hadn't truly looked at me the entire conversation. "But?" I asked.

"There is no but." Her eyes blinked. Blinked again. Then the tears poured out. She put her hands to her face. "Oh, Minnie, he's dead. He'd dead, and now I'll . . . now I'll never . . ." Sobs overtook her body. Her shoulders shook and her knees were quivering.

"Come with me," I said, and tugged her back down the hall into the front office. "Hi," I said to the startled secretary. "Sorry, but Leah just got some bad news. Could someone please watch her classroom for a few minutes? No, she'll be fine soon, right?"

Leah nodded through her tears. "Sally, I just need a couple of minutes. I'll be back in the room by ten thirty. They're doing a project and should be fine, but if you could just . . ."

By that time Sally was out of her chair. "Use the front conference room," she said, locking the office door. "And take your time. Your kids are easy."

"Sally's the best," Leah said, which, through her tears, sounded more like "Sall-Sally's the b-b-best."

I towed her to the tiny adjacent room, sat her in a chair, and temporarily abandoned her to find tissues. Sally had a box on her desk, so I borrowed it and took my time returning to Leah, waiting until the sobs had somewhat subsided.

"Here." I handed her tissues and sat across from her, trying not to think how much the room felt like the sheriff's office interview room. While she mopped her eyes and blew her nose, I asked softly, "What's the matter, Leah? Seems to me like you need to talk to someone, and if you want, it can be me."

Leah looked up for just a flash but long enough for me to see that her eyes were swollen and red. "You're right," she said, and it came pouring out of her like a flood.

A disjointed flood, because I had to ask her to backtrack here and there to get the timeline right, but eventually she took a shuddering breath and said, "And that's it."

"To recap," I said slowly, "you did a genetic test a few months ago for a class project." When she nodded, I went on. "That's when you found out you were adopted. After a couple weeks of quietly freaking out, you talked to your parents. You've always known your two brothers were adopted, but until then you'd thought you were a biological child. Your parents confirmed your adoption, saying you'd never been told because the adoption wasn't officially legal, and they didn't want anyone to get into trouble."

"It would never happen today." She tore one of the tissues into tiny pieces. "An unofficial adoption? Can't see it happening."

I couldn't, either, but I'd only stopped to take a breath. The story was far from over.

"Your parents refused to name your birth parents, again citing the not-wanting-to-get-anyone-into-trouble reason, but because of that, you suspected that at least one of your birth parents, if not both, still lived in Chilson."

She gave the tiniest of nods, and I continued.

"Since then, you've been on the lookout for family resemblances in everyone of a certain age who you come across." My voice cracked; the image of Leah searching the faces of strangers broke my heart. I coughed and went on.

"A few weeks ago, you were in Henika's and saw a picture of Whippy's parents on the wall. The resemblance between you and his mother is undeniable. Whippy was the only person in the store at the time, and perhaps because of that, he admitted to being your birth father, though he wouldn't say a word about your birth mother."

"Meeting my birth father," Leah said, still ripping the tissue to bits, "meant so much. I have a whole set of half siblings, cousins, and aunts and uncles. We were talking about maybe me meeting some of them, but now . . ." She swallowed. "Now I don't see that happening."

"You never know," I said, but she was right. Without Whippy to explain, a big family reunion was unlikely.

A fresh tear trickled down Leah's face. "And I don't know what's going on with the murder investigation. I don't know anything about it, probably never will, and . . . and somehow that makes everything so much harder."

"Did you see the press release?" I asked. It had come out that morning, stating the cause of death as strangulation.

Leah put her hand to her throat. "Yes, but . . . it's hard. He's my birth father, and I have to hear about him like everyone else does. It's . . ." She bit her lip and shook her head.

Though I couldn't understand exactly what she was feeling, I did understand that she was struggling and that I might be able to help. I leaned forward and took her hand. "Leah, I know the detectives at the sheriff's office. I don't know who's doing the investigating, but I'll find out what I can."

"You'd . . . you'd do that for me?"

I thought of that day on the bookmobile, her face white and wan, and I looked at her now, tearstained and a general mess.

"Anytime," I said, and pushed the box of tissues over to her.

Chapter 4

Rafe was not going to be thrilled with the idea of me involving myself with yet another murder investigation, but he'd understand. At least I was pretty sure he would.

As soon as Hunter and I had returned to the library and finished the unloading and reloading of books, I put Eddie in my car and drove the two of us to the sheriff's office. It was just after four in the afternoon, so past the end of the day shift, but I'd texted Deputy Ash Wolverson, and he said he was working on a grant application but would talk to me if I helped him with the application's required narrative section.

I parked under the shade of a maple tree whose leaves were nearly all the way out, left the windows open a crack, told a snoring Eddie to be a good boy, and headed inside.

Ash pushed the interior door open. "Before I even ask what you want, you're going to help me."

"No problem." I flexed my fingers. "Let me at it."

He ushered me down the hall to his office. "You've done grants before, right?"

"My dear Deputy Wolverson," I said, sniffing as snobbishly as I could, "I'm assistant director of a small-town library. What do you think I do all day long? Read books?"

"You know, I've often wondered about that."

I gave the comment the attention it deserved, that is, I ignored it, and once again wondered what it was that created chemistry between two people. Ash's verbal dig was something Rafe might have said. They'd been good friends for decades and had similar temperaments and personalities. Rafe was a good-looking guy by anyone's standards, but Ash, with his square jaw and dimples, was a couple steps past that.

A while back, I'd dated Ash, but it hadn't lasted long, as there'd been no sizzle between us. No spark. The whole thing was puzzling, and I'd given up trying to figure it out. Rafe and I were getting married, and Ash had just proposed to his girlfriend, Chelsea. Things were working out, as they tended to do, given enough time.

I plopped myself in the spare chair in Ash's office. "Is this the grant you want me to look at?" I asked, nodding at a pile of papers. Ash was an experienced deputy and was training to be a detective. Knowing that I was coming in, he wouldn't leave any papers on his desk that were confidential, but it didn't hurt to make sure.

"That's it." He sat heavily. "Everything I've written sounds stupid. I'm embarrassed to send it in like this, but the deadline is midnight tonight."

I picked up the stack of papers, which turned out

to be an application to the Michigan State Police for training equipment. I gave them a quick once-over. "Is this a new grant? No? Good. Have you ever applied for it before?"

Ash shook his head. "No. Well, at least I haven't. Don't know if anyone else here has."

Oh, the inexperience of the inexperienced. "Can you find out?" I asked. "If you've been awarded one of these before, you can use the old application to model the responses for this one."

"But . . ." He shook his head a second time and reached for his cell phone. "Why didn't I think of that?" he muttered, fast-typing a text message.

"Because you've never done this before," I said. "But now you have, and you'll know what to do next time."

He gave me a pained look. "Not going to be a next time."

I laughed, but I knew exactly how he felt. Grant applications and, worse, grant administration could be time-consuming and painful in many ways, but they were a way to obtain funding for things a tight budget wouldn't cover, and these days, almost all budgets in the public sector were tighter than they'd ever been.

Ash's phone pinged with an incoming text. "And?" I asked.

He smiled. "Hal says we've applied twice and were awarded once, about five years ago." He tapped his computer monitor to life and moused around. "Bingo!" His printer hummed to life and began spitting out a new pile of papers.

"Do you still want me to . . . ?" I tapped his current application.

"No, I'd say your work here today is done. And thanks. You've saved me a ton of time."

"Au contraire." I settled down comfortably into the chair, not an easy thing to do, because chairs in sheriff's offices do not tend to be designed for people of an efficient size. "This is the perfect opportunity to spend that same allotment of time answering my questions."

"About what?"

I waited.

Waited some more.

Eventually, he looked up from the printout. "Questions about what, Minnie?"

I smiled. "Not going to talk to you when more than half your attention is elsewhere. Put that down, and I'll be out of your hair faster."

With an exaggerated sigh, he squared up the papers, stapled them, and put them on top of the other pile. "There. Happy?"

I gave my own sigh. "You are sounding more like Hal every day." His supervisor, Detective Hal Inwood, routinely spoke in sentences as short as possible. Saving his words for what, I wasn't sure.

Ash laughed and leaned back in his chair. "You didn't intend that as a compliment, I'm sure, but I'm going to take it that way."

"Do what you have to do," I said. "And you should know why I'm here."

"Let me guess. You want to know about Whippy Henika's murder."

"The murder was in the city limits. Is the sheriff's office investigating or are the city police? Or are the state police taking over?"

"The city police were more than happy to hand it to us. They don't have the personnel to do a murder investigation." He stopped, then said, "Hal and I have been working on it."

Which was why he was coming down to the wire on the grant deadline.

He gave me a look. "You know I can't talk about active investigations."

"Sure," I said, since I knew that and absolutely understood the reasons why. However, that didn't mean I couldn't try and jiggle a little information out of him.

Besides, I'd promised Leah that I wouldn't tell him that Whippy was her birth father, so both of us were keeping information back. I'd told Leah that at some point, the police might have to know, but she'd begged that it be later, not sooner and not until absolutely necessary.

"Do you have any suspects?" I asked.

Ash kept quiet.

"I can't see a guy like Whippy having any enemies, can you?"

"Not going to work, Minnie."

I would have said you couldn't blame me for trying, but I'd found that some people considered reaching too far a character flaw. Some people did, in fact, blame you for trying and held it against you for a long, long time.

"Can you tell me anything?" I asked. "There are so many rumors. It would be great to squash some of them, and I could if you gave me something solid."

Ash leaned back and slung his legs up across the

corner of his desk. "Why do I get the feeling this isn't the only time you're going to be in my office asking questions about Whippy's murder?"

No idea, other than the numerous cases of precedent. "Whippy is missed," I said. "By so many people. Wouldn't it be best to tell them something?"

"That's why press releases were invented. One went out today. Didn't you see it? Gives the time and cause of death, and asks that anyone who has information to come forward."

Any second now I was going to start calling him Hal Junior. "Okay, but beyond that. What if you'd like to ward off the most inaccurate rumors? What if you'd like to get some unofficial information out to the public?"

He rubbed his chin, making a bristly sound. "There could be benefits."

I kept my triumphant smile on the inside and stayed quiet, as there was no gain in disturbing the thought processes that were circling around in his pretty little head.

"All right," he finally said. "I need to clear this with Hal, so don't say anything until I give you the all clear, okay?" At my nod, he said, "We are exploring every avenue of investigation, but there are indications that this is a burglary gone wrong." He held up a hand. "Don't ask what indications, because I'm not going to tell you."

I thanked him for the information, wished him luck with the grant application, and headed outside, thinking so hard that I forgot I'd driven to the sheriff's office and was halfway down the block when I heard a distinctly feline howl.

"Sorry about that, pal," I said, panting a bit as I

got in the car. "But . . . I'm not sure what Ash told me made much sense."

Because why would a burglar burgle a candy store this time of year? The mass of tourists wouldn't arrive for more than a month, so there wasn't much cash inside. And the candy store didn't sell anything very valuable; Whippy made a profit only because of the large volume of goods he sold.

So why, in early May, would anyone break into Henika's?

That evening, when Rafe and I were wandering around the backyard contemplating summer landscaping projects, I got a text from Ash saying that he'd had approval from Hal to share the burglary info.

I texted him back a thumbs-up and immediately told Rafe everything Ash had said. The only thing was he didn't share my concern about the motive behind the break-in.

My beloved shrugged. "Maybe it's because people who steal stuff aren't all that smart."

"Some of them are." I leaned forward to smell the blooms on one of our lilac bushes. Since the blossom buds were still tight and didn't show even a hint of pastel color, there was no floral scent. Even though that was what I'd expected, it still managed to be a bit of a disappointment. So much happiness in life depended on the management of expectations, and someday I'd get a better handle on mine.

"Besides," Rafe said, "why else would anyone kill Whippy? He was a good solid guy who sold candy for a living. What kind of enemy could he possibly make?"

"All sorts of them for all sorts of reasons."

"Realistic ones?"

Well, no. Not so much, as the chances of Whippy being a spy or in the witness protection program had to be none to zero. "He, um, could have been really busy one day, gotten distracted, and shorted someone on change or overcharged them."

Rafe slid me a look. "And that's a motive for murder?"

"By itself, no. But what if this person stopped in to talk to Whippy about it, they got talking about the incident, Whippy said he didn't remember it, and this person exploded with rage."

"Uh-huh. You going to call Ash and tell him that? Or Hal Inwood?"

I was not. "I'm just saying that a burglary in Whippy's store seems unlikely. Even Mitchell's store seems a better candidate for breaking and entering. Some of the toys in there are way spendy."

"That was only one," Rafe said.

"One what? Oh, right. I was coming up with reasons for Whippy to have an enemy."

A northwest breeze popped up, bringing with it chilly air from the still-cold Janay Lake. I crossed my arms against it. "There is something about Whippy that's a secret, but it's something personal, from a long time ago, so I don't see how it could have anything to do with his death."

"Okay." Rafe pulled off his flannel top shirt, worn untucked and unbuttoned, and handed it to me. "Here. I'm fine in my T-shirt and you're all goose bumps."

I took it gratefully. "Today, on the bookmobile, I found out this thing about Whippy."

He straightened the shirt's collar. "And?"

"And it isn't my secret to tell." Rafe had rolled up the shirt's sleeves; I unrolled them, creating sleeves that left the cuffs dangling six inches off the ends of my fingers. Perfect. "But I do need to tell you something. Because of this thing I found out, I promised the person who told it to me that"—I stopped and took a deep breath—"I'd talk to the sheriff's office and find out what I could about the investigation."

"Okay," Rafe said. "For the path to the gazebo I cross my heart and hope to die to make this summer, do we want pavers? Or what do you think about pieces of flat limestone?"

"Hang on." I stared at him. "You don't care that I'm going to be involved in another murder investigation?"

"Dear heart." He slung his arm around my shoulders and kissed the top of my head. "There was a murder in our town of a man we knew and respected. Of course you were going to get involved, one way or another. I'm only surprised it took this long."

The next morning I was still trying to figure out whether or not I should be annoyed at Rafe for his comment about my involvement with murder. I wasn't, because being annoyed at Rafe was a complete waste of time, as he paid little to no attention to anyone's annoyance level, but was there reason to be?

Graydon, coffee mug in hand, knocked on my office doorway. "Good morning, Minnie. You look deep in thought. Any chance that some of those thoughts are solutions for the book bike?"

I smiled and nodded at my guest chair, which just half an hour ago I'd cleared of books, catalogs, magazines, and newspapers. Sometimes serendipity is a real thing. "Any chance you can ask me a different question, one that might get you an answer we'd both like?"

My boss laughed and sat in the chair. "Sorry to tell you this, but Trent's asking for progress reports."

Wait, what? I'd thought my deadline was the next board meeting. I whirled around and looked at the wall calendar. My mom bought me one every year for Christmas; this year's choice featured baby animals. This month's photo was an adorable little giraffe, but at this particular moment, it seemed to be smirking. "The next board meeting isn't for almost three weeks."

"Sure, but you know Trent. He doesn't like surprises."

I understood the feeling. It was my often-stated opinion that there were two kinds of people in the world: those who would enjoy being given a surprise party and those who wouldn't. Rafe was a happy member of the first group, and I was a card-carrying member of the No Surprise Party party, or would have been if we ever organized ourselves.

"I don't understand," I said. "He'll get the report in the board packet ahead of the meeting, just like everyone else."

Graydon leaned forward, and I clued in to the fact that he was giving me a Mentor Moment. He was about to tell me something important, and I should pay attention.

So I did.

"All board members," Graydon said, "like to get a peek under the tent."

"The tent being . . ."

"Everything we do." Graydon gestured at the building around us. "It's what we live and breathe twenty-four seven, so we don't realize how much we know that they don't. Giving them glimpses of our day-in-and-day-out lives makes them feel part of things. More involved, more engaged."

I sort of got it but sort of didn't. "They're on the board. Of course they're involved. They're the ones who make the big decisions."

Graydon nodded. "You bet. But wouldn't it be better if they felt like they were part of the team? If they understood, down to the bone, what all of us do every day?"

"Okay," I said slowly. "But wouldn't that take a lot of time? On their part and ours?"

"Sure would." He sat back, sipping his coffee.

My brain was coming around and grasping what he was saying. "So, to make sure everyone on the board is happy, we need to spend a lot of time making sure they're happy."

Graydon smiled. "Now you're catching on. This is what they call board management, and if I had any voice about the curriculum for library science degrees, I would make sure there was a course for it."

I slumped a little. "So, it's not enough to just do your job?"

"Never has been, never will be." Graydon stood. "Cheer up. There's more than three weeks until the next board meeting. Plenty of time to have a couple of casual contacts with Trent about the book bike."

He smiled at my groan, then said, "Minnie, please think about this conversation. You have a tremendous amount of potential, and I don't want you to make the same mistakes I did."

Graydon had made mistakes? I perked up. "Any chance I'll get to hear about those?"

"Always a chance," he said. "And it would get a little better if you e-mail me your favorite time this week for us to sit down and talk about the five-year strategic plan."

This gave me another little perk. "You bet. I have lots of ideas." The last time the board had worked on strategic planning, our then boss hadn't included me in the process. Well, except for picking up the hard copies from the printer, which I didn't count.

"Write them down," Graydon said. "Bring them to our meeting."

I flourished a pen and pad of paper. "On it, boss."

Ideas for the strategic plan spilled out of me the rest of the morning, into the afternoon, and continued as I started the walk home. Expanded technology. More outreach. Stronger youth programming. More diversity in funding sources. The current plan, the one that would expire at the end of the year, was as dry and serious as the then library director had been. It did the job but wasn't exciting in any way, shape, or form, and as far as I knew, no one except Graydon and me had looked at it since its creation.

"Pictures," I murmured. "Graphics."

Including some images would make the new plan far more appealing than the current text-only version. And with a little bit of arm-twisting, I could get Pam Fazio to make suggestions. She'd sworn off design work for the rest of her life, but she loved to spin out ideas for other people to develop.

I was also thinking about Graydon's advice, about board management, about how to get the board to feel more involved in the library's day-to-day operations. Then it occurred to me that, the day before, I'd done that very thing, by having coffee with Carolyn Mathews and asking her about the book bike.

Maybe I *could* do this board stuff. And Linda Kopecky, another board member, liked coffee. I could meet up with her at the Coffee Corner or maybe the Round Table and . . . and then what? If I kept on with the restaurant invitations, I'd spend a lot of money and a lot of time. "Break room," I said to myself. That's what I'd do, starting with Trent. I could pour him a cup of coffee, and maybe I could convince my coworker and friend Holly to whip up a batch of her famous brownies.

I nodded, pleased as punch for developing a plan so quickly, which I would pass by Graydon before starting just to make sure I wasn't doing something stupid. Smiling, I looked up and focused on my surroundings.

"You are so stupid," I said out loud.

My thoughts had been so inwardly focused that I hadn't been paying that much attention to where I was walking, and my feet had ended up taking me where they'd taken me so many times over the years—to the boardinghouse.

Well, I was more than halfway there at this point, so I shrugged and kept on. I hadn't seen much of Cousin Celeste since she'd returned from

her warm winter trip. Maybe she had a minute between her long list of preopening chores, and we
could catch up.

I rounded the corner, already looking forward to
the fresh lemonade she always had at the ready, and
slowed. What were all those white pickup trucks
doing out in front? The landscaping company she'd
hired drove green vehicles, so what was going on?

Then I saw the workers and what they were carrying.

And knew exactly what was happening.

I stared, not believing what I was seeing. "Aunt
Frances is not going to like this," I muttered, shaking my head. "Not one little bit."

Chapter 5

By the time I arrived home, my outrage had not diminished. If anything, it had grown in intensity.

"Let me get this straight," Rafe said, his head in the refrigerator. "You're upset because your cousin Celeste, the person who bought the boardinghouse from your aunt lock, stock, and barrel is painting her own property."

"Of course not." That would be silly. Painting wood siding was part of regular maintenance, and the fact that Celeste was having it done before the house showed visible signs of peeling meant that she was doing an excellent job taking care of the old building.

"So what's the problem?" Rafe backed out of the fridge and, since his arms were laden with food, shut the door with his elbow.

"The problem," I said, enunciating each consonant cleanly and clearly, "is she's painting it a different color."

Rafe put milk, eggs, Tabasco sauce, mushrooms, and green peppers on the kitchen island. "Still not seeing the problem."

"But it's always been white!"

"And?"

"And it's always been white!"

Rafe pulled a scary-long knife out of the block and started cutting the pepper into bits sized properly for omelets. "Tell me again why you're upset?"

How could he not understand? "White is the color it should be! It doesn't need to be any other color. Nothing else will look right. White is just the boardinghouse's color." I knew I wasn't making much sense but kept going anyway. "Changing things for the sake of change is pointless. Some things should always be kept the same. That's what traditions are all about."

"Tradition, huh?" Rafe pushed his pile of peppers to the side of the cutting board and started in on the mushrooms. "Some people would say the same thing about weddings. That they should be in churches."

"Wait. You want to get married in a church?" Churches had not been on the list of accepted wedding venues we'd given to Aunt Frances. My mother would go ballistic if we didn't have a church wedding downstate in the Dearborn church my parents had attended for forty years, and we wanted to have the wedding in Chilson. And who knew what dates would be available, and there was no way we'd be able to find a reception venue downstate this late and—

"No," Rafe said, still cutting the first mushroom.

"What I'm saying is that the boardinghouse is Celeste's to do with as she pleases."

"Sure, but—"

He talked over my objection. "It's hers. If she wants to paint it pink with purple polka dots, there's nothing you can do."

"I know that."

"Then why are you all wound up?" he asked.

"Because . . . because . . ." He didn't understand. Just didn't. "Never mind. If you don't get it, there's no way I can explain it to you." I slid off the stool and made a decision. "I'm going up to change," I said stiltedly. The plan was to do yard work after eating, and I was still in my library clothes.

"Dinner in twenty minutes," he said.

I grumped a reply, felt a little ashamed of how I'd been behaving, but not enough to do anything about it, which made me feel even worse.

At the bottom of the stairs, I stopped, since there was a roadblock. "And what do you think?" I asked Eddie, who was seated like a cat statue in the middle of the stairway. I stopped and counted; there were six steps below him and six above. "Did you know that you're in the exact middle?"

Eddie stared down at me and gave a silent "Mrr."

I had no idea what that meant, so I had to guess. "Staying out of the painting argument, are you? You do realize that, since I fed and watered you all by myself for years, opting out of a disagreement between Rafe and me is like treason."

My cat blinked and didn't say a thing.

"Fine," I said, and went up, going around Eddie like a stream flowing around an immovable rock.

I hung my jacket and pants in the closet, tossed my shirt into the laundry basket, and pulled on sweatpants and a T-shirt, muttering to myself the whole time.

"Sometimes traditions are there for a reason. And when there's no reason for them to go on, sure, it's time to change things up. But some things are meant to be the way they are. Having the Fourth of July fireworks on the Fourth of July. Singing along when you hear 'Bohemian Rhapsody.' Drinking out of red plastic cups at parties. Kristen and me having dessert on Sunday nights."

"Mrr," Eddie said, sitting in the middle of the bedroom doorway.

"Oh, sure, now you have an opinion?" I opened my dresser drawer for a fleece pullover. "Or are you criticizing, because Kristen and I haven't always had dessert on Sunday nights and won't until the twins are a little older." I sat on the bed to tie my shoes. "Plus, we switched up the dessert all the time. Crème brûlée mostly, but not always, and even then it had different toppings and even different flavors, depending on what Kristen felt like making."

Eddie didn't say anything.

"Okay, fine." I sighed and gave my shoelaces a final adjustment. "You're right. You always are. Celeste owns the boardinghouse, and she has every right to paint it whatever color she wants. And the color wasn't horrible." I thought back. "Kind of pretty, really. What would you call it? Pale peach? Or course, you're a cat, so—"

"Mrr."

I stood and looked around. Two seconds ago,

Eddie had been in the doorway. Now he was . . . "Where are you?"

"Mrr."

"You are so weird," I said, looking into the bathroom. Eddie was sitting with his front half in the sink and his back half on the counter, sniffing at the faucet. "I'm just glad you don't know how to turn the faucet on all by yourself."

Eddie looked at me over his shoulder, and I was sorry I'd put the idea into his little kitty head. "Never mind." I picked him up and cuddled him close. "I'll make sure you have all the water you need, okay?"

He purred, and I carried him all the way downstairs and into the kitchen. I held Eddie up for Rafe's inspection and said, "He wants me to apologize."

"For what?" Rafe flipped an omelet.

I reached up to kiss his cheek. "For being ridiculous about the painting thing."

"Oh, that. Yeah, you were being kind of weird. But I get it. The boardinghouse was where your parents sent you all those summers when you were a kid. Places like that get in your head and stay there forever. When it changes, it's like the ground is shifting under your feet."

"See?" I told Eddie, giving him a little squeeze. "Rafe understands me even when I don't understand myself. Am I the luckiest person in the world, or what?"

Eddie squirmed free of my arms, all four paws managing to reach the floor at the same time, emitting an *oof* as he hit. He then flopped on the floor and curled himself into a meatloaf shape.

"Or what, I think he said." Rafe plated our omelets and slid them across the island's counter. "Because if you were truly lucky, a fairy godmother would show up to do the dishes."

"True." I pulled up a stool, picked up my fork, and dug in. I hadn't been a big omelet fan until I'd eaten one cooked by Rafe. These days, we had omelets for dinner at least once a week. I had no idea what his secret ingredient was, but if I ever learned, I might be in danger of having to cook, so I was happy to leave it as top secret information.

"Speaking of mothers," Rafe said, "mine is about to start bugging us for the date of the reveal party."

"And you know this how?"

"Dad."

I nodded. That made sense. Over the years, Rafe and his dad, Rick, had developed a kind of texting shorthand. It was a jumble of letters, numbers, and emojis that left me baffled. I was half convinced none of it meant anything, but communication did seem to be achieved. "It's months until the wedding. Why does anyone other than us need to know so far in advance?"

"No clue." Rafe paused, his fork about to plunge into his omelet for a fresh bite. "Here we thought having a venue reveal party would be fun."

"Next time we get married, we'll be better at it," I said comfortingly. Clearly, we were bad at this. No wonder we'd jumped on the offer of Aunt Frances to be guinea pigs for her wedding planning business. "But the photographer is set, right?"

"Yup."

"And Kristen is set with the catering."

Rafe shook his head. "The Blonde won't be set

until the day of the wedding. She'll keep changing her mind and changing her mind until the last possible minute."

This was true, but we'd given her a budget and told her to do whatever she wanted, so we had no grounds for criticizing. "Carte blanche, remember?" I asked.

"Sure, but that doesn't mean I can't give her a hard time."

Whatever. "She also said she's going to work with Cookie Tom on the wedding cake. No," I hurried to say as Rafe started to look apprehensive. "They both promise it won't turn into a spectacle. They'll be good."

"So they say now," Rafe said gloomily. "We'll have to keep an eye on them."

This was also true. Both Kristen and Tom had a tendency to get carried away at events, and neither Rafe nor I had a desire for anything about our wedding to go viral.

I nodded. "I'll keep them in check. And my dress is all set." I'd seen one in a magazine that I'd fallen in love with and ordered it online. Mom had freaked out that I'd bought it without her, but I'd mollified her by having it shipped to a Dearborn bridal salon and would be driving down in early June to get a fitting. "You and the guys are wearing dark gray suits"—mostly because they all happened to already own one—"and the bridesmaid and matron of honor have agreed on M.M.LaFleur dresses in this gorgeous color called deep sea." Each of them would probably end up with a different style, but they'd also end up with a lovely new dress they'd be able to wear for years.

"Flowers?" Rafe asked.

I shrugged. "Aunt Frances has that figured out. And the minister from my parents' church is coming north for the weekend, so that's all set. DJ?"

"Thought I told you weeks ago. Tank said he'll do it."

My fork came to a stop. "Your friend Tank?"

"You've heard of 'TJ the DJ'? That's him."

I had indeed heard the name, but that could mean a lot of things. I made a mental note to look online for reviews. "That," I said, "just leaves one thing for us to do."

"Reveal party date. And because I love you so much, I got that all figured out." He reached for his tablet, which was sitting on the counter, and tapped it live. "Using the magic of the Internet, I made one of those meeting invite things with a list of dates and sent it out to our core group."

"Interesting," I murmured, looking at the list. "How is it that the bride wasn't included in that e-mail?"

Rafe froze. "Oh. Um. I never . . . I don't . . ."

I laughed and gave him a kiss, because hearing Rafe at a loss for words was priceless. "It's fine. I love that you did this." Besides, our phone calendars were synced, so he would have seen any conflicts before sending out the invite. "Looks like we have a date," I said. "Memorial Day it is. A perfect start to the summer."

We bumped fists and returned to eating. But there was one more topic to cover before we moved on to the continuing gazebo-design discussion.

"Um, Rafe? Remember what I said, that because of a promise to a bookmobile patron, I was going to talk to Ash about Whippy's murder, and you said you weren't surprised?"

"As if it were yesterday."

Just as if. I pressed on. "So would you be surprised if I wanted to do more than ask Ash what he can tell me?"

The previous night I'd called Leah and passed on what I'd learned. She hadn't *said* she was disappointed it was so little, but I could tell she was, and I'd felt horrible for disappointing her.

"More?" Rafe eyed me. "More like what?"

Find a killer, of course. "Mostly make sure that Ash and Hal are looking down every avenue of investigation that's out there. Sometimes they get stuck in a rut and need a bounce to get them out." With my toes, I gave my snoring cat a gentle nudge.

"Mrr!"

"See? Eddie agrees."

"Well, if he thinks it's a good idea, who am I to say it's not?"

Surreptitiously, I dropped a piece of sausage on the floor. And smiled.

In a classic case of serendipity, the next night we'd already arranged to have dinner with Chelsea Stille and Deputy Ash Wolverson. Wednesday night wasn't normally a night we went out, but due to deputy attrition, Ash was scheduled to start pulling some extra shifts, and this was going to be the last time for a couple of weeks that everyone was free.

In the name of having an uninterrupted dinner, we'd decided to meet outside of Chilson, down in Grayling, at Spike's Keg O Nails, and I made sure

Rafe and I arrived early enough to visit the new bookstore in town, Hidden Nook Booksellers. Once we were all seated at Spike's, Rafe and Ash ordered Spikeburgers without even looking at the menu, and I went for the turkey cucumber sandwich. Chelsea was new to the place, and after some menu perusal and consultation with our waiter, she settled on the smelt basket with star fries.

Orders taken care of, we settled into the easy conversation of good friends. Rafe took a slug from his beer and said to Ash, "Can't believe you've never brought Chelsea here. Where else haven't you taken her?"

"The Mystery Spot," Chelsea said promptly.

Ash made a rude noise. "Never going to happen. If you want to go, you're going on your own."

"I've never been, either. Girl trip." I held out my pinky finger and Chelsea held out hers. We shook solemnly, and I was once again so very pleased at how things had turned out.

Chelsea was almost exactly my age, taller than me, of course, and had lovely straight brown hair that behaved impeccably. She had the friendliest smile around and possessed a sense of humor that let her find the funny side of almost everything. Both of these characteristics helped immensely in her job as office manager at the sheriff's department. Though Chelsea hadn't lived Up North very long, the engagement ring on her finger meant she'd made at least two commitments: one to Ash and one to Chilson.

"This summer," I vowed. "We'll take a full day. Eat breakfast in Pellston. Pasties for lunch somewhere. Maybe stop in Mackinaw City for dinner on the way back."

"Deal." Chelsea grinned. "No boys allowed."

"Boys have better sense than to go to the Mystery Spot," Ash said into his beer.

Pushing back from the table, I looked left and right and up and down.

"What are you doing?" the love of my life asked. "Lose your marbles again?"

"Someone paired 'boys' with 'good sense' in the same sentence. I'm hoping no one gets hurt when the lightning strikes."

Chelsea laughed; Rafe and Ash ignored me.

I smiled. All was well with the world. There was just one thing I wanted to establish, and I wanted to do it straightaway. "Need a favor," I said, gesturing at three of my favorite people in the world. "From all of you."

"Anything," Chelsea said, her eyes sparkling.

"What is it?" Ash asked.

Rafe eyed the bottom of his beer mug and looked around for our waiter.

"Can this evening be free of wedding talk? Aunt Frances is still out of town, and my cell is going nuts with people asking questions I can't answer." That day my mom had called, the florist had called, the photographer had called, Tank the DJ had called—even Kristen had called. It was as if texting had never been invented.

"Deal," Rafe, Chelsea, and Ash said so perfectly timed I suspected there'd been a rehearsal.

"Any other topics that should be off the table?" Chelsea asked.

I glanced at Ash and found that he was looking at me with a set expression on his face that—since I'd spent a lot of time with Eddie and knew how to read faces—all too obviously said, *Do not talk about the murder.*

"Nope," I said cheerfully, smiling directly at Ash. "Everything else is fair game." The boy was spending far too much time with Detective Hal Inwood. For his sake, for Chelsea's sake, and for the sake of their future marriage, he needed to lighten up, and I was just the person to help with that. "Did anyone else hear about what Rianne Howe said to Myles What's-his-name, you know, that new insurance agent, out on the sidewalk in front of her store?"

"That's Benton's?" Chelsea asked, naming the general store that had been family run since its birth in the late 1800s.

The rest of us nodded, and I launched into the entertaining tale of the fortyish and petite Rianne dressing down the twenty-something hotshot from downstate who thought he knew everything about Chilson because he'd spent two weeks here one summer, and so he thought it was okay for him, now that he was a local, to park in the city lot and take up two spaces with his new car.

Just when I got to the best part—when Rianne had described his precious possession as a bucket of bolts that would drive like crap in the snow—Ash's phone flashed and rattled.

He looked at the screen. "Hal," he said, picking it up, saying, "Deputy Wolverson," into the phone as he stood and walked to the front door and outside.

"Hazard of the job." Chelsea watched him go. "I'm starting to get used to it. Hope he'll have time to eat," she added, because our waiter had just appeared, her arms laden with our food.

Before all the plates had landed, Ash was slipping back into his seat. "I'll have to eat fast," he said, ignoring the potato chips and going straight for the protein.

"Anything you can tell us?" I asked, because no one else was.

"There was a break-in at a store downtown," he said around a mouthful of burger. "The city police picked up the guy and are bringing him to the jail."

Okay, but why had Hal and Ash been notified? "And?" I asked, again because the other two were leaving the questioning to me.

"And it's Toby Guinn."

Instantly, I went back to seeing Toby stare through the window of the jewelry store. "Was it the jewelry store that he robbed?"

Ash's brows furrowed over the top of the burger bun. He chewed, swallowed, and said flatly, "Yes. How did you know?"

I shrugged. "Seems obvious. A jewelry store is bound to have a lot of valuable things inside. What other downtown store would be worth breaking into?"

His eyes narrowed.

"But this was a city arrest," Chelsea said. "Why are you and Hal involved?"

I waited, but Ash kept chewing. "Because," I said, "the city police are short-staffed. They don't have the capacity for a big investigation. And the sheriff's office thinks Whippy's murder was a burglary gone wrong. So if Toby broke into one place, it's possible he broke into the candy store."

Chelsea glanced from me to a statue-like Ash,

back to me, then back to Ash. "You think he killed Whippy?"

"Maybe. We're looking into it." Ash used a napkin to wipe his mouth. "Sorry, babe, but I have to go." He stood, and Rafe and I murmured that we'd be happy to take Chelsea home.

Ash thanked us, gave his fiancée a quick kiss, sketched us all a wave, and was gone.

"Toby Guinn," Rafe said. "Wish I could say I'm surprised."

"You know him?" Chelsea asked.

"Had him when I was a student teacher."

I remembered what Rafe had said that day we'd seen Toby, that Toby had never understood that life can be hard work.

Rafe toyed with a potato chip. "No matter what I did, I couldn't get him interested in anything. Back then I thought it was because I was a crap teacher."

"And now?" Chelsea asked. "Now what do you think?"

Rafe grinned. "That I was a crappy teacher. Why do you think I went into administration?"

We laughed, and turned the talk to other things, but the rest of the night, Rafe wasn't quite himself, and I knew he was thinking that he'd failed Toby Guinn.

Chapter 6

The next morning, peering up at the dark clouds and in spite of the forecasted rain, I decided to walk to the library. After all, I was wearing a raincoat and carrying an umbrella. And it wasn't that far, so how wet could I get?

So I set off, and ten minutes later, the skies opened up. Thirty seconds after that, from the knees down, I was wet to the skin.

"Should have worn the rain boots," I grumbled, but had I? No, I had not. Instead, I'd decided to be like Rafe and assume everything would be fine. Why that always worked for him but not for me was another of life's great mysteries, right up there with why we always got snow the day after swapping the car's snow tires for summer tires.

"Minnie Hamilton, you get in here right now!"

It was Pam Fazio summoning me from her store's front entrance. I splashed over and stood in the covered space dripping. Before I could say a word, she towed me inside.

"You're soaked. Keep standing on the entry mat, and take off those shoes and socks. Now come on back and take off those sopping pants. I'll get you a blanket to wrap around yourself while your clothes roll around in the dryer. Yes, I have a dryer. It's how I fluff up the linens before displaying. I'm not about to iron them all."

In short order, I was sitting in one of Pam's back room chairs, my lower half covered with a red-and-black plaid blanket, sipping coffee and accepting her friendly abuse.

"What were you thinking," she demanded, "walking on a day like this?"

I shrugged, having already decided that I was not going to admit I'd been trying to be more like Rafe. "Didn't see the weather forecast." A blatant lie, but self-preservation was important.

"Well, I wanted to talk to you anyway. Have you and Rafe announced where you're going to have your wedding?"

I slid down into the chair, a red velvet slipper chair that was waiting for an empty spot out front. "Memorial Day," I said into my coffee. "I'll send you an invite if you want to be there for the reveal."

"Thanks, but I'll be working. Everyone's looking forward to the wedding, though," Pam said. "It's going to be the social event of the year."

"Oh, sure." I rolled my eyes. "Of the decade, even. Say, not to switch subjects"—although I desperately wanted to switch the subject—"do you know what's happening with Whippy's store? I saw the police tape is gone."

Pam's face turned down in unaccustomed lines of sadness. "They took it down yesterday, Ash

Wolverson and that Detective Inwood. They were in there half the day, and when they left, they took the tape off."

Huh. Ash hadn't mentioned anything about that last night. But then, he wouldn't have. "Is the store going to reopen?"

"No one knows," Pam said. "Do you want to hear the rumors?"

Not in the least. "The sheriff's office is following a lead that it was a burglary gone wrong."

"You heard about the robbery at the jewelry store, right? So, they think Toby Guinn is the killer?"

"Yes, I heard about the jewelry store," I said. "Murder investigations take a long time, though. We might not hear anything for weeks or even months."

But last night, when he was leaving the restaurant, Ash had a look of being on the hunt and closing in on his prey.

And I wasn't at all sure he was on the right track.

"Minnie, can I talk to you?"

I looked up from the reference desk's computer screen slowly, because I was deep into reading the strategic plan from another library—as Tom Lehrer said, it's not plagiarism, it's research—and focused on the woman in front of me.

"Leah," I said, surprised to see her outside her elementary school during the week. "But it's only Thursday. The kids learn all there is to learn for the year, and you get to start summer early?"

She smiled. "I'll have to suggest that to the principal next time I see her. Talk about a motivation technique. But no, it's an in-service day and I finished early. I was hoping to talk to you," she said, glancing around.

Though most of the tables were empty, a few were occupied. Jim Kittle had his genealogy research spread out in front of him. Amanda Bell was studying books on tying fishing flies, and off in the corner, Mrs. Noss was reading books in her attempt to make a travel decision. She and her husband were touring the world alphabetically, and they'd made it to the letter J. "One country per letter," she'd told me years ago, then whispered, "although we had to cheat with the letter I. There are just too many."

I was getting the idea that Leah meant a talk in private. "How about my office? And I'm going to top off my coffee. Would you like a cup?"

Leah demurred, saying it was too late in the day for her, so I carried only one mug down the hall. I gestured for her to sit, settled behind my desk, and asked, "What's up?"

She nodded at the door. "Is it okay if I shut this? Great. Thanks." She did the deed and sat down. "It's just . . . after the other day, when I told you about Whippy, I've been thinking."

"I haven't told anyone," I said as reassuringly as I could. Was she having regrets about telling me her secret? If so, that was understandable but also a little late. "And I won't, not unless you say it's okay."

"Oh. No, that's not it." Leah rubbed her face with her hands. "I trust you." She closed her eyes. "I just need to think how to say this out loud."

I waited. Took a sip of coffee. Waited some more. Drank more coffee. Then, when I was about to get up and make sure she was still awake, her eyes opened.

"A few months ago, my husband and I got divorced." She gave a small sigh. "We'd been married for eighteen years. Dated all through high school, got married right after I graduated from college."

It wasn't an unusual story. I nodded, encouraging her to go on.

"But the last few years hadn't been that great. We were never able to have kids—combination of factors on both our sides, the doctors said—and we drifted away from each other. We'd been living more like roommates than a couple, doing more things separately than apart. I looked around one day, asked myself why we were still married, and couldn't come up with any answer other than habit."

"So sorry," I murmured.

"Thanks." She blinked rapidly a few times. "Kurt didn't get it. He didn't see anything wrong with the way things were. But I didn't want that any longer. And he . . ."

She trailed off and showed no signs of starting up again.

"And?" I prompted gently.

"When I told him I wanted a divorce, he didn't take it well. I figured he'd get used to the idea soon enough, but he . . . didn't. He wouldn't even talk about what to do with the house, so I packed up my things and left. Anyway . . ."

She tipped her head back, looked at the ceiling, then back at me. "There are two things I wanted to tell you. First is that Kurt is the only person other than you who knows that Whippy was my birth father. We were still together, just barely, when I found out."

"The second thing?" I asked.

"Right. The second thing." Her hands went up

again, rubbing her eyes, rubbing her cheeks, pushing on the muscles in front of her ears. "The second thing is that, when I stopped at the house the last time, to drop off my keys, Kurt was there. He wasn't supposed to be, he was supposed to be out at a job. All I wanted was to drop the keys in the toolbox in the garage—that's where we always put an extra key. But he was there, and . . ."

Leah looked at me, her eyes red and raw. "And he came into the garage. Watched me, not saying a word. It was creepy and weird and awful. Then when I was walking away, he yelled after me. He said . . . he said he'd make me pay for what I'd done to him."

She took a deep breath. "Minnie, what if that wasn't just one of those things people say when they're mad? What if he meant it? What if he's the one who killed Whippy?"

That evening, Rafe had to attend a school board meeting, so he picked up something to go from Fat Boys Pizza, leaving Eddie and me to fend for ourselves dinnerwise.

"Hey, look at what you get tonight." I rattled the bucket of dry cat food. "Cat kibble, fresh from the source. Yum, yum!"

Eddie, perched on the one kitchen windowsill that wasn't quite wide enough for him, gave the bucket a disdainful look, then transferred that same look to me.

"You think my dinner is going to be any better?" I raised my eyebrows. "This is a reversal of fortune, going backward to the bad old days, when I had to feed myself all the time." A number of those feedings had included meals at the boardinghouse, meals at Chilson's lower-end restaurants, and occasional recipe trials from Kristen, but still.

I filled Eddie's bowl, made sure it was mounded the way he liked it, or at least the way he'd liked it that morning, and opened the refrigerator door to consider my options.

"There's chicken," I said, "but that's for the stir-fry Rafe said he was going to make tomorrow. There's stuff to make a salad, and cheese to make a grilled cheese sandwich, but that sounds almost like cooking."

I poked through the fridge's other contents. Pretty much anything in there would require cooking more than three ingredients, with accompanying utensils and cookware. Bleah. "Then again, if this is throwback night, why not take advantage?"

"Mrr."

"Glad you agree." I grabbed the milk jug, shut the fridge door, and opened a cabinet. "Toasted Oats or Raisin Bran? Let's go with the box that has more in it . . . Toasted Oats it is. We can always have popcorn later if we get hungry."

"Mrr."

"Well, there you go." I pulled out a bowl and utensil, poured cereal and just the right amount of milk, and sat at the kitchen island. Too late I realized I'd made the tragic error of sitting down to a solo meal without a book.

"Looks like we get to talk," I said, angling myself so I could see Eddie. "But not very much, because I don't want the cereal to get soggy."

Eddie gave an excellent impression of being frozen in place.

"Right. So the big question is, what do you think about what Leah said?"

After the Kurt-as-killer theory had been put out there, Leah had given me some facts. Both Leah and her ex-husband were forty years old, and both had gone to high school in Petoskey. She'd done two years of community college before going off to Central Michigan University and had come home every weekend because Kurt hated her being away so much.

"He sounds like the worst kind of control freak," I said to Eddie, slurping a little on the milk, "but no matter what Leah said, it feels like a big stretch to think he killed Whippy to get back at her. Still, I promised her I'd find out what I could about what Kurt was doing on the night of Whippy's murder, and—"

"Mrr!!"

"Not your turn yet." I scooped up the last O's of cereal, chewed, and swallowed them down, then put the bowl on the floor. "Now it's your turn."

Eddie gave me a glare, sat on the windowsill long enough to demonstrate that I was not in his good graces, then jumped down and sauntered to the bowl.

As I listened to the *lap-lap-lap*, I watched him spatter tiny drops of milk on the floor. "I thought cats were supposed to be neat and tidy." He didn't reply, so I continued thinking out loud.

"What do we know about the murder itself? Since Ash hasn't been willing to share, basically nothing."

Eddie continued to spatter.

"That forces me to move on to sheer speculation."

Luckily, that was something I was completely comfortable doing. "We know that Whippy was Leah's birth father, but that's been true for as long as Leah has been alive, so how could that have anything to do with his murder?"

Eddie polished off the last of the milk, then sat and stared at me.

"No, I'm not giving you more. The vet says milk is bad for cats." What he'd actually said was a lot of milk was bad and that giving Eddie a little was fine, but Eddie didn't need to know that.

Good and bad, I thought. Subjective concepts. Good for one person could be bad for another. "Bad things can happen when old secrets come out," I said. "Whippy seemed okay enough with acknowledging Leah, though. Who else could be hurt by a revelation of Leah's adoption?"

I stopped. The answer was suddenly obvious, but I didn't want to say it out loud, so I whispered the words: "Her birth mother." To solve Whippy's murder, would I have to find Leah's birth mother?

That was a can of potential worms I didn't want to open.

Not one little bit.

Chapter 7

Predictably, Julia thought the idea of a book bike was hilarious. Primarily because of the area's terrain but also because of its creator.

"Trent Ross." She squinched her face shut in a clear effort to demonstrate deep thought. "Nope," she said in a tightly strained voice. "Can't see it." Her face and voice smoothed out. "You're kidding, right? You have to tell me you're kidding. There is no way Mr. Buffed Fingernails has ever fired up a TIG welder."

I almost asked, "A what?" but kept quiet. If I asked what a TIG welder was, she'd either tell me or make something up, and there was no way I'd know which. And I almost asked why she had such a poor opinion of Trent's mechanical aptitude. After all, just because he dressed like an attorney even though he was retired didn't mean that he didn't mind getting dirt under his fingernails. But instead of either of those questions, I asked, "Buffed fingernails? Is that a real thing?"

Since I was driving the bookmobile around a curve, I couldn't look over, but I knew in my bones that she was rolling her eyes. Dramatically.

"Puuh-leeeese," she said, drawing out the word into two extremely long syllables. "How is it you got to your age without knowing anything about fingernails?"

By which I understood that she didn't know exactly what the buffing thing meant, either. I smirked, having scored a small point (not that anyone was keeping score, but I was winning), and said, "Cody at the bike shop has it now and is making sure it's roadworthy. That's not the problem."

"Then what is? No, wait, let me guess. The problem is Mr. Ross wants to hold a press conference to announce the generosity of his gift."

"What is it with you and Trent?" I flicked on the turn signal and slowed to pull into a township hall parking lot, our first stop of the day. She didn't answer, so I said, "At the next board meeting, I need to present a report on how the book bike is going to be incorporated into the library's outreach effort. I'm looking for ideas on making that work. Solid ideas," I added quickly before she could get going, Carolyn Mathews–style, on ridiculous ones.

"Solid ideas." Julia popped her seat belt buckle and leaned forward to open Eddie's door. He didn't move an inch, as he was snuggled up with his pink blanket in the back of the carrier, emitting Eddie-size snores. "Solid," she said again. "Hmm."

She hummed tuneless songs as we readied the bookmobile, but she didn't say anything until I went to open the door. "I have an idea," she declared in the accent of English royalty, rolling consonants that had never been rolled before. "Let us ask our patrons for ideas."

The first visitor of the day, seventy-ish Mrs. Dugan, was already climbing the bookmobile steps. "Ideas for what?" Her eyes were bright with anticipation.

On the inside I was shrieking at Julia something along the lines of *What were you thinking? People have no clue what it takes to run an outreach program! If we ask their opinions and don't implement them, we'll end up with hurt feelings all over the place!* But since I couldn't say that out loud, I pasted on a smile and explained.

Mrs. Dugan's eyes went even brighter. "A book bike? And you want our ideas? How wonderful!" She beamed and clapped her hands.

Throughout the day, we saw the same reaction over and over. "There wasn't any idea I haven't already considered," I told Eddie as I put him in the car that afternoon. "Not that you heard any of them. Or were you faking those snores?"

"Mrr," he said sleepily.

A daylong Eddie nap did not bode well for a full night of human rest, and I was really hoping some quality sleep would let me wake up with a resolution to the dilemma of whether or not to find Leah's birth mother. "How about a long walk around the block when we get home?" I asked, pulling out of the library parking lot. "Or an hour-long game of catch? How about . . . hang on."

I parked outside the toy store, told Eddie I'd be back in a flash, and hurried inside. "Hey, Mitchell," I said. "I need some help."

Mitchell, who was standing in front of a shelving array and holding a computer tablet, gave me that same beaming smile I'd seen all day long. "You're asking me for help? For real?"

"As real as it gets." I explained about the book bike. "You," I said, nodding at him, "have a unique way of thinking. If anyone can come up with an idea that works, it'll be you."

"Huh." He rubbed his chin. "Guess that's a compliment. Give me a couple of days. If I come up with anything, I'll let you know. Say, I went past the boardinghouse yesterday. That new color is pretty sharp, don't you think?"

I gave a vague answer, then asked, "Do you know what's going to happen to the candy store? Is Whippy's family going to reopen it?"

Mitchell's face had been open and sunny; now a cloud fell over it.

"No one knows for sure," he said. "But someone put up a sign on the front door. A big one you can see from the street. It has one word: 'Closed.'"

Mitchell's mention of the boardinghouse had forced me to remember the paint. Up until that second, I'd thought I was being adult enough to accept the twin realities of ownership change and property rights, but his offhand mention resurrected memories of childhood summers that lasted forever, summers when Kristen and Rafe and I swam at the city beach, when I'd climbed backyard trees, book in hand, and read until called in for dinner. All of those memories included a white boardinghouse, and now Mitchell had slapped peach paint in my face.

It was wrong of me to hold that against him. I knew that, of course I did. And someday the rational part of my brain would catch up with the emotional part, and I'd forgive him.

"Until then," I said to Eddie, "I think it's best if I avoid going by the boardinghouse. Celeste keeps texting me to stop by, but I can put her off for a while. Maybe until Aunt Frances gets home?"

It was also wrong of me to keep news of the Peach Paint from my aunt. "Coward," I said. "That's what I am. A yellow-bellied coward who doesn't like change and is afraid of confrontation."

"Mrr!"

By this time we were back at the house. I glared at Eddie. "You didn't have to agree so quickly. I thought we had a bond." I opened the wire door. Eddie trotted out, across the wood kitchen floor, and out of sight.

Rafe was sitting on a kitchen stool reading the newspaper. "Agree about what?" he asked, turning the page of the sports section. In the *Chilson Gazette*, the sports section was one hundred percent about school sports. Rafe said it was part of his job to keep up with the sports news, and for all I knew, he was right.

"That I'm the coward of Tonedagana County."

"Old news. Everybody knows."

Happily, he didn't ask *why* I was a coward. "Are you done with the paper?" I asked, because he was now perusing the "Items for Sale" section of the classifieds, a dangerous thing because we needed absolutely nothing. "I have a question for you."

"Forty-two," he said.

I looked over his shoulder. I was pretty sure he was reading the ad for an upcoming auction and made a mental note to make sure we were busy that day. "Fun answer, but not applicable. Do you know Kurt Wasson?"

As a homegrown local, Rafe was one of my go-to sources for information. It wasn't one of the many reasons I'd fallen in love with him, but it was a handy bonus.

He put the paper down and looked at me. "Sort of. Why?"

I put my backpack on the kitchen counter and unzipped it, pulling out the detritus from my lunch of peanut butter and jelly, potato chips, and apple. "Leah Wasson, the elementary school teacher who I've been working with for bookmobile stops, told me she used to be married to him. She said he isn't dealing with the divorce very well."

Rafe watched me pitch the apple core and wash the plastic containers. "And you're worried he might, what? Be a stalker or something?"

"Hope not. But you never know. Forewarned is forearmed, and all that."

"Is Leah worried about him hurting her?"

"Didn't sound like it."

Rafe nodded. "Okay. I knew there was a divorce. Principals talk about their teachers. Hard to believe, right? I know Kurt from a softball tournament a few years back and because he's a plumber. Used to have his own company, but a couple years ago he started working for North Lakes Plumbing. Got tired of the paperwork is what I heard."

All good information. I wasn't sure any of it was useful, but you had to start somewhere. "You hear a lot of things," I said. "Which makes me wonder where you hear them. It's not like the middle school has a water cooler."

He gave me a look of disbelief. "You want me to reveal all my secrets before we're married? Are you nuts?"

"Nuts about you." I made my voice all sweet and syrupy.

The love of my life made a rude snorting noise. "You're just trying to butter me up so I'll feed you."

I didn't see any problem with that. Then, since I did see a problem with something else, I said, "Got another question for you. An ethical one."

"Is this a bookmobile thing or something about Whippy?"

Both, but I couldn't tell him that. At least not yet. "What if, to fulfill a promise, I had to look into someone's past, a secret past. Should I or shouldn't I? What if I found out something I didn't want to know?" And couldn't forget.

Rafe's gaze sharpened. "Minnie, what are you talking about?"

I hesitated. "I can't tell you. Like I said, this isn't my secret to tell." I thought about what I could and couldn't say. "To right a current wrong, I think I need to find out an old secret that someone wants to stay hidden."

After a moment, Rafe's arms went around me, holding me tight. "Whatever it is you're talking about," he said, "I know you'll do the right thing. But you have to make me one promise."

"What?" I asked, comforted by his warmth, his love.

"That you'll be careful."

"Promise," I said.

And I meant it. At the time anyway.

I was constantly making minor tweaks to the book-mobile's schedule, trying to see what worked best for the people we were hoping to reach and what the staff could sustain long term. In addition to the weekdays, Hunter, Julia, and I had committed to staffing the bookmobile six months of an every-other-Saturday schedule just to see what happened.

"It's all about the metrics," I said to Hunter.

He braked to avoid coming up too close behind an SUV towing a boat and said, "Metrics. That's what people with lots of college degrees call numbers, right?"

I ignored the jibe. "It's a balancing act to find the sweet spot that lets us serve the highest possible number of people and not work ourselves to the bone."

"Then just when we find it," he said, "something changes, and we have to figure it out all over again."

"Life in a nutshell." It made me tired if I thought about it too much, so I moved on to thinking about Leah and Whippy. About Whippy's murder and who his killer might be. And just as Hunter parked us at the first stop of the day, the unused parking lot of a shuttered gas station, I came to an obvious conclusion.

I needed to find out more about the circumstances of Whippy's murder.

"What do you think?" I murmured as I un-latched Eddie's door. I didn't hear or see any indication of cat movement, so I leaned down and peered inside.

He was sitting sphinxlike, staring at me with un-blinking eyes.

"Stop," I said. "You know how that creeps me out."

Hunter, already setting up the back computer, said, "Is he giving you that look? The one that says you are so stupid, why couldn't I have adopted someone who was at least half as smart as the aver-age cat?"

"That's the one." I reached into the carrier and patted Eddie on the head. Not a single purr. "He's in a mood today," I said.

"Maybe it's the weather." Hunter pointed at the front windshield.

A cold front had moved in, bringing with it thick low clouds, spatters of rain, and a chill breeze that, if you looked at the thermometer and not the calen-dar, had you reaching for knit hats and mittens on the way out the door. It was far more like March than May, and no one, but no one, was going to be happy about it.

"The bookmobile is a refuge," I said. "Which means no weather talk today. It's wretched and mean and we all know it, but none of us has the power to make it better, so let's focus on something else, yes?"

"Mrr!"

"Always good to have the Eddie seal of ap-proval." I nodded. "Now what we need is a diver-sion topic, something to catch people's attention and steer them away from"—I glanced outside, my own attention caught by what I could have sworn were snowflakes drifting down, and determinedly averted my eyes—"from any outside unpleasant-ness. We live Up North, and these things happen. We need to deal with it in a positive way."

Hunter sat at the back computer and took the mouse out of the drawer. "Who are you trying to convince?"

"Everyone," I said promptly.

He laughed. "You're probably right. And I have an idea for a non-weather topic. How about—"

The door opened, and Rene Kinney came up the steps.

I exchanged glances with Hunter. Rene was not the cheeriest of patrons at the best of times, and now we were going to try and keep her from complaining about the weather?

"Good morning, Rene," I said cheerfully.

She was tall, somewhere in her fifties, with brown hair cut in a straggly way that looked a little like an expensive haircut but more like she cut it herself with a pair of dull scissors. Today, she had on jeans worn at the knees and a coat with fraying knit cuffs and was stuffing one blue glove and one black glove into the coat's pockets.

"What's so good about it?" Rene asked.

I kept smiling and tried to think of a reply. Rene was a bookmobile patron, and we were here to help her.

"We're not dead yet," Hunter said. "Which is better than a lot of people."

Still smiling, I said, "Kind of a low bar, but I suppose you have to start somewhere." I took the stack of books Rene had ordered and gave them to Hunter to check out: nonfiction mostly, woodworking and gardening books, with two Maeve Binchy novels.

Rene shrugged. "Not sure why you have to start at all."

Literally minded people could certainly make conversation difficult. I was about to give up when Hunter said, "Well, I'd sure rather be here than dead, and I bet Whippy Henika would say the same thing if he could."

Rene's face twisted into a grimace. "Henika. Everybody's saying what a nice guy he was." She made "nice guy" sound like cursing. "And everybody's going on and on like it's the worst thing in the world for him to be murdered." She puffed out a spiff of air. "For some people, it's the living that's hard, not the dying." And she was gone before Hunter or I could come up with a response.

"Um . . ." Hunter scratched his ear. "Is it just me, or did she sound like someone who might be a danger to herself?"

I'd been thinking the same thing and was also thinking about responsibilities and overreach and duty. And when I was done with all that thinking, I used the twenty-year rule: Twenty years from now, what will I wish I'd done today? "I have a psychologist friend. I'll talk to her and see what she recommends."

Hunter nodded, and I went back to thinking.

Why had Rene been so unsympathetic about Whippy's murder? That was not a normal reaction. She'd sounded almost hateful. Rene often came across cranky, but not to that extent. Could she have had something to do with Whippy's death?

I watched her battered sedan—primarily silver but with a hood and trunk lid that came from a whole different part of the color wheel—lurch onto the road and realized something else.

Rene was the right age to be Leah's birth mother.

Chapter 8

When the bookmobile route was over, I took Eddie back home, where he continued to sleep in the carrier even after I opened the door.

"You are so weird," I said. "Adorable but weird."

Though his ears twitched at "adorable," he didn't move.

"Okay, then." I got up off my hands and knees. "Rafe and I will be back later. Not sure when, so don't stay up worrying about us. We'll be fine. I'm sure of it."

You'd think that cats, out of the entire animal kingdom, would grasp sarcasm, but either Eddie didn't get it, or he did and chose not to let on.

Ten minutes later, I posed the question to Rafe. "What do you think?"

"Abouts cats and sarcasm? No idea."

We were now in his pickup truck driving to a residential construction site. Soon after our discussion of Kurt Wasson, Rafe had snapped his fingers and said, "You know what? I have a buddy who's

building a house out in Wicklow Township. After
getting builder estimates, he decided to do most of
the work himself."

I'd hoped the guy was single or had a very patient significant other. The process Rafe had described was how he'd done the renovations on our
house. Yes, he'd saved a tremendous amount of
money, but he had also taken years. And if you
counted basement and attic work, it still wasn't done.

Rafe had pulled out his phone and started texting. "Anyway," he'd said to me, hitting the Send
button, "my buddy is hiring out the electrical and
plumbing, and if I'm right . . ." His phone had gone
ping and he'd peered at the message. "And his
plumber is Kurt Wasson."

"You are amazing," I'd murmured, and given
him a kiss. The kiss had led to other interesting
things, and all else had faded away.

Now I looked at Rafe and asked, "Who is this
buddy that we're going to meet? Am I supposed to
know him? Because at this point I don't even know
his name."

My beloved launched into a story about his
buddy Bob Schroeder that I sort of listened to but
sort of didn't. I'd heard enough Rafe stories to
know that all I really had to do was listen at the
beginning for the pertinent facts and then pay just
enough attention to realize when the story was
about to reach its conclusion.

When Rafe stopped talking, I summarized.
"Bob is a friend of your buddy Jeff, and you met
him when both of you were helping Jeff rip drywall
out of his basement after an unfortunate incident
with a leaking faucet."

"If you want to skip what happened when we hauled the old drywall to the landfill, then, yeah, I guess that's about it."

"Do we know what Bob does for a living?"

Rafe slowed his truck, turning onto a rutted gravel driveway. "Hasn't come up."

It occurred to me, once again, that men and women were not the same. Sometimes it was hard to believe we were even the same species. I opened my mouth, then shut it. What was there to say?

The house in front of us, Bob's future home, was two stories with a full front porch and an attached garage. The shingles were on, the house wrap installed, and maybe half the gray clapboard had been put in place.

Two pickups were parked in front: one shiny and black, the other white with NORTH LAKES PLUMBING painted on the doors.

Rafe parked behind the white truck, and we climbed out. The theoretical point for the visit was to talk to Kurt about doing a project at our house, and I said, "Did we ever decide what kind of plumbing project we're thinking about?"

"Thought you knew," he said as, hand in hand, we stepped onto the wide porch.

The front door was opened by a stocky man in his mid-forties who wasn't much taller than I was. Rafe said, "Hey, Bob. What's up?"

They shook hands, and introductions were made as we entered the foyer.

"Kurt's upstairs," Bob said. "Go on up. I'm in here fussing with the office built-ins." He tipped his head to the right.

Rafe's attention deserted me and went straight

in that direction. An active woodworking project was something he had little power to resist. I understood; I was the same way with a bookstore.

"After," I said, tugging on his hand. "Promise."

Upstairs, we followed muffled plumbing-type noises and found, in what I assumed would be the future master bathroom, a man wearing a Detroit Tigers baseball cap sitting on an upturned bucket, pulling a faucet set out of a cardboard box. He looked about forty, Leah's age, and wore jeans, work boots, and a dark blue long-sleeved T-shirt that buttoned at the neck.

He looked up as we came in. "Niswander, right? Bob said you might stop by. How you doing?"

Kurt Wasson's voice was deep, like one of those radio guys who did late-night shows for romantic music requests, and as he talked, he put down the faucet and stood. Discounting the thick-soled work boots, he couldn't have been more than five foot six, which was probably an advantage for a plumber since they often had to fit themselves into small spaces.

Rafe shook his hand. "This is Minnie Hamilton, my fiancée. Our house is about a hundred years old, and we're thinking about getting some additional plumbing work done." He nodded at me, and I detected a small smirk.

Hah. As if I couldn't dream up a construction project at the drop of a hat. "That's right," I said. "Rafe is doing the basement finishing work, but plumbing isn't his thing. We were wondering what it might take to get a utility sink installed next to the washer and dryer." Ideas were suddenly coming thick and fast. "And it would be great to have a sauna, but we're not sure where we could fit one in. And do you install water conditioners?"

"Hang on there, Tex." Rafe put his hand on my shoulder. "Let's not get carried away."

"Carried Away" was my middle name, but I nodded. "Sure. We can start with the utility sink."

Kurt asked Rafe a few questions, then said, "That's not a very big job. Even if you approved a quote, it's going to be low on the priority list for my boss. Can't promise it'll get done before the end of the summer. We're doing those new condos in Chilson, and they're taking longer than anyone figured."

"End of the summer?" My voice came out a little squeaky. "That's months from now."

He shrugged. "What can I tell you? We're busy. But I tell you what." He reached into a back pocket and held out a business card. "My cell number is on there. I'd have to look at your place to get you a solid price, but for a cash job, I can do it on my own time in the next few weeks. No reason to get North Lakes involved."

Though he was clearly giving the card to Rafe, I took it from his hand. "Wasson?" I asked, reading. "Are you related to a Leah Wasson? She's an elementary school teacher."

His face, which had, up until that time, been pleasant enough, closed down tight. "Not anymore," he said, and turned to face Rafe. "Let me know on that sink." He pushed past us and was gone.

"Did you think that was weird?" I asked Rafe.

We were driving home, windshield wipers swiping

back and forth, clearing our vision momentarily each time. He slowed as a line of wild turkeys took their own sweet time crossing the road. "Got to say, I don't think much of guys who troll for their own work while on the job for someone else."

I nodded. Since I wasn't part of the plumbing world, I didn't know where the ethical line was, but if we talked to Mr. North Lakes Plumbing, I doubted he'd be happy. "And he sure didn't want to talk about Leah."

"That's no surprise," Rafe said.

"No. Still, wouldn't a more normal reaction be 'She's my ex,' and leave it at that?"

"Is there a normal reaction to divorce?"

He had a point, and the rest of the way home, we came up with divorce anecdotes ranging from complete career changes to selling everything and moving to Baja, Mexico, to live on a boat.

"Speaking of boats," I said as he parked the truck in the garage, "I'm going to pop in and see how Corey and Isabella are doing. You want to come with me?" As there was an important baseball game to watch, he did not, so after a quick study of the clouds—Minnie the meteorologist—I decided the rain was over for the time being and walked over to the marina.

I'd expected a sentimental pang or two, but I must have used all those up when we'd helped with the move-in, because all I felt as I neared my houseboat was pleasure. From everything I could see, the Moncadas were taking care of things as if they were the owners, not just renters. The deck was swept clean, the outside windows were washed, and there were even tiny houseplants perched on the windowsills, something I hadn't done for years because of cat inclinations.

I stood on the dock at the houseboat's gate. "Anyone home? It's Minnie." There was no response, so I called out a little louder. "Isabella? Corey?"

"No one's home."

I jumped at the disembodied voice. "You have got to stop doing that."

Eric Apney, whose big powerboat had shared a dock with me the last two summers, poked his head over his gunwale and grinned. "What, and ruin one of the great pleasures of my life?"

"How old are you?" I asked. "Never mind. Clearly not old enough to know better."

By this time I'd accepted his waving invitation and stepped aboard his boat. Eric, known as Dr. Apney to many downstate folks needing cardiac surgery, had already retreated to his glassed-in sitting area, plopped himself at a dining chair, and was pushing a bag of tortilla chips across the table. "If you want anything to drink, you know you have full refrigerator rights here."

Instead, I took a plastic glass from a cabinet and ran it full of water from the tiny bar sink. "When did you get up?" I asked, sitting and reaching for the chips. I'd noticed that his boat had slid into its slip a couple of days ago, but I hadn't seen Eric himself until now.

"Yesterday. Showed up in time to get dinner at Hoppe's," he said. "How was your winter? You and Niswander set a date yet for that wedding?"

I caught him up with the wedding plans, which didn't take long, then asked, "Have you met Isabella and Corey?"

"Who?"

An uneasy feeling started gathering somewhere in my midsection. "My houseboat renters."

"Right." He nodded. "Chris told me their names. No, I haven't met them."

Chris Ballou, the marina's manager, had vowed, hand on heart, that he'd do the introductions. That he hadn't done so was proof positive that the man didn't actually have a heart.

"Have you seen them?" I asked.

Eric shrugged. "I've seen lights. Chris said they're doing restaurant work. Their schedules are probably nuts. Might take a while to run into them."

I nibbled at a chip. I shouldn't be concerned; it was the middle of May. Only a few of the boat slips were occupied. There was plenty of time for Isabella and Corey to grow accustomed to marina life. They had weeks and months to meet people, make friends, all of that. But if so, why did my insides have this tiny knot of concern?

Eric took a chip and dipped it deep into an open jar of salsa. "Chris told me something else. That Whippy Henika was murdered. He can't be right on that, can he? Who would kill a guy as nice as Whippy?"

Something went *click* in my head.

Maybe my unease about Isabella and Corey wasn't due to an easy slide into marina life. Maybe it was because I was remembering the questions they'd asked about Whippy's murder. Because I was remembering the way Corey drew Isabella close, protecting her. Were they so concerned about the murder that they might leave Chilson forever?

* * *

Rafe, as I'd expected, scoffed at my notion that the Moncadas might bail on Chilson because of Whippy's death.

"You're basing this on what? A few questions?" He was holding the ice cream scoop with one hand. With the other he held up fingers; two, then one. I nodded at the one, and he put a single big mound of Mackinac Island Fudge into a dish. He gave himself two scoops, and I topped them both with whipped cream, chocolate sprinkles, and a maraschino cherry. The clouds had blown off, the sun had come out enough to dry things up, so we took our desserts onto the back patio.

"It wasn't just the fact of the questions; it was how they asked them."

"How was that?"

And since I couldn't articulate precisely what I meant—mainly because I didn't know what I meant, other than feeling concerned—the conversation turned to other things. But I was still thinking about it on Monday morning.

"Maybe it wasn't the questions themselves," I told Eddie. Rafe had already left, and I was doing the breakfast dishes before I headed downtown to meet up with Pam Fazio, an arrangement we'd made via text the day before. "It was the fear underneath the questions. I heard it even if Rafe didn't."

Eddie, who was sleeping on a fuzzy blanket next to the heat register, yawned and curled himself into an Eddie-size ball. So much for his input.

I was still wondering about it when I walked up to the Coffee Corner. Pam was already sitting at a sidewalk table. After she'd abandoned corporate life, Pam had vowed to have her morning coffee outside every single day the rest of her life. As far as I knew, she'd done so, if you considered her glassed-in front porch as outside during times of rain and snow, which I did.

"Be right there," I said, and three minutes later I sat down across from her with a happy amount of caffeine. "Is it a generational thing?" I asked.

"Probably," she said. "But it might be nice to know what we're talking about."

"Exactly." I tipped my coffee at her and tried to think of something to say that would make at least a little bit of sense. "Talking. Do younger people talk faster than we do?"

Pam, who was twenty years my senior, raised one eyebrow. "How young? There was a two-year-old in the store the other day talking so fast I wasn't sure what language he was speaking."

I shook my head. "Never mind. Off topic." Sort of. "We're supposed to be discussing a downtown donation for Whippy. Have you talked to Colleen about it?" Colleen, Whippy's wife, was one of Pam's good friends.

"No." Pam sighed. "I mean, yes, I've talked to her, but I didn't want to bring this up. Too soon."

Though I understood that completely, if we were going to ask downtown people for donations, we needed to do it before the summer season got rolling. "His obituary mentioned donations to the community foundation. We could just do that." The obituary also noted his crossword puzzle habit and his love of the outdoors and the Detroit Red Wings. It had also mentioned that a memorial service would

be held in July, and I'd already added it to my calendar.

"Sure," Pam said, "but I think it would be a nice
remembrance to come up with some kind of project."

That was a great idea, and I said so.

"Wasn't me." She shook her head. "It was my
sister. She did that for her father-in-law. They contacted the town where he lived and asked about a
gift. There was a list of things to buy, preapproved
by the city council."

"Do we have anything like that here?" I looked
around as if a list might magically materialize.

"Nope. But the county's park system does." She
sounded a bit smug, but it was a well-deserved
smugness.

"You are brilliant. How do we want to do this? I
suppose we could bring a list when we go around
asking for donations. Or just tell people some of the
things on the list and say we'll choose whatever best
fits the final collection amount?" I frowned, thinking of more possibilities. "But what if we want to
buy two of something? Or two different things?"

Pam tossed a wadded-up napkin at me. "Stop.
You are making this way harder than it has to be."

"I've heard that before."

"Such a surprise. All we have to do is say we're
collecting for a capital donation to the parks, and
we'll send a photo of what's purchased to everyone
who donates."

"Genius." I looked at her with admiration.

"Thank you, thank you," she said, nodding gra-
ciously. "Now. We have to make sure to approach
everyone, but let's make it easy on ourselves and
just talk to the people we come across. After a

week, if we haven't hit everyone, we can make special stops."

From my backpack, I extracted the list of downtown businesses I'd assembled. "I uploaded this to the cloud so we can both keep track, but do you see anyone I missed?"

Pam scanned the names, then looked up. "Here comes one now," she said, putting the paper down. "Hey, Dan. Happy Monday."

Dan Calhoun, owner of the store next to Whippy's, nodded. "Pam. Minnie. Working on something, are you?"

"We're starting a collection," I said, "for a tribute to Whippy. The county parks department has a list of things they need, and we're taking donations to buy something in his memory."

"Count me out." Dan glanced at the list of names. "Maybe I'll be the only one who doesn't donate, but no way will I give any of my hard-earned money to glorify Whippy Henika!"

By that time, he was almost shouting. He gave us a hard glare, then stalked off, his hands in fists.

Pam and I, our mouths gaping open, stared after him.

"What was that all about?" Pam asked.

"No idea."

But I was going to find out.

Chapter 9

By the time I needed to head up to the library, Pam and I had donations from half a dozen business owners and pledges from a dozen more.

"Not a bad morning's work," Pam said, holding up her fist for a knuckle bump. "Well done, us."

I smiled. It had been rewarding to see how many people were willing to donate. So far, Dan Calhoun was indeed the only holdout. "I'll update the online list at lunch today."

Which meant thoughts of Whippy and murder and Toby Guinn and Kurt and Dan and Rene bounced around in my head all morning long, going from one to the other at the speed of Minnie's brain.

When the end of my working day started to draw nigh, I popped upstairs to Graydon's office, asking if he minded me leaving a couple of hours early.

He looked up from his computer screen. "Only if you commit to working two extra hours later this week. Oh, wait. You're salaried for a forty-hour week but regularly work at least fifty. Never mind, then. Fly and be free." He twiddled his fingers at me, and I left, thinking once again that I had the best boss in the world.

I hurried home, grabbing a donation commitment from Cookie Tom on the way, and jumped in my car without even going in the house. What I needed to do was talk to Leah again. I had no idea where she lived, so I hoped to catch her as she left the school.

When I pulled into the school parking lot, the buses were rolling out. I parked in an empty slot and tapped the steering wheel, deciding on next steps. I didn't have her cell number, so should I go in or wait outside? How long did teachers stay in their classrooms after the kids had left? There were so many things I didn't know.

Once again, procrastination paid off. I'd just unbuckled my seat belt, having decided to go in, when Leah came outside. She was carrying two canvas totes that had to be on the heavy side, given the pained way she was walking.

I jumped out of the car and hurried her way. "Need some help?"

"Minnie! What are you doing here? If you could open the back end of my car, the key fob is in that bag there . . ."

I unlocked her small SUV and fiddled with the fob buttons, raising its back door without making the car alarm go off—hooray!—and Leah pushed the bags inside. "Wow, this parking lot is farther from my classroom than I thought!" She flexed her hands. "I almost lost all feeling in my fingers."

"Lots of homework to grade tonight?"

She laughed. "No, I'm getting a jump on the end-of-the-year classroom cleanout. That was a bunch of winter books and project materials I'm ready to get rid of. There's a group of homeschooling parents who are always interested in new materials." She took her keys back. "I have to go back in for another load."

"Happy to help. I was hoping you had a minute to talk about . . . about Whippy and the, um, the situation."

Leah looked around and saw what I had seen, a group of teachers walking toward the parking lot.

"Sure," she said. "It's nice out. Let's go over here."

I followed her to a playground sized to make five-foot me feel big. With a wide inside smile, I sat on a belt swing and toed myself back and forth, back and forth.

After a few contented arcs, I said, "I don't want to upset you, so if you don't want to talk about this, you'll say so, right?" I waited until she nodded. "Okay. The biggest question I have is why you and your ex-husband are the only ones who know you've been in contact with your birth father." Well, Leah and Kurt and now me, but I didn't correct myself. "Why haven't you told your parents?"

Leah, who'd sat in the swing next to me, turned in a circle, rubbing her swing's chains against each other in a metallic screech.

"It's my dad," she said finally. "Mom and Dad are in their seventies, and Dad's health is a mess. Heart problems, digestive issues, high blood pressure, vertigo." She sighed. "Mom does her best to take care of him, but it's wearing her out. They moved downstate to be closer to the university hospital just after my divorce. The last thing I want to do is make things harder for them, and I'm afraid . . ."

Her voice trailed off. But I knew where she was going.

"And you're afraid telling them you've met your birth father would be an additional stressor. Might even be something that puts your dad's health on a downward path."

Leah was leaning forward, far enough that her hair covered her face, hiding her expression. "I can't tell them right now," she said quietly. "Maybe not ever. They're great and I don't want to hurt them. What would be the point of telling them? I don't see how anything good could come of it."

"Sure," I said. "I understand."

And I did. But I also understood something else, that Leah was determined to keep her parents in the dark about her contact with Whippy. Could that have anything to do with the murder? I didn't see how, but . . . maybe?

I looked at Rafe across the grocery store's selection of bananas. "There's something I need to tell you."

"You don't like bananas and never have? Now you tell me." He picked up the bunch he'd just placed in our cart.

"Put those back. I like bananas just fine." As long as the skins weren't green or dotted with more than half a dozen spots of brown. "It's about—"

"Hello, Minnie. And you must be Rafe." Carolyn Mathews, the new library board member I'd had coffee with the other day, smiled at us. "Fancy meeting you here."

I made the introductions and said, nodding at her, "So, you finally found time to get a haircut? Looks nice."

"Had a family photo shoot last weekend, and my daughter said I had to get an updated look or she would just die of embarrassment." She fluffed her now super-short brown hair, making some of the fine strands stick out with static electricity. "Not sure it's an improvement, but I'm told I'm now stylish, so there's that."

Rafe said, "Mallory is your daughter, isn't she? And Spencer is your son. Nice kids."

She blinked. "How did . . . Oh, that's right." Her face, which had gone tight, brightened. "You're Mr. Niswander. Of course. The things I forget these days! You two are getting married soon, aren't you? July? No, that's my niece." She shook her head. "I've shoved too many things into my head. Retrieval is a problem."

Laughing, I said, "We need mental search engines. Rafe and I are getting married in September."

"Lovely time of year for a wedding," she said, smiling approval at our choice. "And now I have to find something to feed the family that doesn't involve actual cooking."

"The deli section?" I asked. "We went there first. The broccoli salad looks great, and there's always macaroni and cheese."

Carolyn smiled. "A woman after my own heart." She bustled off, and Rafe and I went back to fruit selection. I was sure that during our conversation with Carolyn, two additional brown spots had formed on the bananas Rafe had chosen. Feeling slightly guilty, I plucked them out of the grocery cart, put them back on the heap, and chose a better bunch.

Rafe eyed the rejected bananas, glanced at the ones in our cart, then shrugged. "Anyway. You had something to tell me?"

I started to say something but stopped and looked around. Though there weren't many shoppers, there were enough to make me rethink the timing of this conversation. "It's a confidential thing," I said.

"My favorite." Rafe grinned. "Was somebody at the library bad? Let me guess. It was Lloyd Goodwin. He finally got tired of Josh jingling the coins in his pants pockets and snapped. He whacked Josh over the head with his cane until Josh promised to never do it again."

Imagining the kindly and nearly eighty-year-old Mr. Goodwin using his cane on anyone exceeded my powers of imagination. "No," I said. "Let's wait until we're outside."

And so it wasn't until we were loading the truck's rear seat with groceries that I said, "Okay. It's about Leah Wasson." On the playground swings, I'd asked her how she felt about me sharing the identity of her birth father with Rafe. I'd told her I'd understand if she didn't want me to but that I didn't like keeping secrets from him. She'd been quiet a moment, then nodded, saying that she trusted Rafe to keep a confidence.

Rafe looked at me. "This sounds serious."

"It is."

After the groceries were in and the cart was tucked into its slot, we climbed into the truck and I started talking. It took time to tell the whole story from start to finish, partly because I kept forgetting important pieces and had to backtrack more than once, and at the end, the groceries were away and we were sitting on the living room couch.

"So," I said, gusting out a deep breath, "to summarize: Whippy was Leah's birth father. She doesn't know who her birth mother is. And she's not telling her parents about any of it."

"To protect her dad," Rafe said.

I snuggled up to his side. He put his arm around me, and I sank into his all-around warmth. "Yes."

"Leah is a good person."

I nodded, feeling the flannel of his shirt move up and down my cheek.

And we held each other tight.

I woke the next morning with a brand-new idea. "What do you think?" I asked Eddie. It had taken me a few minutes to find him, but an Eddie-size cat can't stay invisible forever. He'd insinuated most of himself underneath the warm fuzzy couch throw blanket at the foot of the bed, and the only reason I'd found him was because his right hind leg had been left out in the cold.

"Mrr."

His voice was muffled, coming as it was from underneath a thick layer of fleece.

"You're not depriving yourself of oxygen, are you?" I lifted the blanket and peered underneath. Eddie lifted his head and peered back.

"Mrr."

"I'll take that as you being fine." I replaced the blanket, making sure to cover his back leg. "Did you hear anything I was saying the last five minutes? Because even though I didn't know where you were, I assumed you were listening."

What I heard next was the unmistakable rumbling of Eddie purrs.

"So much for us having a bond." I patted the blanket's head. "Don't forget, we have to leave in a few minutes. I'll be in my office all day working on the strategic plan and on the book bike proposal. It'll be you and Julia and Hunter in the bookmobile, so I hope you—"

Eddie scooted out of his warm nest, jumped to the floor, and galloped away. Seconds later I heard the unmistakable sound of my cat's body sliding into his carrier and thumping into its back wall.

"So I hope you won't miss me too much!" I called out.

"Mrr!" he called back.

"Back at you," I said, and then, once I got to the library, spent a regrettable amount of time wondering whether or not Eddie and I were losing the magic in our relationship. It wasn't anything I could ask anyone ever, because I was sure it would sound even loonier out loud than it did in my head, so I kept mentally chewing it over and feeling silly the entire time.

"What's the matter?" Holly Terpening—library clerk, mother of two, fellow thirty-something, and good friend—came into my office, holding out a brownie-laden napkin. "Here. Whatever it is, this will make it all better. New try at the old recipe, includes butterscotch chips."

I'd been staring at my computer screen with my chin in my hands, but as the scent of still-warm brownies wafted my way, I sat up straight and held out my hands. "That smells fantastic. Thanks. Say, do you have a minute?"

Holly sat in the open chair. "I have to unlock the doors at ten, so I only have a few minutes. What's up? Wait, let me guess. Josh got behind with updating the firewall software, and now we have a ransomware demand of half a million dollars from a thirteen-year-old in an Eastern European country no one has ever heard of."

I laughed. Holly and Josh had a very sibling-like relationship, and to the best of my knowledge, neither one had ever missed an opportunity to dig at the other. "Nothing to do with the library."

"Oh?" Holly frowned. "That brownie is just sitting there getting cold. Eat."

"Enabler." I took a bite and made happy groany noises. "And I love you for it." After another bite went into my stomach, I said, "It's about adoption." My middle-of-the night insight was to ask questions of people who I knew had dealt with adoption, and Holly was first on the list.

"Wow, that was not where I thought this was going." Holly sat back and studied me. "You and Rafe are . . ."

"What?" I felt a brownie crumb fall off my upper lip. "No! I mean, who knows, maybe someday, but not now. We're not even married yet, we're not thinking about children." Hadn't even talked about kids, other than approving the general idea of having a couple. Someday.

Holly smiled. "You're so cute when you're embarrassed."

"Stop that." I put my hand to my cheek. Sure enough, there was heat. For crying out loud. "My adoption questions are the other way around, about adult adoptees finding birth parents. I know your brother was adopted, so I was just wondering how much you could tell me about how that works."

"Not a whole lot." Absently, Holly twirled a lock of her hair. "After me, Mom couldn't have any more kids, so she and Dad decided to adopt. Took a couple of years from start to finish, if I remember right. My brother's birth mother was from downstate, and she chose Mom and Dad because she wanted her baby to grow up in a small town."

"So he's known his birth mother from the beginning?"

"Sure." Holly nodded. "When he was a kid, she used to drive up here once or twice a year. I don't think he's seen her in a while, but she still sends him a birthday card and a Christmas card. It was an open adoption. I can get you the name of the agency, if you want."

"What about the birth father? Is he in your brother's life?"

"Not really. There were a few birthday cards and presents early on, but I don't think my brother has had anything from him in years."

"Do you think this is a typical experience for people who were adopted?"

Holly gave me a long look. "Are you going to tell me why you're asking all these questions?"

I hemmed and hawed. She was not going to take this well, but there wasn't any alternative—not an ethical one, at least. "Sorry, but I can't. It's someone else's thing, not mine."

After a long moment, she nodded. "Yeah, I get it."

"You . . . do?"

"Sure. For lots of people, adoption is a very private thing, even in this non-privacy age of no secrets for anyone, anywhere, ever." She smiled. "All I can tell you about my brother's adoption is how he was adopted." She glanced at my wall clock and jumped up. "We can talk more about this later, but I have to go."

I watched her hurry away, thinking that she was probably right. I did some quick browser research on my phone regarding adoption and came to the same, and in retrospect not very surprising, conclusion: Every adoption was a story, and every story was unique.

Which led me to . . . what?

Nothing, really. But there was one hard conclusion I'd come to: that if I learned the identity of Leah's birth mother, I didn't have to share the knowledge with anyone. I could keep the secret to myself.

The big question was whether or not any of this had anything to do with Whippy's death. Leah was still reluctant to tell the police that Whippy had been her birth father, so looking into the possibility of a connection was up to me.

Chapter 10

I spent the rest of the morning doing my best to shove information into my brain—looking on the Internet for strategic plans from other libraries, looking at plans from completely different kinds of entities, while also trying to remember if I'd learned anything about strategic planning in graduate school. (News flash: Either I didn't learn anything, or I didn't remember.) But thanks to search engines and friends at other libraries, I found new ideas all over the place. By noon I was actually getting a little excited about it, in a geeky library sort of way.

With possibilities galore bouncing around in my head, I jogged up the stairs and knocked on Graydon's office doorframe.

He looked up, a little dazed, from a stapled set of papers. I inched forward to see what he was working on. Ah. It looked like the contract for next winter's snowplowing services. Something absolutely necessary but heavy with details about gas prices, snowfall amounts per plow, and road salt substitutes. I almost asked if he was having fun with it but decided it would be rubbing salt—Hah! Salt, get it?—in his wounds, so I kept my happiness that I was the assistant director, and not the director, all to myself.

Graydon laid the contract on his desk. "If you're here to ask about leaving early again, you should start looking for another job."

I heaved a dramatic sigh based on Julia's best. "Okay, but you're going to miss me."

His face froze in place. "That was a joke," he said. "Please tell me you're joking."

"Okay, I'm joking."

His shoulders slumped just as dramatically as I'd sighed. "Thank goodness. I don't know who else I'd get to work as hard as you do for as little money as you earn."

"And who else would get as excited as I am about the strategic plan?" I asked, smiling.

"You are? I mean, that's great." Graydon tapped the contract. "The prices for a renewal snowplowing contract went sky-high. The Finance Committee meets tomorrow, and I'm going to recommend that we do a request for proposals." He looked at the papers and grimaced. "And you know what that means."

What it meant was a lot of work. For Graydon. His happy assistant said, "If you want, I can keep working on the strategic plan by myself. I can put together a draft and get it to you next week."

He nodded. "Thanks. Let's do that." I started to leave, but he said, "How about that other thing you're working on?"

"Other thing?" I blinked.

"Your presentation to the board."

Still no reaction from Minnie's side of the desk.

"On the book bike."

"Right," I said brightly. "On it. I'm absolutely on it." Not literally, of course, because I was pretty sure the bike was still in Cody's shop. I'd been holding out a forlorn hope that the bike wouldn't be roadworthy and that I could forget the whole thing. Sadly, Cody had texted me the other day that all it needed was a little maintenance. The wheels had to be trued up and the brakes greased, and if I was okay with waiting a couple of weeks, he'd do it for free.

I harbored a small, forlorn hope that the two weeks would turn into months. But it turned out that Cody loved the book bike concept. Was excited about getting it on the road and seeing it in action. I'd pressed him to make sure all the bike parts were in good working order and that I'd be fine with waiting months—years, even—if that's what it took to get the right parts, but he'd shaken his head and said he'd get it roadworthy before Memorial Day if he had to drive downstate for parts himself.

Omitting the bits about me hoping for a long delay, I told all that to Graydon.

"Sounds good," he said. "So this afternoon, I take it you'll be working on the board presentation."

My inside self drooped into melancholy misery. My outside self said, in perky tones, "You bet. Totally my plan."

Graydon laughed. "You are a horrible liar. Get out of here."

The opinion that I did not do well in the lying department was one I'd heard many times before.

Although I could see uses for improved lie-telling, I didn't anticipate me spending much time working on it. "I'll show you a draft early next week."

"Book bike has priority over the strategic plan." His attention was already back to the contract, but without looking up, he added, "And if you keep making that face, it might freeze that way."

I laughed, wiped my expression clear of its grimace, and headed downstairs to the break room, because somehow, it was already time for lunch.

"Hey." Holly looked up from the sandwich she was eating. "Question for you. We had a slow morning out front, so I got to thinking about this morning and the adoption stuff."

"Okay." I opened the refrigerator, took out my leftovers, and put them in the microwave.

"Does this have anything to do with Whippy's murder?"

Whatever button I pushed on the microwave was the wrong one. Loud beeps filled the small room, and I stabbed at the control panel frantically until they stopped. "Um, why do you ask?" Out of the corner of my eye, I saw her shrug.

"No real reason. It's just that you've been involved in finding murderers before, so I wondered."

Since I knew full well my lying limitations, I said, "As far as I know, there's no connection." Which was the truth. Not anywhere near the whole truth, but the truth nonetheless.

Holly was about to ask more questions, so I said, "Graydon is starting to push me on the book bike presentation."

I had, in fact, started working on it. I'd asked folks on the Association of Bookmobile and Outreach Services LISTSERV for ideas and trolled the Internet for ideas all over the world. My ABOS buddies had recommended developing policies, which wasn't my idea of fun, but I saw the need and added the task to my to-do list. Still, I needed to tailor whatever we did to our resources and needs, and one way to do that was by talking to everyone.

"Do you have any ideas?" I asked.

"Lots," Josh said, coming into the room. "Which ones do you want today?"

"About the book bike." I opened the microwave door and stirred the contents of my container. "How to make it work for us. What would be perfect would be for someone on the staff to volunteer to try it out, see how it goes. What do you think?" I asked, turning around, then muttered, "You have got to be kidding."

Because the room was empty.

My friends had fled.

The more I thought about things, the more I thought I needed to work harder to help Leah. "Right now," I said to Rafe over a massive pile of shredded bark, "I don't feel as if I'm getting anywhere."

The landscape guys had been told to offload our order next to the driveway, but they must not have understood what the word "next" meant, because all five cubic yards of it was smack in the middle of the driveway, right in front of the garage door. Until it was moved, Rafe couldn't get his truck into the garage, and I couldn't get my car out.

Rafe had called his guy at the landscape company and been told it would be two days before they could get back. So he said we'd move it ourselves and negotiated a price reduction. Not a big enough one, given the number of blisters that were forming underneath my work gloves, but I supposed that physical activity was good for me. Somehow. Probably.

"Okay," Rafe said. "Tell me who's on the suspect list. And why each one is on it."

I put my shovel down and counted on my fingers. "Toby Guinn, the burglar, because Whippy caught him in the act. Kurt, Leah's ex, as a way to punish her. Rene Kinney, no known motive, but she clearly hated Whippy. Dan Calhoun, again no known motive, because he also seemed to have a problem with Whippy."

Rafe leaned on his pitchfork. "Seems like you have some motivations to figure out."

"Investigations have to start somewhere," I said.

"And what's your starting point?"

I'd already decided. "Kurt Wasson. That's who Leah is pointing to, so I want to work on him first. Maybe it'll be easy to find an alibi for him, and he'll be the first suspect crossed off the list." I mimicked doing so.

Rafe returned to pitching bark. "What if it's not easy?"

Since I fully expected that it wouldn't be, I was ready. "Then I'll work harder. Dig deeper."

"How about some digging right here?" Rafe used his chin to point.

Sighing, I picked up my shovel, but with both of us working, the job really didn't take that long. And as a bonus, while shoveling, I planned my next investigative step.

"The Internet is a powerful thing," I said to Eddie, flexing my fingers to ease the shovel-induced stiffness. Rafe was in the shower to rinse off, so I was taking the opportunity to implement step number one.

"Mrr!" Eddie jumped on the kitchen stool next to me.

"Hey, quit that." I batted away the white paw that was tapping at my laptop's keyboard. "Not a cat toy. Now. Let's see what we can find, eh?"

"Mrr."

"Glad you agree."

First was the easy stuff. After a few minutes of poking around the usual suspects—Facebook, Twitter, and Instagram—I came to the reluctant conclusion that Kurt Wasson was one of those people who didn't do social media.

"Good for you," I said. But in a sarcastic way, because a single post on Facebook about where he'd been the night Whippy died would have been helpful. Still, my efforts weren't over yet. Not by a long shot.

One website told me there were only three men named Kurt Wasson in the whole country. "Happy day," I said. If he'd been named Bill Smith, the job would be a lot harder. I did a general search and came up with a few hits about his now defunct plumbing business.

"You are so dumb," I told myself, and opened a review website for contractors. "North Lakes Plumbing," I said, typing in the name. "Think we'll find anything worth finding?"

"Mrr," Eddie said, jumping down.

"You're probably right. Still, it doesn't hurt to look. Hey, what are you doing? Get off the counter, what are you— No, getting in the sink doesn't count as getting off the counter." I walked over, picked him up, and dropped him onto the floor. "Now stay there."

"Mrr!"

"Love you, too." I went back to the computer. "Let's see what we have here." I scrolled and clicked, scrolled and clicked. There were some complaints about plumbing projects taking too long and a few people grousing about final bills being higher than the estimates, but in general, the company had good reviews.

The anonymity of the posts was frustrating; if even a few of the customers had left their real names, I might have been able to track them down and . . .

"Hang on." I drummed my fingers on the counter. Maybe I was doing the typical Minnie thing and making this harder than it needed to be.

I took Rafe's phone from the counter and looked for the phone number of his friend Bob. Unfortunately, Rafe had twelve guys named Bob in his contact list, most of them with no last names.

"Seriously?" I showed the phone to Rafe, who had just returned downstairs. "How do you keep them all straight?"

"Do you really want to know?"

"I want to talk to the Bob who's building that house we went to. About Kurt."

Rafe scrolled through his Bobs. "Here you go." He tapped the number. "Have at it," he said, handing me the phone.

"Hey, Bob," I said when he picked up. "This is Minnie, Rafe Niswander's fiancée . . . Doing fine, thanks. How about yourself? Say, if you have a second, I have a couple more questions about North Lakes and Kurt. Okay, great. I work for the library, and we're always interested in quality contractors, so I was wondering if you know how much commercial work they do. I could ask them myself, but I think talking to customers gets a more honest . . . Oh, good . . . Okay . . . That's great information. Thanks."

I handed the phone back to Rafe.

"What's the matter?" he asked. "You look like you just swallowed an Eddie hair."

"According to Bob," I said slowly, "just before he was killed, Whippy hired North Lakes to do a job at his store. And Kurt was doing the work."

"This time it's going to be different, right?"

"Mrr," Eddie said.

"Please tell me you're not just saying that. Tell me you really mean it. That this time you are not going to get all freaked out. Tell me that you and the twins are going to work together to forge a lasting and permanent relationship, because otherwise it's going to strain a friendship that has lasted for decades, and I'm sure you don't want that to happen, do you?"

"Mrr," my cat said softly, ducking his head and rubbing it against his front legs.

"Glad to hear it." My confidence that he'd understood a single word I'd said was in the zero to don't-be-ridiculous range, but I appreciated his response.

"Now, I have the entire day off—yes, I can do that every once in a while in the middle of the week because I'm the one who makes the schedule—and this morning Kristen is bringing Eloise and Cooper,

I mean Lloyd, over. This afternoon I have other plans. No, you won't be involved in the afternoon events, but I promise to tell you everything that happens."

My rambling narrative, as so often happened, soothed Eddie to the point that he was snoring. I wasn't always sure how to interpret that. Was my voice a calming influence, or did he just find me boring?

I gave him a long patting pet, and he added a low purr to the snore, something that I wasn't sure was possible.

Before I could pull out my phone to find out, the doorbell rang. On the plus side, Eddie didn't so much as twitch. On the downside, I could hear indications of an unhappy infant coming from the other side of the door.

"Can you take her?" Kristen said, thrusting a baby carrier at me. "Cooper is fussing. He'll be fine if I take him for a walk. I'll be back in five minutes."

I gaped at her retreating back. "Umm, Kristen?"

"Five minutes!" she called, and was out on the sidewalk.

"Um." I looked down at the tiny human. "So how are you doing, Eloise?"

Her eyes, the bluest of blues, blinked at me. She waved one impossibly small fist in my direction.

"Right." I leaned out, looking for Kristen, but she was already out of sight. Five minutes. I could do five minutes. Though I was certain I'd never been alone with a baby before in my entire life, I was fairly sure even I couldn't permanently mess up a kid that fast.

"Your mom is headed toward the marina." I shut the front door with my foot and dabbed at the tiny bubbles forming at the corner of Eloise's teensy mouth with the corner of her yellow blanket. The second I did so, I froze. Was that okay? Could I do that? I needed to tell Kristen what I'd done when she got back. She'd probably want to wash the blanket right away. What if I'd spread germs around? What if I'd infected Eloise with something horrible?

I looked down at Eloise, and she looked up at me. Clearly, I was supposed be doing something, but I had no idea what.

Fighting down panic, I said, "This is probably supposed to be a deep dark secret, but I'm going to break the bonds of friendship. Promise you won't tell your brother, okay? This has to stay between us girls."

Eloise wasn't crying, but she wasn't exactly cooing and smiling, either. Maybe if I kept on with my rambling babble, she'd do an Eddie and fall asleep.

"Excellent. The vow of silence is a good touch." I carried her into the living room, set the carrier on the coffee table, and sat on the edge of the couch. "So here's the secret." I looked left and right in an exaggerated manner. I couldn't remember what Kristen had said about the age of babies when they started focusing on objects and tracking them but figured better safe than sorry.

"Your mom," I whispered loudly, "is afraid of boats. Yep. Terrified. Always has been. She wouldn't even go on the docked houseboat if she could avoid it. What I don't know is why she's so scared. She says she was born that way. Maybe that's true, but maybe something happened when she was too little to remember. I've never thought about asking her parents," I mused. "Although . . . when you get a little older, maybe next year, maybe you could ask. They might give you a straight answer, and—Eddie, what are you doing?"

I could see the tips of my cat's ears rising, Batman-like, above the far side of the coffee table. Then I saw the top of his head, his eyes, whiskers, and finally his chin. "Eddie," I said sternly, "you be good."

My cautionary tone went right over his head. The *thump* as he landed on top of the table startled Eloise. Her wide eyes opened even wider and her little mouth opened in an O.

"Oh, boy." I leaned forward and reached out. "Eddie. Down."

He backed away from my grasp and scooted around to the other side of the table. "Mrr?" he said, approaching Eloise's carrier, positioning himself just far enough away that I couldn't reach him.

Eloise, who had been vaguely studying me, turned her head and found herself facing a creature who weighed more than she did, who was covered with fur, and who was staring at her with an unblinking yellow intensity.

The result was inevitable.

I helped Kristen install both her wailing daughter and her sleeping son back into her vehicle. "Sorry about that."

"What happened?" Kristen asked. "Do you know?"

I hesitated, not wanting to tell on Eddie but also

not wanting to keep anything important from my best friend, especially not anything about her children. So what was important about the little episode? "New place, new faces. You know I don't know nothing about no babies."

She laughed at the *Gone with the Wind* misquote. "Past time for you to learn, I'd say."

I shut the door and waved all three of them off on whatever their next adventure might be. The adventure I'd scheduled next—if you can schedule something like that, which I was fairly sure you couldn't—was a trip to the Tonedagana County Courthouse. If you knew where to look on the county's website, you could find court dockets, and ever since Ash had said they were investigating Toby Guinn, I'd been keeping an eye on what was going on in district court. This was the day he was being arraigned, and I'd decided to attend. I'd also decided to make it a double-duty stop and see what I could find out about birth certificates.

On my way out of the library, I'd stopped at the front desk, and Donna, seventy-something part-time library clerk, part-time marathon runner, and source of a vast amount of random knowledge, had said I should go to the clerk's office for any and all governmental information. "If the clerk's office doesn't know," she'd said confidentially, "they'll know who does."

And so, at a long oak counter scarred with generations of scratches, I learned from a woman who reminded me of my mother that you couldn't just walk in and get someone's birth certificate.

"Unless they're dead, of course," she said. "Then anyone can request a copy."

It made sense. "So you have to be the person on the birth certificate, one of the parents named on it, or the person's guardian?"

Sheryl, for that was the name of my new friend, nodded. "Or the person's attorney."

"How about adoption information?"

She gave me a hard questioning sort of look, so I quickly added, "I work at the library and I get questions like this all the time." Essentially true. "So I thought I'd come here and learn the facts from the source instead of trusting the Internet."

Laughing, she said, "Bless you. But adoption is complicated."

No surprise there. "How so?" I asked.

"Well, there are open and closed adoptions, and there are multiple adoption agencies for both kinds. To get closed adoption records, you have to be the adopted person, the adoptive parents if it's a minor, a biological parent, or a biological sibling. Whoever it is should probably contact the court where the adoption happened."

"Um, court?"

"Family Division of the Circuit Court," she said, nodding. "Adoption day is one of the happiest days on the court docket."

Which was when I remembered seeing pictures in the newspaper of smiling parents, kids, court staff, and judges. I made a mental note to try to see that in person someday and thanked her for her time, adding, "And if anyone asks me anything government-like, I'll tell them the clerk's office is the place to go."

"We're here to help," she said cheerfully, and

looked behind me. "Good morning. How can I help you today?"

I stepped back from the counter and let the fifty-ish man take my place. The wall clock said I had ten minutes until my next scheduled event. Plenty of time, assuming that I remembered how to find the district courtroom.

And one or two wrong turns and a short unexpected tour of the county's Equalization Department later, I read the sign for proper court decorum posted on the door. For the tenth time, I checked to make sure my cell phone was off—because annoying a judge was not on any of my written or unwritten to-do lists—and entered.

The only empty seat was on a bench at the very front of the courtroom, with a much better view of the proceedings than I wanted. I hesitated, then slid in next to a woman with short salt-and-pepper hair who was sitting with a woman about my age and a man of about thirty. Whippy's wife and children.

The judge sat at a high desk, her short blond hair a stark contrast to her black robe. Reading glasses were perched on the end of her nose, and she was studying the young man in front of her. He was standing at a small podium, looking as if he'd lost every friend he'd ever had, and dressed in an orange jumpsuit that managed to sag in every direction.

"Are you Tobias Robert Guinn?" the judge asked.

"That's me."

"Please respond yes or no."

Toby swallowed. "Um, yes. Your Honor."

"Please state your address and phone number." After he did so, there was some tapping on a computer tablet, then she asked, "Do you understand the charges made against you?"

Another murmured yes from Toby.

"I'm now going to read each of the charges. For each one, the court needs to hear how you are going to plead, either guilty or not guilty. Do you understand?"

"Yes, ma'am."

She gave him a long, measured look, then nodded sharply. "All right then. The first charge is breaking and entering at the Tonco Convenience Store at 1513 Everett Street, Chilson, Michigan, on the night of April twenty-fifth. How do you plead?"

"Guilty, Your Honor," Toby said.

"The second charge is breaking and entering Lake Street Computers, 424 Lake Street, Chilson, Michigan, on the night of April twenty-eighth. How do you plead?"

"Guilty," he whispered.

The charges seemed to go on and on, but finally the judge looked up from her tablet. She took off her glasses and looked directly at Toby. "Mr. Guinn, the final charge against you is breaking and entering at Henika's Candy Emporium, 213 Main Street, Chilson, Michigan." She cited the date of the break-in, then asked, "How do you plead?"

The courtroom went quiet. Everyone was staring at Toby, waiting, watching, listening.

"Yeah, I stole stuff from those other places," he said. "But not from the candy store. That's, like, my favorite place ever since I was a kid. I'd never steal from Whippy." He rubbed at his eyes and I caught

a shine of tears. "I mean, that was the night somebody killed him, right?"

"Mr. Guinn," the judge said tersely. "I need to
hear you state your plea."

Toby stood tall, took a deep breath, and looked
straight at the judge. "Your Honor, I plead not guilty."

After the arraignment, I texted Ash that I was on my
way over to the sheriff's office and that I had to talk
to him. I must have sounded firm, even via text message, because he met me at the front door and, es-
chewing the interview room, took me back to the
office he shared with Detective Hal Inwood.

Ash waved me toward a vacant chair and held out
two empty mugs, raising his eyebrows. I nodded and
he vanished, reappearing less than a minute later
and handing me the one with added cream. There
are advantages to being friends with an ex-boyfriend.

I wrapped my hands around the ceramic mug,
remembering the strained faces of Whippy's wife
and children. "It was awful," I told Ash, shutting
my eyes. Which, instead of pushing away the memory, brought it back to life. "When Toby pled not
guilty to breaking and entering at the candy store,
Whippy's wife started just . . . just shrieking."

"The prosecutor called me half a second after
you texted. He said that same thing."

I opened my eyes and stared at the dense carpet.
After coughing away a catch in my throat, I sipped
my coffee and hoped it would give me strength and
calm. Or at least something that resembled strength
and calm to anyone who couldn't see my insides.
"What happens now? Is Toby going to be indicted
for murder, too?"

Ash leaned back in his chair. "At this point it's in the hands of the prosecutor's office. We'll work with him on putting together evidence for the breaking-and-entering trials. And we'll continue working on the murder investigation. It could take months, you know."

I did. The wheels of justice rolled on inexorably, but they didn't tend to roll very fast. "You would have charged him with Whippy's murder if you thought he was guilty, right?"

He eyed me through the rising steam of his coffee. "What are you getting at, Minnie? Do you think Toby is innocent?"

I did. Or at least I wasn't ready to assume he was a killer. "Just seems like a big leap from burglary and theft to murder. I mean, I could maybe see it if he'd been robbing people, but it wasn't even that."

Ash half smiled. "Look at you, all up on criminal justice terms."

It was only because I exerted the full strength of my character that I refrained from rolling my eyes. "It's pretty basic to know that robbing is taking something from a person and that burglary is entering a building illegally to commit a crime."

"Sure, but people are always mixing them up."

Whatever. But since I did not want this conversation to slide sideways into me getting all annoyed about male condescension—an annoyance that I, of course, had every right to feel—I tucked my emotions away to pull out later on an as-needed basis. "You know," I said, "Toby seemed sincere when he said the candy store was his favorite place. He admitted to the others. Why wouldn't he admit to that one, too?"

Ash laughed. "Big guess here, but I'll go out on a limb and say it's because if he admits to that, he's a huge step closer to being indicted for murder."

"Sure, but—"

Ash cut in. "Minnie, people in jail lie all the time. It's what they do."

"I get that." And I did. The people who ended up in county jails and in state and federal prisons didn't tend to get there by being honest and upright human beings. I sighed. "Sorry. It's just . . . does Toby have any specifics about why he couldn't have done it?"

"Minnie, you know I can't tell you that." His tone had the finality of a door shutting hard and being locked at the knob, dead-bolted, and chained.

I sipped my coffee and considered my immediate future. If Ash was going to go all serious detective on me, how was I going to get more information about what was going on? How was I going to help Leah if I couldn't get Ash to tell me anything that wasn't already public knowledge?

Then I remembered something.

"Dan Calhoun," I said, snapping my fingers. "Or Danny, if you're from here."

"He owns the T-shirt shop, right? What about him?"

"Was his store one of the ones Toby broke into?"

"No. Why?"

"Because the day of the—don't laugh—Trout Lily Festival—" I frowned. "Hang on. I told you not to laugh, and there you are, doing what I told you not to."

"Hard . . . not to," he said, still laughing. "Funniest thing ever, watching all those guys pull their boats into the launch parking lot, looking for where to register for the trout fishing contest. Classic. And no saying you don't think it's funny; I see that smirk."

I straightened out my face. The mix-up had been a Real Problem for some people. "Mitchell is still annoyed about it."

"Couple of years ago, Koyne would have been eating this up; now he's Mr. Business." Laughing even harder, Ash tapped his ear. "What's that I hear coming? Yup, watch out, everyone. The zombie apocalypse is nearly upon us."

While it was okay for Rafe and me to continue to be shocked by Mitchell's transformation, I found myself irritated by Ash's attitude. Of course, that could have been irritation heightened because of his refusal to talk about the investigation.

I ignored Ash and said, "At the festival, I saw Toby and Dan Calhoun together, talking."

"About what?" Ash asked, his eyes suddenly alert.

Mentally, I put myself back in time. Rafe and I had been talking with Pam Fazio and Dan. Then Dan had walked away and met up with Toby. Then . . . nothing. I shook my head.

"They were too far away to hear," I said, and Ash's interest level evaporated. "But," I remembered, "their body language wasn't friendly. Dan was kind of looming over Toby, and Toby was looking at the ground. Neither one of them looked happy."

"Going to need more than that," Ash said.

"Since Dan's store wasn't one Toby broke into, maybe Dan was the mastermind behind the thefts." I could feel my thoughts clicking, my words coming faster and faster. "Maybe Dan was checking out the stores first, telling Toby which ones to break into.

Maybe Dan was the one in Whippy's store that night. Maybe Whippy saw Dan in his store, and Dan is the killer, not Toby."

"And maybe," Ash said, "Moriarty is the mastermind, and we need to give Sherlock Holmes a call."

"Nice literary reference, but—"

"Hang on." Ash held up a hand. "I'll talk to Hal. It might make sense to interview Mr. Calhoun."

Might? On the inside, I scrunched my face at him. *Might?* Really? There was only one thing for me to do. Learn a lot more about Dan Calhoun. "Is there anything else you're going to tell me?" I asked.

He hesitated, then flipped open a file on his desk. "There is one thing. This was found at the murder scene. I showed this to Colleen Henika and her children, but none of them recognized it. The killer may have dropped it, or"—he shrugged—"a customer could have." He pulled a piece of paper from the file and pushed it across the desk. "Do you know who this is?"

I stared at the paper, which had a single color photo printed on it.

A baby photo. A girl, if the pink ribbons were any guide. With straight light brown hair and a smile that looked exactly like Leah's.

Chapter 11

Ash let me snap a picture of the photo. He made me vow, hand on heart, that if I figured out the baby's identity, I'd tell him straightaway, and I was absolutely fine with that. I'd connect with Leah as soon as I could, and if the baby was indeed her, I'd haul her into the sheriff's office myself.

After I left Ash, I stopped at the front desk to chat a bit with Chelsea, Ash's fiancée. The two of us made plans for the four of us the Saturday after Memorial Day. Hiking at the state park if the weather cooperated, card playing if it didn't, and cooking on the grill no matter what. "Subject to law enforcement needs, of course," Chelsea said. "And any middle school or library emergencies that might turn up."

"Understood," I said, and waved as I headed out the door and up the hill, thinking about middle school and library emergencies. Rafe, as principal, could get pulled away for a number of things. Student accident or illness. Teacher accident or illness.

An emergency meeting of the school board. But what library emergency could possibly make me leave my friends?

By the time I walked through the library's front door, I'd come up with two. One, something had happened to my boss. Two, something had happened to the building. Fire or pipes bursting and flooding everywhere or a horrific windstorm that broke windows and crashed trees into the building hard enough to tear great gaping holes in the roof and walls.

"Is something wrong?" Holly asked.

I whipped around to face my friend. "What makes you think there's anything wrong?"

"You. Staring up at the ceiling like that. You see a spiderweb?" She stood beside me and peered upward. "I don't see anything."

Since I wasn't about to admit I was looking for signs of pending roof failure for no good reason, I said, "Guess it was a trick of the light." Then, before she realized that since the day was starting out as one of those cloudy dreary days and there was no light trickiness to be had, I said cheerfully, "And what I really need is another cup of coffee. Any chance Kelsey didn't make it?"

Holly laughed. "None. Have fun with that."

I took a winding scenic route to the coffeepot, first upstairs to check on Graydon (who was on the phone when I did a slow walk past his office, and he sounded perfectly hale and hearty), then back downstairs to find Gareth Dibona, our custodian, the maintenance and all-around fix-it guy.

"Hey," I said, poking my head in the door of his lair.

Years ago, Gareth had managed to shoehorn a desk from the old library into a storage room corner. On top of the desk was a tidy stack of work orders, a computer that he used to manage the building's HVAC system, and absolutely nothing else. Either Gareth was the most organized maintenance guy ever, or all the stereotypes about them were wrong.

"How's everything looking today?" I asked. "Any problems we should warn Trent about before the next board meeting?"

Gareth looked away from the computer screen. "The VAV box above the conference room is sticking again."

I sighed. Heavily. "You know I have no clue what that means, yet you said it anyway."

"Well, yeah. How else am I going to keep this cushy job?" He grinned.

"Just so long as the roof doesn't fall in."

"No chance of that," he said, yawning and stretching his arms. "This building will last another hundred years, easy."

If Gareth wasn't worried, I wasn't going to, either. Yet . . . "What about the what's-it box? Is fixing it going to be expensive?"

Shrugging, he said, "What isn't? But it's budgeted."

"Good to know. Oh, by the way, I'm about to make a new pot of coffee."

He brightened. "I knew there was a reason I liked you."

"And here I thought it was because I listened to you talk about VAV boxes."

"That too."

With my concern about the two theoretical

library emergencies completely alleviated, I made my way to the break room. Since there was less than one mug of Kelsey's thick espresso-like brew left in the pot, I quashed all guilt and dumped it down the drain. I poked around on my phone while the fresh coffee dribbled down, and I learned two things.

One, that VAV stood for "variable air volume," which didn't leave me any more informed than when I didn't know what the acronym stood for, and two, that the website for Dan Calhoun's store was in dire need of an update. The "About" page referred to the store's twentieth anniversary, which had been more than three years ago, and even I could tell that the colors of the T-shirts you could buy were soooo ten minutes ago.

I guess the out-of-date website had more to do with the death of Dan's wife and almost nothing to do with Toby Guinn, the burglaries, or with Whippy's murder, but it was another piece of information to put into my tiny little brain.

But I had learned something from the website: Dan was not a Chilson native. For some reason I always thought he'd grown up in the area. Figured he'd gone to elementary school, graduated from high school, and—

"You're brilliant," I said out loud.

Because I'd thought of a way to, very quietly, discover the identity of Leah's birth mother.

My eating habits varied tremendously when I took the noon-to-eight shift at the library. Sometimes I ate a big lunch before going to work and had popcorn for dinner. Sometimes I had a brunch-type meal at home, and Rafe had dinner waiting for me at the end of the day. Sometimes I didn't eat anything except a bowl of morning cereal until I needed to leave the house, had no meal prepared to bring with me, and to avoid wasting away to a mini-Minnie, would stop for a sandwich either on the way in or when I took a break in late afternoon.

A couple of hours after I had my flash of brilliance about Leah's birth mother, I stopped at the front desk and told Holly that I needed to run out for some food.

"Forget to eat again, did you?"

Not exactly, but I didn't want to share too much about my true plans. Though Holly was a good friend, her understanding for my tendency to involve myself in other people's problems wasn't the deepest. "It's my new weight-loss strategy."

"Good story," she said, nodding. "I don't believe a word of it."

"And here I thought I was getting better at that fibbing thing."

Holly laughed. "You are still the worst liar I've ever met. Better work on that, now that you're getting married."

I smiled, but as I headed out into the murky dimness of the overly cloudy day, I thought about her offhand comment. Was it true? Did married people lie to each other on a regular basis? Was my marriage doomed before it even started because my ability to lie was pretty much nonexistent? Sure, I could be vague with the best of them, wasn't bad at ambiguity, and deflection was a skill I'd honed over the years, but telling outright untruths wasn't a strength.

Still thinking about my weaknesses, I opened the door of the *Chilson Gazette* offices and saw that its proprietor was sitting behind a desk pounding on a computer keyboard and frowning mightily.

"Hey, Camille," I said. "If you're on deadline, I can come back later."

Camille Pomeranz pushed herself back from the desk. "Nope. The more I keep poking sticks at this article, the worse it gets. What's up?"

"Question. Does a successful marriage mean you need to be a good liar?"

Camille, a fiftyish African American woman, had been married forever to a software engineer. The two of them had moved north a number of years ago, and other than my friends Barb and Russell "Cade" McCade, I couldn't think of a happier long-married couple.

She narrowed her eyes to thin slits. "Is that why you stopped in? Marriage counseling? Because I am not going there."

"Well, fine," I fake-huffed. "Moving on to my next question. Do you still have that archive of high school yearbooks?" A couple of years ago I'd done some hunting in the *Gazette*'s back issues and noticed the shelves upon shelves of the Chilson High School *Northern Lights*.

"Like those things are ever going anywhere." She laughed.

Exactly why I was there. "Can I take a look?"

"My casa is yours to do whatever you want with. But no blaming me if you have to take a shower afterward."

"Thanks. And duly noted." Once again, my boring library attire of neutral dress pants, unstructured jacket, and dressy T-shirt worked in my favor. As whoever it was said, function over fashion. "Do you know why there are so many copies up there?"

"No idea. Donations, I'd guess. You'd think one for each year would be enough, but once upon a time, somebody decided we should be the yearbook repository." She sighed heavily.

I nodded in sympathy. A Chilson-based publisher had gone out of business decades ago, and I was pretty sure every year someone donated more copies of their books to the library. Though we'd long since accumulated a full set of every book they'd ever published, it was hard to disappoint the shiny faces.

After thanking her, I climbed the narrow creaky stairs and used my phone flashlight to find the switch that turned on the long tubes of overhead fluorescent lights.

I blinked at the sudden burst of illumination and wended my way through the metal shelves filled with newspapers, books, boxes, and pieces of equipment whose function I could only guess at. The yearbooks were at the very back, and I tipped my head sideways to read the spines.

Whippy's obituary had said he'd been fifty-six. After using math and hardly any fingers, I found the appropriate shelf and counted six copies of the yearbook from his high school graduation year.

"Careful what you ask for," I murmured, and pulled one out. I first flipped to the senior photos and confirmed that William Henika had graduated that year. Whippy hadn't had a single hair on his head, but William sported a head of wavy center-parted hair that looked light gray in the black-and-white photo.

Blond? Whippy had been a blond? Not something I would have guessed.

With a slightly shifted worldview, I checked the end pages for signatures, but the pages were still pristine. So not helpful. I'd been looking for a yearbook crammed with handwritten comments and quotes and anecdotes, hoping to find something that indicated who Whippy might have been dating back in high school.

I put book number one back and moved on to book two. Same thing. Book three? Same. Book four had a scattering of notes, but nothing beyond "Have a great summer" and "School's out forever!"

"Still not helpful," I said. But maybe it wasn't a thing in Chilson to write long notes in yearbooks. Maybe my high school was the only one that did that. Or maybe it was just my friends. But since I was here, I might as well keep on looking.

Book five was also blank of personal notes, and I opened the last copy with little hope that I'd learn anything from the entire endeavor.

Yup. Blank.

I muttered my annoyance and started to put the book back on the shelf, then stopped. Maybe I'd learn something from looking through the yearbook itself. Anything was possible, right?

Since I was a person of order, I started at the front, reminding myself to look for the eighteen-year-old William, not the fifty-something Whippy. I paged through the yearbook, seeing lakeshore photos and candid photos. Class photos with William listed as being a member of the basketball and baseball teams. Sports photos, band photos, teacher photos . . . I flipped faster and faster. I was learning nothing, and—

And then I found it. Way in the back, just ahead of the advertisements, was another page of candid photos. Only this time they were captioned. And this time there was a photo of an impossibly young Whippy and a pretty young woman, hand in hand, gazing raptly into each other's eyes.

"Will and Lill," the caption said. "Three years and going strong!"

But Whippy's wife was Colleen. I imprinted the image of the girl's face in my memory, hurriedly paged back to the class photos, and scanned name after name until—there she was.

Lillie Siler.

"Are you Leah's birth mother?" I whispered to the photo.

But the only reply was the hum of the light fixtures.

Since I'd spent all of my mealtime at the *Gazette*, when I got back to the library, I ate a protein bar out of my emergency food stash and told my stomach to keep quiet, that I'd get it a nice big meal for dinner.

For once, my stomach actually paid attention to what my brain said, and I made it until eight with hardly a grumble. I locked the doors, did a building walk-through to check for stragglers, slid on my spring jacket, grabbed my backpack, and walked over to Fat Boys Pizza.

"Hey, Minnie."

I turned and saw two men sitting at the counter. Both were tall, wiry, and had the look of people who didn't consider that all the cautions about wearing sunblock applied to them. "Hey, Chris. Skeeter, when did you get here? I didn't know you were up already."

Chris Ballou managed Uncle Chip's Marina in the summer and worked at a marina in Georgia in the winter, hence his perpetual tan. Skeeter, whose real name I'd never heard, told story after outlandish story about his off-season occupation. No one knew exactly what he did for a living, but then again, no one actually cared.

"Yesterday," Skeeter said. "Say, Chris here is telling me you and Niswander still haven't told anyone where you're going to have your wedding reception."

"We're having a small party on Memorial Day. We'll tell everyone after that." I inched toward the register, where I could see my veggie sub was waiting.

"Sounds like something Niswander would say." Chris nodded, then tipped his head sideways at Skeeter. "Since we know you, and we know Niswander, we bet you don't have a place reserved at all, so we figured it was our job to come up with the perfect spot."

"Your job?" I asked, somehow not surprised they would think so.

"Well, yeah. Who better?"

Pretty much anyone.

"Anyway," Chris said, "it took a few beers, but we have the answer. Want to hear?"

"Giddy with anticipation," I said.

"That old barn out on Adams Road. You know, the one with the fieldstone silos? Barn weddings are a thing, right? And I know the property owner. It's been empty for years, and I bet he'd let you use it for next to nothing."

"Um . . ." There were so many thoughts in my head competing to be said first that they created an audio logjam. "That's an interesting idea," I finally said. "I'll talk to Rafe. Thanks for thinking of us."

"See?" Chris elbowed Skeeter. "Told you she'd like the idea."

Skeeter looked at me through half-closed eyes and smiled. "No way she wouldn't, right?"

"What I said." Chris thumped the counter. "When is it again? Got to make sure I leave the whole weekend open."

I cited the date, trying to remember if Chris and Skeeter had made the guest list, and started wondering if people still eloped. And if we eloped, who would be angriest: my mom, Aunt Frances, or Chris? Clearly, it was time to shift the subject.

"Say," I asked, "have you heard if Whippy's store is going to open this summer?"

Chris, who typically heard downtown gossip before it reached the status of full-blown rumor, shook his head. "The family's not saying anything other than they don't know yet."

"Makes sense. I get it." And I did. It wasn't much more than two weeks since Whippy's death; making an important decision in so short a time would be brutal.

Happily, the young lady at the register had put my order under the warmer. I paid and picked up the long white bag, but as I turned to go, I saw

Carolyn Mathews sitting at a booth in the back corner.

I hesitated. If she'd seen me and I didn't say hello, she might think I was rude. Having a library board member consider me unprofessional was way down on my list of things to do, so I walked over.

"Carolyn," I said. "Hi. How are—"

She jumped. Truly and literally jumped. "Ohh . . ." Papers slid off the table, onto her lap, and onto the floor.

"I am so sorry." I crouched down and reached out to gather up her documents.

"Stop," she snapped.

I pulled back, hands up. Right. She was a hospital administrator. She was probably reading private medical documents. Confidential papers. "Sorry. I wasn't thinking. HIPAA rules, right?"

Carolyn leaned down and swept together all the loose documents. "Yes, of course. HIPAA. Exactly. Sorry, Minnie. I didn't mean to be so abrupt."

"Don't worry about it. My fault." I pointed to one last paper, which had managed to waft itself under a nearby table. "There's an outlier."

She stood and picked it up. "'Outlier' is the word," she murmured, and sat back in the booth. She set the paper down on top of the pile and looked up at me. Intensely. And for so long that I started to squirm on the inside.

"I can trust you."

She'd made it a statement, not a question, but I nodded anyway. "Yes. You can."

She nodded at the other side of the booth, and I sat.

"I like you, Minnie," she said. "You're smart.

Capable. Intelligent. Empathic. Funny. All things we need in leadership positions."

More squirming on Minnie's part. "Thanks. I appreciate you saying so."

"Just being truthful. I want to help young people like you, and I believe one of the ways I can help is by being honest about the realities of being a leader. It can be hard. Very hard. You're going to get criticism from people who've never known you, and as a woman, you'll be criticized for things no one would ever criticize a man for doing."

I nodded. Some of this I'd already experienced.

"Case in point." Carolyn handed me the top piece of paper. "This came in my office snail mail. I didn't have time to read my mail today, so I was catching up with it just now."

In block letters, with black ink, someone had written, *TIME FOR YOU TO DIE.*

I looked at her, my eyes round with shock.

"Nice, eh?" She smiled.

"You have to tell the police," I said. "That's a clear threat. A death threat." And beyond creepy. "That's against the law." At least I was fairly sure it was.

Carolyn shook her head. "No, I'm not going to waste their time. I've received letters almost this nasty in the past, and I'm sure I will again. When you have the power of hiring and firing, getting letters like this can be part of the job. Ugly, isn't it?"

I stared at her, appalled. "You sure you won't go to the police?"

"What would they do?" She shook her head. "No. I keep them, though. In a special file."

I wondered what she labeled that particular file

but decided not to ask. "Is there anything I can say that will convince you to talk to the police?"

"Nope," she said cheerfully. And nothing else I said budged her from that position.

When I left to walk home, I made a personal vow to keep a special eye on Carolyn whenever I could. If she wouldn't take extra care, I'd have to do it for her.

I multitasked on the way home, walking and eating my sandwich whenever the sidewalk was straight and I wasn't crossing streets. Efficient was what it was, and it kept me from eating a lukewarm dinner, but I did arrive with hands gooey from Italian dressing.

Rafe opened the door. "Why did you ring the doorbell? It was unlocked."

I held up my sticky hands, one of which was holding the empty food bag. "Turns out I can do two things at once. But not three, because that would mean I thought to get napkins at Fat Boys."

"Future wife," Rafe said, "you can be very weird."

"What does that say about you?" I sent him an air kiss and went into the tiny half bath tucked under the stairs to wash my hands. When I came out, I went upstairs to change out of library clothes and into ancient running pants and a fleece pullover that had at least two colors of paint on it. By the time I got halfway down the stairs, I heard two male voices instead of the one I'd expected, and by the time I reached the bottom of the stairs, I figured out that Ash had stopped by.

In the kitchen, Rafe was leaning against the counter and Ash was sitting at the island. "Long time no see," I said to Ash. "What's up? Wait, don't tell me. You've seen the error of your ways about making Toby your lead suspect in Whippy's murder, and you want to apologize for not taking my viewpoint seriously from the get-go."

"Where did that expression come from?" Ash asked. "'Get-go.'"

I ignored the question. "You've realized that none of Toby's previous offenses involved any violence against people whatsoever. That he actually went out of his way not to hurt anyone. He was just—"

Ash interrupted. "He was just looking for the easiest way to steal stuff to make a quick buck, which doesn't prove anything about future intent, and you know I'm not going to talk about this."

"Then I'll leave you two to whatever riveting conversation you were having," I said, putting my chin up.

"The summer softball tournament." Rafe opened the refrigerator and pulled out two cans of Labatt Blue. "We're having the first planning meeting."

"Let the record state," I said, "that I am perfectly okay with you working on planning for a summer softball tournament when there are a zillion things to do to get ready for our Memorial Day reveal party."

"You are the love of my life." Rafe kissed the top of my head.

"A jewel," I agreed.

Ash shook his head. "I still can't believe you left the decision about your own wedding and reception locations to someone else. What is wrong with you two?"

So many things. I smiled and left them to their

softball discussion, which was pointless because the tournament had been running almost entirely on its own momentum since 1987 when Penelope Nash, who currently ran the concessions at the downtown movie theater and probably would for another fifty years, had created a detailed and task-oriented flow chart.

"Boys are so silly," I told Eddie as I walked into the small room that had once served as a downstairs bedroom and was now our home office. Since we both used laptops and tended to work all over the house, the space served primarily as a location for paperwork storage, but it was a nice quiet spot to sit and think, and that was what I wanted to do.

"Mrr."

Well, it was nice and quiet most of the time. Sometimes, however, the room turned into one big cat playground. I watched Eddie jump in one smooth leap to the top of the lateral filing cabinet we'd bought for next to nothing from a landscaping business that had converted their paper files to digital. His next step, of course, was to give a pile of newspapers a push and send them all fluttering to the floor.

"Not sure you needed to do that," I said, leaning back in the castered chair and putting my feet up on the battered desk that had seen Rafe through high school, college, and graduate school. "I'd go pick them up, but you're in a mood, aren't you?"

"Mrr!" He sat, statue-like, and looked around.

"Nope," I said. "Not going to put them back. It's been a long day and I don't have the energy."

"Mrr?"

"What *do* I have the energy for? Right now, I just want to think." A lot had happened since my first cup of coffee, and I wanted to work through it all.

"Toby pled not guilty to breaking and entering at the candy store." I tipped back even farther in the chair, not quite to the point of overbalancing. "Ash thinks that's a play to look innocent if he's charged with Whippy's murder. Which, I'll admit to you if not Ash, is a possibility. But it's also possible that Toby is innocent."

Eddie thumped to the floor.

"Glad you agree. And then there's that letter Carolyn had." Once again, I read the horrific words, and a sizzle of unease ran down my back. "I agreed to keep that confidential, and I will." For now. "But if I see anything or hear about anything that has the slightest whiff of escalation, I'm calling Ash and— *Ooff!* Funny, I don't remember inviting you onto my lap."

He clunked his skull against my chin so hard that my teeth rattled.

"You are such a dork." I kissed his furry forehead. "What I really need to do is meet up with Leah and show her that baby picture. If it's her, that could change everything." But Leah hadn't returned my text messages, so that had to wait.

"The possibly big news," I said, "is I learned that Whippy and Lillie Siler were a serious couple in high school. But I don't know for sure if Lillie is Leah's birth mother." I suddenly recalled Rene Kinney's angry reaction to Whippy's death out on the bookmobile and wished I'd remembered to look for her in the yearbook, too.

Eddie flopped on my lap and curled himself into a cat ball. Absently, I petted him and continued talking out loud, only quieter.

"Now I have to decide what to do next. Do I tell Leah about Lillie and Whippy? Do I find out more about Lillie by myself? Should I do anything at all?" I blew out a breath. "Maybe I should just leave it all alone. What do you think?" I asked, jiggling my legs.

The rumble of Eddie's purr was so low that I felt more than heard it.

Though it wasn't much of an answer, I smiled.

And knew what my next step should be.

Chapter 12

The next morning started badly. Rafe had gone to work early to hold an "after" meeting with the teachers and staff so they wouldn't speculate too much about what had gone on at the school board meeting. He'd nudged me awake, but I'd slept poorly and fallen back into a doze punctuated by fragmented dreams of black-robed judges throwing high school diplomas at me while shouting, "You promised! You promised!" A diploma came close, and instinctively I threw up an arm to protect my face.

"Mrr!"

I blinked and my brain swam to wakefulness. "Sorry, pal." I patted Eddie, who'd tucked himself into the V between my arm and hip. "Didn't mean to disturb you."

He gave me a look and slid off the bed.

"Super sorry, honest," I said, but his pace of departure didn't slow, and I heard the *thump-thump* of a cat going down the stairs as noisily as he could.

Pre-Eddie, I'd never lived with a cat, so until recently I hadn't known they could, if they chose, make as much noise as an elephant. "Or is it just you?" I called. No response, which was what I'd expected.

Yawning, I stretched and slid myself out of bed, which was when I noticed the alarm clock and was suddenly wide-awake and running for the shower.

Not very many minutes later, Eddie and I were pulling into the library's back parking lot, cozying up next to the bookmobile. Hunter was already there, circling the vehicle, doing the outside part of the preflight check.

I glanced at my dashboard clock and smiled as I unlatched Eddie's carrier from the passenger's seat. Even though I was a few minutes late, the bookmobile would leave on time. Clearly, there was more than one benefit to having a second driver on staff.

"Morning, Captain." Hunter opened the bookmobile's door and saluted. "Check is complete. All is shipshape and roadworthy."

"At ease, First Mate. Initiative for commencing work previous to my appearance is noted and appreciated." Then, since I'd hit my weekly quota of formal speak, I said, "FYI, Eddie is in a mood today. Might make things interesting out on the road."

Hunter peered into the carrier. "What do you think, Mr. Ed?"

Through the slots in the gray plastic, we watched Eddie rotate himself so that his hind end faced the carrier's front.

"You know you've accomplished something when you've been dissed by a cat," I said, nodding. "Nicely done."

"Can't wait to tell my wife when I get home."

"She'll be very proud of you."

Hunter grinned, showing the gap between his front teeth. "For sure."

By this time we were all inside and buckled up. Hunter started the engine, looked left and right, and we pulled onto the street.

I sat back and, like I did every time I went out in the bookmobile, felt a huge smile spread across my face. Truly, I had the best job in the world. Not only did I get to be an assistant library director, which meant I got to work on fun projects without having to deal with the push and pull of working directly for a board of directors, but I also got to go out on the bookmobile, spreading the joy of books far and wide, over hill and dale, across winding streams and—

"So, I have something I want to talk to you about," Hunter said.

My happy mood poofed out of existence. He was going to quit. His welding business had expanded so much that it didn't make financial sense for him to keep working for the library. Or the college business class he'd enrolled in for the summer required an internship that conflicted with his bookmobile days. I started to mentally spin out even more scenarios but stopped myself. "Sure," I said as perkily as I could. "Talk about what?"

"Well." He took a deep breath. "I want to try riding the book bike."

My eyes, which had shut in hopes of warding off the pending doom, flew open. "You . . . what?"

"The book bike. You need someone to ride it, right? I do a lot of mountain biking, so I should have the leg strength. I want to try it."

I had not expected this. So much so that I blurted out the first thought in my head. "Absolutely not."

Hunter glanced over at me. "Um, maybe you could think it over first?"

"Good idea." I hummed a few bars of the *Jeopardy!* theme song. "Okay, I've thought it over. Absolutely not. I appreciate the offer. Truly. But you don't have time to give us more hours, do you? I didn't think so. You're the only one other than me who has a commercial driver's license. I need you to drive the bookmobile."

He half smiled. "Yeah, I kind of figured. Just thought I'd offer."

"I do appreciate it. Very much. And I wish I could take you up on it. Unfortunately . . ." I shook my head and sighed. "I'll figure something out."

But no solution came to me the rest of the drive to our first stop at a township hall. We arrived a few minutes early, so after we opened ourselves for business, I sat in the sunshine on the bookmobile steps and pulled out my phone to do a bit of non-library research.

Last night, I'd determined my next investigative step was the obvious one: figure out Leah's birth month, day, and year. If it was within the time frame of Whippy and Lillie's high school romance, odds were good that Lillie was Leah's birth mother. If not . . . Well, I'd think about that if I had to. Luckily, I found it quickly on her Facebook account. Leah had been born in April the year after Whippy graduated from high school.

Because I still hadn't had a return text from her, I sent her a Facebook message, asking her to contact me as soon as she could.

A car pulled into the parking lot, and I slid my phone into my pocket, thinking. Had Whippy and Lillie still been an item after graduation? How on earth was I going to figure that out? Who would remember, other than Whippy and Lillie? And if I found Lillie, would she tell me?

At lunchtime, our route circled back to Chilson. Hunter eased us to a grand stop at the library's main entrance, and I scratched Eddie's chin through the wire door, told him to be a good boy, and vacated the passenger's seat.

"He was quiet all morning," Hunter said. "Thought you said he was in a mood."

Julia bounded up the stairs. "Ah just *love* Eddie moods!" she sang out in her Scarlett O'Hara accent.

"Even the bad ones?" I asked.

"Bless your heart." She batted her eyes. "The bahd ones are my fahvorite kind."

Hunter grinned. "Going to be one of those kinds of days, is it?"

"My deah." Julia pulled her thick braid around, held it up as a mustache, and dropped the Southern accent in favor of one that sounded Eastern European. "What iz thiz bus?" She waved at the bookmobile contents. "Where I come from, we not have thing like it. I must ride along!"

"Mɪɪ!"

The humans laughed, and I felt a pang. In a perfect world, all of us would have gone along on the afternoon route, but since it wasn't a perfect world, I waved them good-bye and determinedly turned my mind to my to-do list as they rolled off.

Halfway to the library's back door, I stopped. I'd

left in such a rush that morning that I hadn't had any breakfast or packed a lunch. With such an empty stomach, there was no way my emergency food stash or the library's vending machine was going to meet my nutritional needs. I pulled my phone from my pocket and looked at the time. If I walked fast, grabbed a sandwich from Shomin's Deli, and ate fast enough to risk indigestion, I could get back to the library by one.

My feet knew I'd made the decision before my brain fully recognized what had happened. "Excellent decision," I said quietly to my feet as I entered the restaurant. There was only one person in line in front of me, and it was someone I'd planned to talk to soon anyway. Two birds, one stone, all that. Life was good.

"Hey, Bianca," I said.

The blond woman pulled her credit card out of the reader and turned. "Minnie. You and Rafe ever have that wedding venue reveal party?"

"Memorial Day," I said, heartily wishing that Rafe and I had never come up with the idea in the first place. "Are you doing takeout or eating here? Because if you have a few minutes, I'd like to talk to you."

Her eyebrows went sky high. "Don't tell me you and Rafe are selling that house." Bianca, one of the most successful real estate agents in the area, was one of the most successful agents because she was always tuned into the slightest opportunity.

I smiled. "Rafe says the only way he's leaving that house is feet first."

"Feet . . . oh, I get it." Her temporarily furrowed

brow cleared. "Like on a stretcher, you mean. But sure, let's sit over there."

After paying for my new standard—avocado and turkey with tomato, a lovely gooey mess of a sandwich—I slid into the wooden booth, sitting across from Bianca. "Has Mitchell recovered from the Trout Lily Festival?" I asked.

That this intelligent, pretty, and financially successful woman was happily married to former slacker Mitchell Koyne was still a source of wonder to many. Then again, there were probably people who thought Rafe and I were an unlikely couple. Love was indeed a mysterious quantity.

Bianca laughed. "He's trying to get appointed to the chamber of commerce board. Yes, that was about the same look I gave him. I told him if he wants to do that, he should ask if he can attend a few board meetings first to see how things work."

"Good advice." At least that's what I tried to say. I might not have said it very loud because most of me was trying to imagine Mitchell sitting in a conference room, agenda packet on the table in front of him, commenting on new business item three. With immense focus, I managed to create the image, but then I tried to hear him make a motion, and it all dissolved. "Hope things work out," I said faintly, and sent the chamber director a wish for good luck.

Our food was brought to us by a young man who didn't look old enough to stay home unsupervised, let alone work in a restaurant, but the sandwiches looked—and tasted—fine, so after a couple of bites I asked, "Do you know what's going to happen with the candy store?" I'd thought and thought about who might know, but I hadn't thought about Bianca until that morning when we'd passed one of her FOR SALE signs. Of course she'd know; she knew the owners and tenants of every downtown building.

Bianca slumped a bit. "No. The whole thing is awful. Whippy's wife is a mess, the kids have gone back downstate, and meanwhile the store just sits there, the stock getting dusty and nothing getting ordered for summer."

"The Henika family has owned the store forever," I said. "If Colleen sold, she'd probably make a lot of money."

"The place would sell like that." Bianca snapped her fingers, French-manicured fingernails shining in the light. "And you-know-who would be first to write an offer."

"Um . . ."

"Danny Calhoun," Bianca said. "He's wanted to expand his store for years. He can't expand west because he's on the corner, right? The only way he can get bigger without moving is to go east, and that's Whippy's store."

"He's wanted to buy Whippy's store for a long time?" I asked.

She nodded. "Every winter for the past ten years, he had me talk to Whippy about selling. And every year, including this one, Whippy said no. That he wouldn't know what to do with himself if he didn't have a store to run."

I took another bite of sandwich. And now, with Whippy gone, Dan might finally get the retail space he'd coveted for so long. Could that be motive enough for murder? I didn't want to think so. But . . . maybe.

* * *

As soon as she finished her sandwich, Bianca glanced at her watch. "Sorry, Minnie, but I have to go. I'm showing a house out on the point in half an hour, and the owner was adamant that all the windows be opened for fifteen minutes to get the fresh lake breeze smell inside."

She put air quotes around "fresh lake breeze," and I laughed. The point was full of massive residences that normal people called mansions. Most of them had been constructed in the late 1800s as cottages for summer people from Chicago who steamed up Lake Michigan to spend the hot months in cooler climes, hauling north trunks of clothes and bringing maids and cooks who slept in uninsulated attics.

Though those days were long gone, the houses remained. Many still belonged to descendants of the original families, but every once in a while, a house came on the market for prices far beyond the reach of the ninety-nine percent. People selling or buying out on the point tended to have drastically different worldviews than the rest of us, and vastly different expectations about service.

"No way would I have the patience to deal with requirements like that," I said. "Realtors earn their fees."

Bianca smiled as she gathered up her lunch detritus. "All in a day's work. And every job has parts that aren't any fun, right?"

After she left, I finished my sandwich and tried to come up with the parts of my job that were less than enjoyable: The occasional cranky patron. Kelsey's way too strong coffee. The annoying president of the Friends of the Library group.

But all of those were minor irritations. No, the worst thing about my job was something that was my own fault: Eddie hair. Keeping the bookmobile as free of cat hair and dander as possible was a constant chore, and I was continually trying to improve the methodologies.

I got up and tossed my lunch leavings into the trash, smiling on the inside. If cleaning up after my own cat was the worst part of my job, I had to be the luckiest person in the world.

The child at the register said, "Have a nice rest of your day."

"Thanks." Instead of walking out, I stopped and looked at him. Upon closer inspection, I could see facial signs of adolescence—acne and chin fuzz—so he must be older than he looked. "Maybe you can help me," I said, shifting into investigator mode.

All the downtown business owners knew one another, so it stood to reason that the employees did, too, at least to some extent. In my head, I quickly read through the suspect list: Dan Calhoun, Kurt Wasson, and Rene Kinney. Plus Toby Guinn, because if Ash thought he'd done it, there was probably a good reason, and even though I thought he was wrong, there was always the worst-case scenario that I'd eventually be forced to admit he was right.

But that day wasn't anywhere on the horizon, and here was an opportunity to gently explore for information. I smiled, hoping my brain would figure out appropriate questions as I talked, gave him my name, and said, "I work at the library. Do I remember seeing you there working on research projects?"

Marlow, for that was the name on his tag, shook

his head. "Nah. I do all that stuff online. I go to Mitchell River Academy."

Which was a small charter school just outside town. So much for using the "Your principal (or former principal) is my fiancé" card to persuade him to talk. "I hear that's a great school. Are you interning here?"

"Yeah. I want to be one of those chefs, you know, like on TV. My mom and teachers say I need to start with the basics. I do front lobby stuff one day a week and work in the kitchen on Monday afternoons. The school set it up."

It sounded like an excellent approach to vocational training. "Do you like restaurant work?"

Marlow's face, which had been flatly polite, lit up. "Yeah, I do. It's different every day, you know? I don't have to sit in a freaking chair all the time, and I get to make something people want."

He sounded remarkably like Kristen when she'd walked away from a career in biochemistry. "You're lucky," I said. "To find out so early in your life what you want to do. Some people never figure it out." Inspiration struck, and I said, "Like the guy who runs the T-shirt shop. Dan Calhoun. I think he'd gone through a couple of careers before he started his store."

"Yeah? Never been in there. I mean, why would I? I don't need a Chilson T-shirt. I live here, right?"

That hadn't been my point, but I persevered. "And then there's people like Kurt Wasson. He's been a plumber up here all his life, but he's gone from working for himself to working for North Lakes Plumbing. Got tired of the hassles of owning a business. Do you know him?"

"Nah. Seen their trucks around, though. Couple of weeks ago that gift shop around the corner had a leak in their basement. I was working in the kitchen that day and left late because I was helping Reva and Corey with a new recipe. It was like six o'clock and there was still a truck there. Hi, can I help you?"

Marlow's question was posed to the couple who had just walked in the door. I gave Marlow a nod good-bye, and headed straight to Lake Street Gifts. I spun a quick story about checking up on plumber references and confirmed that, yes, they'd had a basement pipe burst.

"Water everywhere," the woman said, spreading her arms wide. She looked about forty, with short hair just starting to gray and a face that looked like it wanted to smile. "It was horrible. The basement is too musty to store stock down there, but we still lost packaging supplies and seasonal decorations. Took the guy hours to fix it, and I'm not looking forward to seeing the invoice."

"Did the plumber's name happen to be Kurt?" I asked. "Kurt Wasson?"

"That was it. Kind of a short guy. Nice enough, I guess, but not a talker. Far as I know, he does good work." She smiled. "The basement is still dry anyway, and . . ." Her smile faded away.

"And?" I prompted.

"It's just something . . . something I don't like to think about." She sighed. "That leak was the same day Whippy Henika was killed."

I called Holly to tell her I was running a few minutes late and marched into the sheriff's office with a list of bullet points in my head. If Ash wouldn't listen to me, I'd go over his head and talk to the sheriff. She and I weren't friends, exactly, but there had been a time when she'd kept Eddie overnight, and once you'd seen someone in the early morning light, hair tousled, wearing a ratty bathrobe, and cuddling your cat, you formed a certain kind of unbreakable friendship.

I went up to the glass window and blinked at the unfamiliar twenty-something woman. "Hi. No Chelsea today?"

"Sorry. She took the afternoon off. I'm Jennifer. What can I do for you?"

"How about Deputy Wolverson. Is he available?"

She shook her head. "Sorry, he's also out this afternoon."

"Good for them. Hope they're having a good time somewhere." But now what was I going to do? "Is there any chance Sheriff Richardson has a few minutes? My name is Minnie Hamilton, by the way, and it's about Whippy Henika's murder."

"Oh. Um." Jennifer looked around, but the office stayed empty and unhelpful. "Well, I just started this week, so, um . . . hang on a minute, okay?" She left the room, and I inched over to the only available reading material—flyers pinned up inside the locked glass display case.

I perused information on obtaining a burning permit, read a memo on telephone scams, and was working through the agenda for the next county board of commissioners meeting when the inside door opened.

"Ms. Hamilton. To what do I owe the pleasure?"

I tried to keep my face clear of disappointment.

Probably failed. "Detective Inwood. How nice to see you."

The tall thin man in his mid-sixties tipped his gray-haired head and sighed. "Nice? Yet I'm told you asked for Deputy Wolverson or Sheriff Richardson."

There were lots of reasons for that, and we both knew all of them. I swallowed a semi-belligerent response of *Do you want to hear what I have to say or not?* and instead said, "Five minutes, and I'm out of here."

Hal Inwood gave me a long, considering look, then nodded.

"Five minutes starting after I sit down," I amended, and was shocked to detect the smallest of smiles on his craggy face.

"Five it is." He ushered me into the closest interview room. We sat on opposite sides of the much-scratched table, and I started talking fast, because he'd already noted the time on the wall clock.

"About Whippy Henika's murder. I know Toby Guinn is your, whatever you call it, your person of interest, but I've learned some things that could take your whole investigation in a different direction."

"Unlikely," Detective Inwood said. "But proceed."

How kind of him. What was it about this guy that bristled every negative emotion I had? And how was it that the infuriating Hal Inwood could stay married to the wonderfully cheerful Tabitha for so many years? I pushed it all away and kept talking.

"Dan Calhoun owns the store next to Whippy's. Did you know he's wanted to buy the candy store for years? You might want to talk to Bianca Koyne about that. She said he's wanted to expand his business, doesn't want to move from his location, and for ten years has been pressuring Whippy to sell. Could be a motive for murder in there, don't you think?"

I heard the snarkiness in my voice and took a breath. No point in riling Mr. Former Downstate Detective any more than I had to.

"And there's Kurt Wasson," I went on. "No, I can't give you a motive, but he's a plumber, and he was doing emergency work on a gift store just around the corner from Whippy's store the night of the murder. Plus," I said quickly, because I could see Hal's pending objection, "the place where Kurt works was doing some contracted work in the candy store. Whippy had one of those keyless coded entries"—a fun fact anyone who walked down the alley could have learned—"and I bet Kurt was given a code to get in."

Detective Inwood eyed me. "So one of your suspects has a motive, but you haven't placed him at the scene of the crime. Though the other could be placed near the crime scene, there is no motive."

My mouth opened, but Hal was still talking.

"Let me give you a few details from the medical examiner's report. It's already public knowledge that Mr. Henika died from strangulation. I will not disclose the item used to commit the murder, but I will tell you that the report indicates that the killer was approximately six feet tall."

Six feet . . . I took a deep breath and let it out slowly. Kurt Wasson wasn't anywhere near that height. But Dan Calhoun was.

I leaned forward. "You need to interview Kurt Wasson. Maybe he saw something that night. Maybe he—"

Hal stood. "Your five minutes are up, Ms. Hamilton. Thank you for coming in."

Next thing I knew, I was out on the sidewalk, the door of the sheriff's office shutting behind me.

"And that's why he annoys me so much," I muttered.

But no matter how often he used his law enforcement techniques to manipulate me, I wasn't going to stop bugging him. Not until I was sure they'd arrested the right person for Whippy's murder.

Chapter 13

H ow tall did he say?"

As he asked the question, Rafe had half of his attention on the red pepper he was slicing and half on me. This concerned me, as I didn't want to take the time to drive to the emergency room and didn't have a book handy to take with, other than the ones on my phone, and reading on the phone always gave me a headache, so it was never the preferred option. Then again, he was showing signs of high knife competence, so I averted my eyes from the potential catastrophe. I had annual emergency first aid training, after all, thanks to what I'd included in the library's bookmobile operations policy, and if something happened here in my own kitchen, surely I'd remember the pertinent parts.

I went back in time a few hours, to the interview room where Detective Inwood had spoken to me so pompously. "He said, and I'm quoting here as closely as I can, that 'the report indicates the killer was approximately six feet tall.' That's all he said."

Rafe swept the cut-up peppers to one side and reached for the head of cauliflower. I had no idea what he was going to do with any of it, but as long as I didn't have to cook, all was good.

"Six feet," Rafe repeated. "Toby Guinn fits that description. Fits right into the case for prosecuting him."

I wasn't buying it. "That has to be—well, I'm not sure 'circumstantial' is the right term, but you know what I mean. There are a lot of people that tall."

"Six feet is not the far end of the height bell curve, I give you that. Still, it does cut down the suspect list."

And that was the disconcerting truth. "Kurt's, what, five foot six? So he's out." I told myself to remember to tell Leah her ex-husband couldn't be the killer and got the feeling that was not going to be a fun conversation.

"Who's left?" Rafe asked.

"Well, Toby's still on there." I got up to wash the cutting board Rafe had put in the sink. "Plus, there's Rene Kinney and Dan Calhoun."

"You have a favorite candidate?"

Of course I did. "Dan Calhoun," I said promptly. "He's wanted the candy store property for years, he didn't want to donate to the memorial fund for Whippy, and you know that since his wife died, he's changed. Doesn't go out as much, more irritable. Now that she's gone, he doesn't have anyone to calm him down or to distract him."

As I was talking, the theory was making more and more sense. "Maybe, living alone, Dan had been getting hyperfocused on expanding his business. That's all he's thinking about, all he cares about. And this time, when Whippy said he wasn't going to sell, Dan snapped. He didn't walk in meaning to kill Whippy. It wasn't premeditated. He just couldn't take it any longer, and—"

I paused. There'd been an odd noise coming from upstairs, which almost certainly had a cat origin. It stopped, so I kept talking.

"And he grabbed something that was sitting right there in the store." I picked up a dish towel and dried the cutting board, thinking about the cases of chocolates, taffy, and fudge. "Not sure what, though."

"Ribbon," Rafe said. "For gift wrapping. They have a bunch of it by the cash register."

Then I saw them, the spools and spools of bright colors, and knew Rafe was right. I hated the idea of Whippy's breath, his life, being cut off by his own ribbons, and hoped the image wouldn't haunt my dreams. Or the dreams of his family. "Yeah," I whispered. "That sounds about right."

"Hey." Rafe wrapped his arms around me from behind, his solid presence a sudden comforting warmth. "Have I told you lately how much I love you?"

"No," I said, putting towel and cutting board on the counter and rotating to face him. "Pretty sure you haven't said anything of the kind for seconds. Minutes, even."

"Time to fix that," he murmured, leaning down to kiss me on the temple, then my ear, then my cheek. "Minerva Joy Hamilton, I love you." He tipped my chin up and kissed my lips gently, lovingly, and thoroughly.

"Well," I said when we both came up for breath.

"That wasn't bad. Maybe we should do it again. Practice makes perfect and all."

"Absolutely." Rafe leaned down and—

THUD!

Rafe and I gave simultaneous sighs. The second noise had sounded a lot closer than the first. "You keep cooking," I said, pulling out of his embrace. "I'll go see what he's doing."

"I support whatever punishment decision you make."

"And you think that will make a difference to his future behavior?"

Rafe shrugged. "Can't hurt."

True enough. I sucked in a deep breath for courage, let it out slowly, and went to investigate. The sound had been a thud, not a crash, so maybe the Eddie damage would be minimal. He wasn't often destructive, if you left off the occasional shredding of paper products, but he was a big cat and could knock things over unintentionally.

I called his name as I entered the dining room. "Eddie? Where are you, buddy? I know you're okay, because otherwise you would have been howling, right?"

"Mrr," came a cat voice from under the dining table.

I went down on my hands and knees. "Nice," I said, looking through the small forest of table and chair legs. Somehow he'd managed to bring a rubber duck from the master bathtub all the way downstairs. "But I'm not sure how you made so much noise with such a small item. Is this a new talent, or one that was previously untapped?"

His yellow eyes glared at me. "Mrr!" he said, and launched himself out from underneath the table, through the living room, and up the stairs.

"Yeah, mrr to you, too," I said. Cats were always mysterious, but some days they were off the charts.

"All right in there?" Rafe called.

I stood up, ducky in hand, and looked at it. "Sure," I said. The bright yellow toy had been among the things that had been moved over from the houseboat last fall. I'd had it for so long that I wasn't sure where it had come from. I had no memory of buying it myself, but since by noon every day I often couldn't remember what I'd eaten for breakfast, that didn't mean much.

"Not that it matters," I said to its smiling face as I took it back upstairs and returned it to the edge of the tub. "What matters is that you reminded me of something I need to do."

Luckily, the duck didn't reply, and when I returned to the kitchen, I didn't tell Rafe about the one-sided conversation. Instead, I said, "After dinner, do you want to go over to the marina with me?"

He looked up briefly, then returned his attention to the grill pan. "Maybe." He flipped the two chicken breasts and, when the sizzle died down, asked, "Any particular reason?"

"To see how Corey and Isabella are doing. They're renting my houseboat, after all, and I want to make sure they're getting the full benefit of marina life."

Rafe poked the chicken with tongs. "You could just let nature take its course."

"I could, but that's not as much fun." I watched

him add roasted red peppers and cauliflower to our plates. "So are you going to come with me or not?"

It turned out that he did, and so, after I'd washed the grill pan and put the last dish in the dishwasher, we walked the short distance to the marina, hand in hand. As soon as we got close, however, we heard a hail from the office's front door.

"Niswander!" Chris shouted. "Skeeter is grilling turkey legs and we're picking the best barbecue sauce. We have eight kinds. Want to vote?"

"Don't do it," I murmured to Rafe. "They'll suck you into their insanity."

My beloved, of course, ignored my caution. He gave my hand a quick squeeze, then headed toward the office.

I left him to his fate and wandered over to the dock where the houseboat was moored. "Anyone home?" I asked as I approached. "Corey? Isabella?"

"Hey, Minnie." Corey, who'd been lying on one of the two lounges in front, stood up, yawning. "Sorry, I must have fallen asleep. Isabella's at work."

I smiled. "I'd ask if you had a long day, but all restaurant days are long ones, aren't they?"

"Truth." He gestured to the other lounge and I sat.

"Had lunch at your place today," I said. "Met your intern, Marlow. Seems like a nice kid."

"So far, so good." Corey nodded. "Good work ethic, knows when to ask for help, interacts well with the customers."

"And wants to be a famous chef," I said, smiling.

"Don't we all." Corey made a wry face.

I wasn't sure about that, but I knew what he meant. I was also impressed that Corey, only a few years out of high school, was already able to assess a new employee so clearly and concisely.

"How are you settling in?" I nodded to the boat next door. "Hope you don't mind, but I asked Eric to give you the inside scoop on living here at the marina."

"Yeah, he's helping us out quite a bit. Thanks."

But after asking a few more pointed questions, I realized that Eric's mentoring consisted of showing the Moncadas the best way to coil lines and telling them the ideal time of day to fill coolers with ice.

Which was all well and good, but that hadn't been the kind of mentorship I'd been hoping for.

"Did you see?" Corey pointed. "The other day Isabella and I both had time off, so we got old toothbrushes and some chrome cleaner and did the railing all round. How does it look compared to when you did it?"

I got up and inspected the sparkling surface. Since I'd never once taken any kind of brush to the railing, it looked a zillion times better than I'd ever seen.

"Looks fantastic," I said. Corey smiled and looked about twelve years old.

"Say," Corey said. "Do you know if they figured out who killed Mr. Henika? We're still a little nervous about being so close to a murder. I mean, that store is just down the street, you know?"

I came to a sudden and hard conclusion: I really wanted this young couple to stay in Chilson. They were fun, hardworking, and an asset to the community. And if what it took to keep them in town was to step up my efforts to find Whippy's killer, then that's what I'd do.

* * *

"What do you think?" I asked Rafe as I walked off the end of the dock and onto the concrete sidewalk. "Or is it just me? Maybe I'm overly sensitive. Maybe I'm seeing things that aren't really there."

"Might be that way." He took my hand. "Then again, it might not."

"So not helpful."

"After we're married, it'll be different."

"Can't believe you said that with a straight face." I looked up and saw his grin. "Oh, wait. You didn't. Never mind."

His half smile went full wattage. "Glad we understand each other."

I gave him a mild hip check. "Back at you. But I'm talking about Whippy's murder. I really don't think Toby did it. What do you think?"

Rafe went oddly quiet. Then, as we approached the house, he said, "Honestly? I want to believe you're right, but I'm afraid that you're not."

Something inside of me drooped. I wasn't sure if it was my confidence or my self-esteem, or what, but if Rafe was so sure I was reading the situation all wrong, then I should listen to him.

"But," he added, "you see things I don't. When people talk, you hear things people don't say. So if you think there's something there"—he nodded— "then there might be something there."

"Trust my instincts is what you're saying."

"You have them for a reason, right?"

It was a point worthy of printing out in a fancy font and taking to the frame shop. And maybe someday I'd do that, but my next investigative task was to roll up my metaphorical sleeves, flex my key-boarding fingers, and see what I could find about Whippy's high school girlfriend. Surely my hunch that Leah's birth mother might be involved was worth some exploration time.

Rafe and Eddie settled on the couch to watch baseball, and I settled in next to them, computer on my lap and earbuds tuned to the soundtrack from *The Sound of Music*, original Broadway cast, because Julia had said my life would be incomplete until I heard it start to finish.

My first Internet site was one that gave an estimate of how many people by any given first and last name there were likely to be in the United States. I checked me first, of course, and was interested to see that there was one more Minerva Hamilton since the last time I'd looked. I wondered where number seventeen had been born, but restrained myself and typed in "Lillie Siler."

"Four of her," I said. Interesting. Finding women wasn't as easy, though, thanks to that maiden name thing. But lots of women used both their maiden and their married names on Facebook pages, so maybe—

"You are so stupid," I said out loud.

Rafe poked me and waited until I took out my earbuds. "Hey. Don't talk about my fiancée that way."

"If she wasn't so dumb, I wouldn't."

"Just keep things kind, okay? Eddie doesn't like it when people make fun of her."

I looked at our cat, who was facedown along the length of Rafe's legs. "I think I'm safe for now." I

put my earbuds back in place, went to the Scovill
Funeral Home website, found Whippy's obituary,
and scrolled through the comment section.

Not every person who posted left their name, but
many did, and it didn't take long to find a comment
from Lillie Davis: "Condolences. So many fond
memories of Will." I wondered if I'd ever remember
to ask someone where—and when—the Whippy
nickname had come about, and also thought about
the odds of Whippy knowing two women named
Lillie.

Slim to none was my conclusion, and I started
the social media search for Lillie Davis. Roughly
two minutes later, I found her on Facebook. Or at
least I found a Lillie Davis whose profile said she
was from Chilson, a critical care nurse, and living
in Cadillac, Michigan.

Hmm. It was less than a two-hour drive to Cadillac, if you assumed dry roads, daylight, and little
traffic, easily a down-and-back trip in one day. But
how should I approach her? How should I intro-
duce myself? How did I—

"Just type," I said, quietly enough that no one
except me could hear, and sent Lillie a stream-of-
consciousness message.

*Hello, you don't know me, but I knew Will
"Whippy" Henika. If you're the Lillie he dated in
high school, I'd like to talk. You might be able to
help find his killer. I'd be happy to meet you this
weekend at a restaurant you choose. Please let me
know. Thanks so much.*

I added my name and a link to my staff bio on
the library website, read and reread the message,
which grew more and more stupid the more times I

read it, then finally just closed my eyes and hit Send. I slapped my laptop shut and yanked out the earbuds. Baseball. Sure. I'd watch baseball for a couple of innings, then see if she replied. It was unlikely that she'd be on the computer right that second. Probably I shouldn't even check until tomorrow. Maybe not even tomorrow night.

Five minutes later, I couldn't stand it and opened my computer.

Message from Lillie Davis: *More than happy to help, but I'm out of town right now. Next Friday in Cadillac at After 26—how about eleven-ish?*

Message from Minnie Hamilton: *Thanks so much. See you then.*

When Carolyn and I had crossed paths at Fat Boys, we'd made plans to meet up once a month for coffee. "And let's start this Friday," Carolyn had said, tapping into her phone. "The earlier we start, the faster it becomes a habit, so why wait?"

My mouth had flapped open and shut a few times, but she was right. There was no reason to wait. I'd figured that, as a hospital administrator, she would have to check multiple calendars before scheduling a non-hospital event, maybe even have her assistant make the appointment. That she had so quickly, easily, and non-fussily created a brand-new standing commitment impressed me and gave me a new standard for decision-making. If there was no point in waiting, go ahead and get things done. Saved time in the long run, and time was the nonrenewable resource to end all nonrenewable resources.

I walked through the sparkling morning air of

late May, thinking about all of that and wondering if it was profound or just an obvious statement of fact. Or was it possible it was so obvious it was profound? Hah. As if. I scrunched my face up into a twist, annoyed by the weirdness my brain conjured up.

Laughter floated down the sidewalk. "You know what your mother would say about that face," said Carolyn.

"Good thing she can't see me, then." I smiled. "Beautiful day, isn't it?"

"Glorious." The older woman turned her face to the sun, soaking in its radiant heat, her short hair shining and her eyes closed. "It's days like this that make me regret my career choices. Why did I decide on a profession that forces me to be inside?"

"Toss it all away," I suggested. "Come out on the bookmobile. We pay hardly anything, and it won't be a full-time job, but we have fun pretty much all the time."

"Don't tempt me." Carolyn's eyes stayed closed. "Tell you what. How about we talk outside on the waterfront? I'll buy if you go in and get our coffees. I don't want to waste a minute of this sun."

Once again, I was taken aback by the speed of her decision-making. I also wanted to take notes on how easily she'd proposed a change in plans. And since it sounded like a fine change, that's what we did.

After waiting for the traffic to clear—which at this time of year was minimal: one dusty sedan, one black pickup with a cracked back window, and one shiny European convertible—we walked across the street and down the hill toward the broad swath of concrete the city had constructed next to the water.

I asked, "Does all that come naturally, or did you develop the skills over years?"

"What, walking and drinking coffee at the same time? I'd have to say it was a learned skill."

I laughed. "No, what you did a couple of minutes ago." Step by step, I listed what had happened. "We'd planned to meet in the coffee shop, right? But you saw an opportunity, straightforwardly pushed out a workable idea, cited a reason for the change, and included a financial incentive for me."

"That's what I did?" Carolyn took another sip of her coffee, sidestepping a man walking three dogs. "Honestly, I just wanted to be outside and dragged you with me."

"But it's how you did it," I insisted. "Reasonably, smoothly, and with room for compromise. I mean, if I hadn't wanted to come out here for some reason, you would have accepted my decision, right?" I waved my free hand at Janay Lake and at the wide walkway, which, on this warm sunny morning, was starting to fill up with people, strollers, and dogs. It was a more than a week until Memorial Day, early in the season for so many people to be around.

Carolyn made a *hmm*-ing sort of noise. "Maybe. But I wouldn't have given up easily. This is the weather I dreamed about all April. Having the opportunity to get out in it on a weekday is a rarity for me."

"Is that the worst thing about your job? Being stuck inside all the time?"

"On days like this, certainly." She smiled at the

sun. "But in all honesty, the worst thing is recognizing a problem, knowing the solution, but not being able to implement it."

"Why not?"

"Depends on the problem. Most often it's a budget constraint. Capital improvements have the potential to be funded through the foundation or from grants, but operations and regular maintenance have to be funded through normal revenues."

I bounced on my toes a little, the eager student ready to learn. "The hospital has a strategic plan, right? I'm working with Graydon on a revised version for the library. What was the hospital's process?"

She glanced at me. "You sound excited. No one is excited to work on a strategic plan. Ever."

"Um, first time for everything?" I grinned and she laughed.

"Who am I to squash the exuberance of youth? I'm glad you and Graydon are working on that. Strategic plans, if they're used on a regular basis, can be a very effective change agent."

Her words were like music. Not that the library needed any significant changes, but someday it would, and it only made sense to get everyone used to referring to a strategic plan now, before there was a need for change and massive upheaval.

"Our process goes like this." Carolyn dropped her empty coffee cup into a nearby bin and started talking, using both her hands extensively.

I listened closely to her description of public visioning sessions, online surveys, employee lunch and learns, and ad hoc committee meetings. She was detailing the timeline when I heard an odd noise. A low buzzing kind of whir. I couldn't identify it at first but then recalled the Trout Lily Festival. A scooter, that's what it was, but scooters weren't allowed on the waterfront, were they? No, they couldn't be. Skateboards weren't, so how could scooters be?

The noise was growing louder and louder, coming close faster than made sense.

Frowning, I turned around. "Move!" I shouted to Carolyn, but she hadn't been paying attention, she didn't know where to move or why, and if she didn't move soon, the scooter would run her over, and how could I get her to see that—

No. There was no time to talk, no time to discuss, no time at all. The scooter was almost here, almost on top of us, almost running us over. I had to move fast and I had to do it now.

Using both hands, I shoved her as hard as I could toward the water, toward safety, and hurled myself in the opposite direction.

Chapter 14

"A re you okay?"
    "Can you stand up?"
    "Did he hit you?"
    Bystanders were suddenly surrounding me. I'd hit the grass face-first but now rolled to my back and saw the concerned faces.
    In answer to the last question, I shook my head. "I'm fine," I said. Was pretty sure of that anyway. Mentally, I explored all my body parts and didn't detect anything out of the ordinary. I started to get up, and a woman on my left and a man on my right helped me to my feet.
    "Take your time," the woman said. "You hit the ground hard."
    "That was a spectacular dive," the man said. "You looked like a runner flat out for home plate. Do you play softball?"
    The man obviously did not know me. I thanked them for their help and looked over at Carolyn, who was still on the sidewalk.

My view of her was blocked by Good Samaritans. I muscled my way between two of them and crouched next to her. "Carolyn? Carolyn!"

She looked over at me. "Ah. Minnie, there you are. I was afraid . . . well, it's good to see you."

I blinked, trying to erase the shock that I was sure was written all over my face. She'd hit the concrete walkway with the side of her head, scraping her cheek bloody. She was gripping her shoulder with one hand, both of her hands raw and red.

"All minor," she assured me. "If you hadn't given me that hearty shove, I'd be hurt much worse."

I swallowed. "Wish I'd pushed you harder. If you'd gone into the water, you wouldn't be hurt at all."

"Assuming I could swim. If I couldn't, I might have drowned." Smiling at my expression, she said, "Just kidding. I can swim." She laughed, then winced. "Don't you hate it when it hurts to laugh?"

I wanted to think that she couldn't be hurt too badly if she could make jokes, but I wasn't so sure about that. "You're a mess. Please tell me you're going to go to the hospital and get checked out."

"So convenient that I work there, yes?" She sat up.

The bystanders, who'd been temporarily silent, started talking again.

"Don't you want us to call nine-one-one?"

"It happened so fast, we didn't have time to get our phones out. All I know is he was wearing jeans, a black sweatshirt, and a black helmet."

"He was on a white scooter. And he tried to hit you. You should call the police."

"No police," Carolyn said.

"But that guy had a bat!" one of them said. "He was swinging it right at your head. If it wasn't for her pushing you out of the way, he might have killed you!"

He'd had a bat? I tried to remember but couldn't. Not for sure. What I'd reacted to had been the noise and the scooter and the speed.

Carolyn and I looked at each other. "Well," she said. "Looks like I owe you a huge debt."

"Should I send you an invoice? Sorry, didn't mean to make you laugh."

As there wasn't much to see, the onlookers started to disperse. One woman kept saying that the police should be called and kept on insisting until I said, "Don't worry, I'll talk to the sheriff's office." After that, she was willing to leave us alone, and Carolyn and I made our way to the nearest bench. "How are you, really?" I asked.

"Minor abrasions and contusions on the right side of the face, both hands, and right knee."

I glanced down and saw the gaping hole in her dress pants.

"The shoulder is of some concern. I'm sure they'll want imagery. And I really don't have time for this, but I know what I'd have any patient of mine do, so . . ." She sighed.

Somehow I'd forgotten. Carolyn was now a hospital administrator but had been a general practice doctor for years.

"That was a direct attack," I said quietly. "And after you got that letter? You really should talk to the city police." And I should run after the other witnesses to get their contact information.

She shook her head. "What are they going to do? Man on a scooter. Jeans, black sweatshirt, helmet. One eyewitness account of a bat, but did you see it?

I didn't, either. There's nothing to say it was a targeted attack. Could have been completely random and probably was. Scooter? Some teenager who just got dumped by his girlfriend out to wreak some havoc."

Maybe. But maybe not. Either way, I couldn't make her go to the police.

We sat quietly. After a long moment, Carolyn turned and gave me a long look. "Being in a position of authority is rewarding in many ways, but there are threats to my leadership. Right now, I cannot be seen as weak. Cannot afford to be perceived as a hysterical woman who cries attack when anyone can see it was an accident."

"But—"

She held up a hand. "I know and you know none of that is true. But for me, for now, if I want to maintain my authority, there are things I have to ignore."

"That . . ." I struggled for words. Couldn't come up with any. "That sucks," I muttered.

"You are absolutely correct." Carolyn gave me a one-sided smile. "On the plus side, I have high hopes for your generation. Things are shifting, my young friend. I want to live long enough to see it happen, but there's a lot of work ahead, so you'd better get cracking."

I laughed. "You're raising the bar pretty high for me."

"You're up to it," she said, nodding. "And now I have to call my husband for a ride to the hospital, because I doubt I can fasten my own seat belt with this shoulder, let alone shift gears. No, it's fine. He can take me. He doesn't have court today."

After the quick call, she told me he'd be in the main parking lot in ten minutes. I helped her to her feet and escorted her up the hill. By the time we made it there, a black SUV was already at the curb. A tall man in a suit and tie got out, and seconds later, they were rolling away.

I watched them drive off, hoping that Carolyn's shoulder was only banged and bruised. The SUV was soon out of sight, and I headed back home to change out of pants that now had grass-stained knees. I paused to wait for a white sedan to pass, then rocked back on my heels. Mouth hanging open.

A scooter had almost hit Carolyn. A white scooter.

Like the one I'd seen when helping Corey and Isabella move into the houseboat.

After I got home, I texted Rafe a concise version of the incident so he wouldn't hear it from anyone else. I put my stained black pants in the laundry bin and pulled on a clean pair of black pants. Eddie, snoring on the bed, didn't so much as twitch a whisker the entire time I was in the bedroom.

"So nice to have this extra time together," I said, kissing the top of his head. "See you tonight." He swiveled one ear, which I chose to interpret as a sign of love and affection, and I blew him a kiss on the way out.

I was pretty sure his snores became a little louder as I left the room, but not completely sure, and I spent the first block of my walk up to the library trying to put myself into Eddie's head.

By the time I reached the second block, I'd given up trying. I barely knew what was going on in my own head, let alone someone else's, and if that someone else was a cat, there was no way I was ever going to truly grasp what went on in there.

So I moved on to thinking about Carolyn, which was a tumbled mess of topics. The immediate was her health, of course, but also her slightly depressing assessment of women in leadership. And then there was that creepy letter, and now the attack. Did she really believe the two things weren't connected? It was possible, I suppose, but not likely, and what if the letter writer decided on another attack? I needed to convince her to—

"Minnie!"

I came to an abrupt stop. Had to, really, because someone was standing in front of me. I blinked away my thoughts and focused.

"Morning, Bianca. Sorry, I was thinking about . . . something else."

"Gee, I never would have guessed. I called your name three times." She laughed. "Someday that habit is going to get you into trouble."

It already had. And since I couldn't seem to stop the regrettable tendency, it probably would again.

"Anyway," Bianca said, "I just wanted to tell you that almost every day I have people asking me about that gorgeous house of yours. Are you and Rafe planning on staying there forever?"

"What? Oh, um—"

She touched my arm. "Prices are sky high right now, and you never know when the market will drop, right? It doesn't hurt to think about selling."

Bianca was in full real estate agent mode, and it took a number of tries to get her to stop talking. "Rafe and I are really happy where we are," I said, backing away. "If that ever changes, I'll let you know, okay?"

In full flight mode, I spun around and hurried off but stopped abruptly. For the first time in almost three weeks, there were lights on inside the candy store, in the back. I hesitated, then went to the front door and tried the handle. Unlocked. I pushed it open. "Hello? Is anyone here?"

Silence, then footsteps clicked across the wood floor. "I didn't mean to leave that unlocked. We're not open and . . . oh, hello. You're Minnie, right? With the bookmobile and the cat."

"That's me." I smiled at Colleen, Whippy's wife. She was in her late fifties, with black hair going gray and bright blue eyes. We'd met a couple of times at downtown functions, and I'd seen her at court, but that was about it. "Hi. Sorry to bother you. I saw the light on and just wanted to make sure everything was okay." As soon as I said it, I wanted to kick myself. Everything was not okay for her and never would be. How could I be so stupid?

She gave a wan smile. "It was time to start dealing with the store's paperwork. I need to get a handle on all that before making a decision about what's next."

If I recalled correctly, Colleen was a dental hygienist and worked in the store only during the busiest summer months. Whippy had been owner, operator, and manager of the store; if she didn't have any interest in retail, selling the store made sense. But the thought of no Henika's gave me a hollow, empty feeling. "Would you like some help?" I heard myself say. "I'd be happy to stop by at lunch. I'll bring a couple of sandwiches from Shomin's."

"Oh." She looked taken aback. "I can't ask you to do that."

"But you're not asking, right? I'm volunteering. Retail finances aren't my thing, but I know how to organize."

"Alphabetically?"

"From A all the way through Z," I said, smiling.

She glanced over her shoulder. "When the police were looking through everything, they might have made it worse, but probably not. Whippy's filing system has always been a mystery. I could use some help back there, that's for sure."

"Then I'll be back at lunchtime. Turkey, roast beef, ham, or veggie?"

Accordingly, I was knocking on the door at noon with ham sandwiches, small bags of chips, and chocolate chip cookies in hand. Colleen let me in, locking the door behind me. "I haven't made much progress since you left," she said. "When the sun came out, I saw how dusty the place was and I just had to clean."

Though I knew what she meant, I had a sad tendency to solve that particular kind of problem by closing the curtains.

"Well," I said, "I'm here for an hour, and I'll do whatever needs doing. Cleaning, paperwork, doesn't matter." Although I'd vastly prefer paperwork. Not only to keep my library clothes intact, but also because maybe I'd learn something. "And I can come back after work."

Colleen blew out a breath. "Let me show you the office. You might regret you offered to help, and I wouldn't blame you."

"I'm used to a messy workspace," I said, following

her through the product-laden shelves to the back. "And my friend Kristen's office, at Three Seasons, is always a disaster. I'm sure this can't be . . ."

My voice faded away. If Kristen's office was a disaster, Whippy's was a cataclysm of epic proportions. I gazed at the heaps of paper, boxes, magazines, and catalogs, and said faintly, "Is it always like this in here?"

Colleen almost laughed. "Since day one. Sure you still want to help?"

"Yes," I said firmly and hunted around for a flat surface that wasn't covered with papers. I freed up a corner of a rolltop desk by moving a pile of five-year-old calendars to the floor, dusted the surface with my hand, and put our lunches on the shiny oak. "There," I said. "Step one complete. Only nine thousand, nine hundred, and ninety-nine to go. Here's your—oh, geez."

When I'd started to open the bag of food, I'd managed to push a stack of papers past their tipping point, and a cascade of white fluttered to the floor.

"Don't worry about it," Colleen said. "I've done that half a dozen times already."

But I was down on my hands and knees gathering up the scattered documents. "Doesn't look good for the librarian to make a mess rather than create order." I straightened the small stack, then lowered my face toward the floor, looking under the desk to make sure I'd recovered everything, and saw one single piece far underneath.

I leaned down, stretched, and with my tippy fingertips pulled the paper toward me. "This little guy almost escaped. Watch, it'll be blank, or it's a sales flyer from 1996 or a—"

"Minnie?" Colleen asked. "What's wrong? You look . . . what does it say?"

But I barely heard her. "We have to go to the police," I said. "Right away."

With a shaken Colleen at my side, I pushed the letter across the interview table. "Read this. Read it and tell me what you think."

Detective Hal Inwood and Ash examined the piece of paper without touching it. "Where did this come from?" Ash asked.

"Whippy Henika's office."

"His office at home or in the store?"

"The store," Colleen said so softly I almost didn't hear her.

The two law enforcement officers exchanged a glance. I wasn't sure what the glance communicated, but something had been said, because Ash's face went from its habitually pleasant expression to something more along the lines of shame.

Belatedly, I realized what I'd done. If I recalled correctly, Ash, the detective in training, had been in charge of the crime scene. If something had been missed, it was Ash's fault.

I hitched forward in my chair. "The only reason I found it was because I'd dropped a pile of papers on the floor and was down on my hands and knees, making sure I'd picked everything up. It was way in the back, right up against the wall."

Hal Inwood gave me a long ice blue look. "While I understand your attempt to deflect criticism from a friend, I find it to be misplaced loyalty. Poor performance is poor performance."

"But—"

Ash shook his head. "Just leave it, Minnie."

I pressed my lips together and sat back. There had to be a way to help him, but that task would have to wait. The important thing now was the letter, sitting flat in the middle of the table, its horrific single-syllable words seared onto the inside of my brain: *YOU NEED TO DIE.* The letters were big and bold, written in a thick black marker in all caps.

Just like the letter to Carolyn.

"There's something else," I said.

Hal Inwood's eyes closed briefly.

It was easy to guess what he was thinking: *Give me strength.* And though it was only a guess, I felt a high degree of certainty that I was correct, and my irritation level rose sharply.

My chin went up, and I thought I saw the tiniest twitch of a smile from Ash. "Yes, there's something else," I said. "I've seen a letter that looked a lot like that one sent to a friend of mine. And that someone else was hurt badly this morning from an attack by a man on a scooter."

"A scooter," Detective Inwood said, dryness dripping from his tone, if dryness could drip.

"Yes, a scooter." I folded my hands on the table so I didn't turn them into fists and pound them. "Witnesses said he was swinging a baseball bat. The only reason she wasn't seriously injured is I happened to hear the scooter coming, and I pushed her out of the way. But she's all bruised and scraped up, and might need shoulder surgery."

Probably not, because she'd texted me that the orthopedic surgeon had said to come back the next week after the swelling went down. Still, you never knew, and not that she was *old* old, but she had to be my mom's age, and Mom was always saying she didn't heal like she used to.

Inwood was frowning. "This happened in Chilson?" He gave Ash a sharp glance. "Call the city. We need a copy of their report as soon as it's completed."

"No report." I did my best to summon a mental force field and surround myself with it. "She didn't want anyone to call the police. She—" Frustrated, I pounded the table with my folded hands. What could I say to make them take this seriously, yet not give them Carolyn's name? It was an impossible situation.

I sucked in a deep breath and let it out slowly. "I'll talk to her again. Try to convince her to talk to the police. She has solid reasons to keep quiet, but it's different now. I'll try to convince her to at least bring in her letter so you can compare it to Whippy's."

"That would be helpful," Hal said, then, before I could berate him for being Mr. Ironic, he added, "If the letters show indications of being written by the same person, the murder investigation could shift."

"We really need it," Ash said.

I nodded. Of course they did. And once I told Carolyn that Whippy had received one, maybe she'd feel differently. Whippy, who was now dead. But what was the connection between Whippy and Carolyn? Or . . .

"What's the matter?" Ash asked.

My mouth opened and shut a few times before I could make myself say the words. "Whippy was a successful business owner, right? And my friend is a successful professional. What if there's some crazy out there? What if more people in Chilson got letters like this? What if more people are in danger?"

The four of us stared at the stark black words.

Hal was the first one to speak. "Unlikely, but possible. Deputy Wolverson, we need to meet with the sheriff ASAP." He rose to his feet. "Ms. Hamilton, please talk to your friend. Mrs. Henika, let me see you out."

As soon as they'd left, Ash and I stood.

"Sorry about dropping you in it," I murmured.

"My own fault. I'm just glad you found the letter at all." He looked down the hall, and I followed his gaze. Hal was holding the door for Colleen, both of them out of easy earshot.

"Technically," Ash said quietly, "Toby Guinn could have attacked your friend. Yesterday we arrested over a dozen people during a drug bust. You know the jail has an overcrowding issue, right? Guinn was released with an ankle monitor and a restriction to stay inside the city limits."

"He was what?" It didn't make sense. "I thought he couldn't afford the bail."

"It was a mistake, but he's back inside. They picked him up late this morning. We're not sure how it happened, and you can't tell anyone. Hal will have my hide if he knows I told you."

"I won't even tell Rafe."

He nodded, then asked, "You really think that guy on the scooter was aiming for your friend? It couldn't have been an accident?"

"No doubt in my mind," I said. "And how about we replace the cutesy 'scooter' with 'small motorcycle'? Because that's what it felt like. He was coming in fast and coming in hard."

Ash gave my shoulder a quick squeeze. "Be careful, Minnie. If you were close enough to keep your friend from getting hurt, this guy might know who you are. You could be his next target."

"If I get one of those letters, you'll be the first person I call."

I'd been joking, because if the killer was targeting successful people, it would be years before he made it down the list to me, but Ash nodded. "Please do," he said, and headed back to his office, leaving me in the hallway alone and a bit frightened.

Chapter 15

I left the sheriff's office, and by the time I reached the sidewalk, I was big-time wrestling with a moral dilemma, one that I had never faced before.

I'd been one of those kids who'd basically always done what they were told. Played by the rules. Stayed out of trouble. Never once had I vandalized a mailbox, stolen a candy bar, or skipped school. I'd grown up into what passed for a fully functioning adult who, with the occasional exception, obeyed laws and complied with rules, regulations, and policies.

But now . . . now I desperately needed to bail on my afternoon library duties and responsibilities. I knew there were people who just didn't show up to work. And people who called in sick when they were actually playing golf. I didn't see how I could do that, though, and be able to ever look my boss in the eye.

There was only one thing to do. I pulled out my phone and called Graydon. "Afternoon, Minnie."

"Hey, boss."

"Every time you call me that, I think I should be wearing wing-tip shoes and suspenders. What can I do for you?" he asked cheerfully.

"Well." Once again, I'd forged ahead with action before developing a plan. One of these days that unfortunate habit was going to get me into serious trouble. I just hoped it wasn't today. "Something came up. Something personal. I hate to do this to you, but would it be okay if I took the afternoon off?"

Silence, except for the clicking of a keyboard. I felt a chill. Graydon was writing me up for a disciplinary action. He was e-mailing Trent about my flagrant violation of the library policy to request time off two weeks in advance. He was checking with the library's attorney to make sure he had grounds to terminate me.

"Hang on," he said finally. "I was in the middle of an e-mail to the regional library director group. About book bikes, of all things. How's that going, by the way? No, never mind. You can tell me later, because you need to take the afternoon off. Hope it's nothing bad."

I blew out a sigh of relief. Why had I thought he might be angry? Graydon was an understanding and reasonable man. And now that I thought about it, when I'd been serving as interim director, I'd okayed an unplanned time off or two for employees. Ash's warning must have rattled me more than I'd realized. "Thanks. You're the best boss ever."

"Sure, sure," he said. "Get me a crown that says so and I might believe you."

"When's your birthday?"

Laughing, he hung up the phone, and I suddenly had a guilt-free afternoon off. I whisked myself home and got in the car without even going in the house, which might have wakened Eddie from his beauty sleep, and we couldn't have that, now could we?

I drove to the hospital in Petoskey. They'd done a major expansion since the last time I was there, and the parking lot layout was so different that my memory was more hindrance than help. Eventually, I found a spot that didn't feel like I would end up in parking lot jail if my car stayed there for half an hour, and I walked into the building.

Once inside, I realized I had absolutely no idea where the administration offices might be. It was possible I wasn't even in the right building.

"You have that lost look. What are you looking for?"

I spun around. A late-middle-aged man wearing a blue jacket was smiling at me. His name tag read ROBERT, and he had the open expression of someone who'd never skipped an afternoon of work in his life.

"Administration offices?" I asked.

Though his directions were lengthy, they were accurate, and I was soon opening a solid wood door and walking into a space that was quiet yet humming with activity. Framed photos of Lake Michigan in all seasons hung high on the walls, with lateral files below. Four doors hinted at additional offices, and the desk in front of me was occupied. A young man looked up and smiled politely. "Can I help you?"

"I'd like to talk to Carolyn Mathews. I don't have an appointment, but—"

"Minnie?" Carolyn appeared in an inner doorway. "Don't tell me you were hurt more badly than you realized. Please tell me you're okay."

I assured her I was fine. "Sorry to barge in like this, but I really need to talk to you."

She looked at her gatekeeper. "Trevor, when's my next appointment?"

Tapping on his keyboard, he said, "Let me double-check . . . yes. Two thirty with the facilities director, in his office."

"Thanks." Carolyn turned back to me. "I can give you ten minutes. Trevor?"

"On it." He tapped some more. "Okay, you're blocked out."

"Thanks." Carolyn swept me into her office and shut the door. Thanks to television, I'd expected a large room with couches and enough extra space to turn a cartwheel. The reality was a cramped office not any bigger than my own, although she did have a lake view.

I sat in the chair she indicated and gave her a quick once-over. Her scrapes had been cleaned and looked much better than they had a few hours ago, although the bruises were starting to come in. "How's the shoulder?" I asked, watching as she sat gingerly.

"It'll be fine. Now. To what do I owe the pleasure? And just so you know," she said, smiling faintly, "Trevor will pound on that door in nine minutes and haul me out of here."

I nodded. "It's about the letter. The threatening one."

"What about it?"

This was the tricky part. Ash had asked that Colleen and I keep quiet about Whippy's letter since the investigation was ongoing. "Another one has turned up," I said, "and the police want to compare it with yours. No, don't worry, I didn't give them your name. But they really need to see it. More people might get hurt."

Carolyn turned in her chair and stared out the window at the long line of blue that was Lake Michigan. Way on the other side of the blue was Wisconsin, but if you didn't know that, you wouldn't know, because from here, the blue looked as if it went on forever.

I waited, my approved minutes ticking away.

At long last, she faced me. "I'll mail the letter to the police with a narrative description and a timeline. If they have questions, I hope you'll be the liaison."

I didn't know that I could even pronounce the word "liaison" correctly, but I nodded. "Thank you."

"Who got the other letter?" Carolyn asked. "Do you know? Never mind. I can see that you do but that you can't tell me. Well, I hope she's okay, whoever she is."

"Um." I glanced at the wall clock. Two minutes left. "I'm just wondering. The letter, the attack. You don't seem all that surprised by any of it. Why?"

She straightened a small stack of papers. "Hospital administrators have to make difficult choices. It's part of the job. Not long ago, our budget projections showed that our revenues aren't keeping pace with expenses, and after discussions with the board, I made the decision to let a number of people go."

"You think it was someone you terminated that sent you the letter. And was on the scooter."

"Who else would it be? So you can see why I don't think my letter and this other letter are related . . . unless the other woman who got a letter also works here." Her voice was suddenly sharp.

"You have to at least tell me that, Minnie. If one of my people is in danger, I need to know."

But I was already shaking my head. "No connection to the hospital."

A light double knock sounded on the door. "That's Trevor," Carolyn said, standing.

"Thanks for seeing me." I got to my feet. "And thanks in advance for sending the letter. If there's a connection between the two letters, the police will find it."

"Or they were sent randomly, and they'll never be able to figure it out." She moved to the door and opened it.

"Please take care of yourself," I said softly.

"I am suddenly hypervigilant." Carolyn smiled. "My sense of self-preservation has been activated. Trevor, shall we?"

The young man jumped to his feet. "On your six." He nodded at me. "I'll watch over her. Judge Mathews, her husband, came in this morning, and the three of us had a talk."

"Most uncomfortable conversation of my life," Carolyn muttered. "Good thing I love that man."

Two seconds later, we were in the hallway. Two seconds after that, they'd outdistanced me and were soon out of sight.

I made my winding way back to the front lobby, made only three wrong turns, and emerged into the afternoon sunshine with new questions running around in my head.

Had Whippy ever worked anywhere but at the candy store? If not, did he have some other connection to the hospital? Had anyone else at the hospital received one of those creepy letters?

I shivered, and I didn't think it was from the chill of the lake breeze.

My phone buzzed with an incoming phone call. I looked at the caller's name and immediately picked up.

"Leah! I've been trying to reach you for days!"

"I had to run downstate," she said. "My dad took a bad turn and was in intensive care for a couple of days."

"So sorry to hear that. Is . . . he doing better?"

"Yes, thanks. Out of the woods, at least for now. So. What was it you wanted?"

I hesitated. She sounded exhausted, but this really couldn't wait. "I have something to show you. Could you possibly meet me for a few minutes?"

"Right now?" she asked, disbelief in every letter of the words.

"Yes. I wouldn't ask, but it's important."

After a bit more cajoling, she agreed to meet me at a gas station outside of Chilson that also served excellent coffee and had a few outside tables. I arrived first, and when Leah arrived, I pushed a cup of coffee across the mesh metal table. "Here. You sounded like you need this."

"Like a life preserver." She took a long sip. "It sure would be great if you had some good news. Like they've arrested someone for Whippy's murder?"

"Not yet. When I talked to the detective yesterday, it sounded like they're still considering Toby Guinn as their most serious suspect."

"Well, that's just silly," Leah said.

"It . . . is?"

"He's a mess, for sure, but the idea of Toby killing anyone is ridiculous."

"I didn't realize you knew him." And I kicked myself for not finding this out earlier.

"A while back, my brother dated Toby's sister." She took another caffeine hit. "They were serious for a long time, so we ended up having family cookouts together. I remember the time a mouse ran across the yard, and Toby insisted that we live trap it and release it in the woods."

It wouldn't mean anything to law enforcement, of course. But I took it as, well, maybe not proof but surely evidence that Toby didn't have killer tendencies.

"What I wanted to show you was this." I'd printed the baby photo on a piece of paper. I took it out of my pocket, unfolded it, and slid it across the table.

Leah's hand shook, spilling coffee all over the paper. "Where did you get this?" she asked, ignoring the coffee running every which way.

"That's you?" I asked, and she nodded. "You're sure?"

She pointed at the photo's background. "That's the fireplace in the house where I grew up. Where did you get this?" she asked again, this time more demanding.

"It was found at the murder scene," I said.

Leah didn't say anything.

I waited.

And waited.

After a short eternity, she sighed. "I have to tell the police, don't I?"

"It'll be okay," I said, and dialed Ash's cell.

Though, as it turned out, he didn't seem to care all that much. "Thanks for the information, Ms. Wasson," he said, just barely loud enough for me to hear, leaning close to Leah. "I appreciate you coming forward. We'll take this into account, but I'm not sure it will change the course of the investigation."

She frowned. "You're not still thinking Toby Guinn killed Whippy, are you?"

"Ma'am, we're—"

"Toby's not a murderer," she said. "There's no way!"

The conversation went downhill from there, and it wasn't long before Ash ended the call. I took my phone back and gave Leah a tight smile. "I'll talk to him later. I'll make him listen."

How, I wasn't sure, but there had to be a way.

Graydon's comment about the book bike had reminded me of the pilot project I'd managed to set up. I texted Donna, the only library employee I'd managed to convince to volunteer, after I got home.

Minnie: *Ready for tomorrow?*

Donna: *Wind sprints and working on my quads the last two weeks.*

Minnie: *And that translates to what, exactly?*

Donna: *Not peak condition, because I did Too Slow for Boston last month, but I'm good.*

Minnie (after remembering Donna's trip to South Carolina for a marathon): *You sure? We can cancel.*

Donna: *And disappoint all those folks? Not a chance.*

Minnie: *Okay. See you at the library at ten.*

Since I wanted to be like my aunt Frances, who didn't worry about anything, I pushed my concerns to the back of my mind and didn't think about them at all until the next morning, when Donna and I loaded the book bike's bright shiny carriers.

"This thing is going to weigh a ton," I said. "You sure about this? The hill up to Lakeview is huge." After many conversations with various folks, a zillion e-mails to the ABOS LISTSERV, and much internal debate, I'd gone up to the Lakeview Medical Care Facility and asked the director what she thought about a book bike. The library's outreach efforts already included Minnie dropping off books twice a month, but I thought the residents might enjoy seeing a book bike being wheeled into the massive main lobby. The director had lit up like a Christmas tree at the idea, so here we were, facing the harsh facts that came with following through.

Donna grabbed the handlebars and moved the bike back and forth. "It'll be fun. And I'd always planned to walk it up. Even these quads"—she pounded her thighs—"can't bring that much dead-weight up that hill."

I looked at the full carriers. "We could take the books out, put them in my car, and then put them in the bike up at Lakeview. I'm going there anyway."

"Cheating," Donna said succinctly. "If this is going to be a real pilot project, we need to do it right."

"Then, bon voyage, I guess. I'll see you up there. Half an hour?"

"It's only two miles. Even if I have to walk all the way up the hill, it won't take me more than twenty minutes, tops."

She spoke so confidently that I was reassured. Donna was one of the most competent people I'd ever met in my life, and she had absolutely nothing to prove to anyone. If she said she could do something, she could.

Accordingly, I was standing at Lakeview's front entrance and checking the time on my phone when she cycled into view. "Seventeen minutes," I called. "And you don't even look out of breath."

"Wind sprints," she said. "They pay off every time."

I made a mental note to find out exactly what a wind sprint was and followed her inside. A small group of residents were gathered in the lobby, and they spontaneously clapped at the sight of the bike.

"It's adorable," said one resident.

"Looks just like the bike I got for Christmas the year I was twelve," said another.

"And there are books inside?"

"Who made that thing? One gear? Coaster brakes? Somebody wasn't thinking."

"How," I said to the man who'd made the last comment, "did I not anticipate that you'd come up with the only criticism."

Max Compton, who had to be nearly ninety, winked at me. "It was either that or hit on your helper. She's a little young for me, but I don't look my age. We could be the perfect couple."

"You and Donna? Not sure her husband would agree."

"Husbands smushbands." From his wheelchair, Max waved a hand knobby with arthritis. "When he kicks off, let me know."

"I'll do that," I said. "Meanwhile, do you want to see these books or not?"

"Sure, if Donna brought better stuff than you do. Here." He pushed aside the blanket covering his legs, revealing a stack of library books. "All yours. Take 'em."

I blinked. Max wanted to return his checkouts now? Now? I'd been after him for ages—the library didn't charge overdue fees to Lakeview residents— and *this* was the time he chose to do what he could have done months ago?

"Of course," I said. Maybe I could get a box from . . . someone. I looked around and grasped that Max wasn't the only one taking the opportunity to do returns. Donna was simultaneously handing out and accepting books and looking a wee bit flustered.

I went to her, and we quickly came up with a plan: Put the returns on a side table and figure it out later.

And so, once all the residents had dispersed, we eyed the heap. "Not something I anticipated," I said. "Didn't think about it once."

"Well, that's the point of a pilot project." Donna tapped her nose. "You know, I think we lent about as many as came back. I know we need to keep the returns separate, so we can check them back in, but I think I can make it work."

She did, using a magnificently easy method of putting the few nonborrowed books facedown, and the returned books faceup.

"Easy peasy," she said, nodding at her handi- work. She took hold of the handlebars. "See you in a few!"

I watched her roll away, thinking once again that I wanted to be like her when I grew up. Competent, confident, and not afraid to show it. I poked my head into Max's room to say good-bye, but he twid- dled his fingers at me. "Go away. I'm reading."

"Love you, too," I said sweetly, and he made a rude gesture.

Laughing, I left him to his book—*Good Omens* by Neil Gaiman and Terry Pratchett—and headed out. Donna, on the bike, would have taken the short cut down a sidewalk not accessible to cars, so I drove back to the library and waited for her. And waited. And waited.

"Something's wrong," I murmured, and checked my phone for the hundredth time. She was more than twenty minutes out for a mostly downhill ride. And she'd sent no message. I knew she had her phone. Why hadn't she texted why she was late?

I jumped back in the car and drove up the hill. I couldn't get on that sidewalk, but I could get close, and I'd park nearby, and I'd run up the hill, I'd find her, and—

A bright yellow flash through the trees caught my eye. I braked to a quick stop at the curb and hopped out. "Donna?" I called as I jogged toward her. "Are you okay? Tell me you're not hurt."

"I'm not hurt," she said. "But I'm not so sure about the bike."

On Monday morning, I told the Saga of the Book Bike to Julia, who said the right things in all the right places, then asked, "Donna wasn't hurt at all?"

"Not a bit. Just past the top of the hill, she realized what was going to happen—gravity still being a thing and all—and she made sure to get out of the way." She'd also run beside it most of the way down, giving the handlebars an occasional shove, trying to keep it from diving nose-first off the bluff. The bike's speed had increased, soon moving too fast for Donna to keep up, and it had eventually bashed into a retaining wall.

Julia lightly banged her fists together and made crashing noises. "You think the returned books were the tipping point?"

I shrugged. "Maybe. But the same thing might have happened even if the bins had been empty. The bike itself weighs about a quintillion pounds."

"Quintillion," Julie mused. "That's a lot."

It was indeed. And even with the books removed. it had taken a lot of muscle—and height—to get the bike to Cody to fix. I'd made a few phone calls, and before long, Rafe, Donna, Josh the IT guy, Gareth the maintenance guy, and I myself had heaved the poor thing up into the bed of Rafe's truck.

I'd given the bent front wheel and the skewed handlebars a long look. Right then and there, I made an executive decision. "No one else," I'd said firmly, "needs to know about this."

Of course, I was now telling Julia, Cody would undoubtedly tell people, and word would spread, but with any luck, it would spread slowly and not very far, and not until the bike returned to roadworthiness.

Luckily, Cody had said that he could pirate a new wheel from an old bike he had in the back and that the handlebars were an easy fix. "I'll have it ready for you in a couple of days," Cody had said. I'd wanted to tell him not to rush, but instead I'd smiled, thanked him profusely, and told him I'd be paying the bill myself. No need for Graydon to see it, no need at all.

"What's the next plan for the bike?" Julia asked, smirking. "Testing its top speed? You could take it up to Ironwood and send it down that ski jump. I know," she said, sitting up. "You could take bets on how fast it could go. Something like that, it would go viral. Make all kinds of money for the library."

"Mrr!"

"See?" Julia said, nodding. "He thinks it's a great idea, too."

Since Eddie would think anything was a great idea if it included cat treats, he didn't qualify as a decision-maker on this topic. Right that second, he was stretched along the dashboard, tail and front legs out, in super-kitty pose. We'd just set up for the first stop of the day, and Eddie had taken roughly a second and a half to assess the lay of the land and reserve the sunniest spot for himself.

"Mrr," he said again, with the last "r" ending in a yawn.

"Okay, maybe he doesn't like the idea," Julia said through her own yawn. "But you can still think about new ways to make money. No reason not to, right?"

"You saying you have a job opening?"

We turned. The day was just the right temperature to leave the door open, so we hadn't heard our first patron of the day come up the steps. Rene Kinney, tall and lanky, was dropping a short pile of returned books on the back desk.

I wasn't sure how she'd jumped to an employment opportunity from what Julia had said, but then I typically didn't understand my own mental leaps, so who I was to criticize? "Not right now," I said. "We were talking about something else."

"Oh." Rene's facial expression went from an interested almost smile to a surly twist. "Figures. Well, if you hear of anything decent, I'm looking.

Unemployment doesn't cover the bills, not by a long shot."

Something went *click* in the back of my brain, and I knew what I had to do next: probe gently when my deepest desire was to switch topics altogether. I took a deep breath. "This was a recent thing?"

"Just a couple of weeks ago." She folded her arms and leaned against the desk. "I was at the hospital in Petoskey, processing payroll. Solid job, you'd think, right? More and more people are moving up here all the time, and people don't stop getting sick. How could a hospital job not be a sure thing? But no," she said in a snarly voice. "It's decreased revenues this, budget cuts that, blah blah blah, and I'm out the door, no severance, no nothing but a kick in the behind."

"Sorry to hear that," I said.

"Yeah, you and me both." She gave a barking kind of laugh. "Last year this time, things were finally working out for me, moneywise. Had the full-time hospital job and picked up part-time work at the candy store, you know, Henika's? Then around Halloween, Whippy tells me he doesn't need me anymore. Okay, I get it, seasonal work, but now this? Kick in the teeth is what it is. Just a kick in the teeth."

"That's tough," I murmured. Because it was.

"Getting fired is horrible." Julia moved to the nonfiction section. "Question for you. Are you familiar with *What Color Is Your Parachute?*"

I watched as Julia tried to get Rene interested in career guidance materials. Watched but wasn't paying all that much attention, because my brain was suddenly thinking very hard about another topic.

Last time we'd seen Rene, she'd been far less than sympathetic to the news of Whippy's death. From that, I'd jumped to a theory that she was Leah's birth mother. It now seemed obvious that Rene's reaction to the murder was because he'd laid her off last fall.

But . . . had her termination from the hospital been a tipping point? Had that second layoff triggered something? Was Rene the connection? Had she written the letters? Had she attacked Carolyn?

Was she a killer?

I inched forward, quietly inserting myself between Rene and Julia, between Rene and Eddie, and vowed to find out.

Chapter 16

Because Rafe and I discussed everything—at least everything that was important . . . well, at least almost everything that was really important—over dinner, I told him what I'd learned about Rene and Whippy and Carolyn.

"I don't know, Minnie," he said as he added salt to the nearly boiling water. Dinner was spaghetti with pesto sauce, and I was putting together a salad of whatever was in the refrigerator's produce drawer. It was going to be heavy on baby spinach and broccoli and light on everything else, but dark colors were supposed to be good for you, right?

"Don't know about what?" I asked.

"People get laid off all the time," he said. "If that was a motive for murder, we'd see a lot more violent deaths."

I didn't disagree. "Yes, but you didn't see her. That 'if looks could kill' thing? It's a saying for a reason."

"Okay. Say she's the one. Didn't you say the person on the scooter was a man?"

"All I saw was someone wearing a black sweat-shirt and a helmet. It was the other people who said it was a man. But I'm not sure how you could tell gender for sure if he—or she—was all covered up. It's more a default assumption that someone on a motorized vehicle is male."

"Fair enough." He dropped the spaghetti into the water and stirred. "Do you have anything you can take to Ash?"

"You mean like actual proof? Something other than conjecture and theory?"

"Like that, yeah."

"Of course not." I ignored his grin. "And I know that correlation is not causation. If I walk in with this, Hal Inwood will listen to me, pat me on the head, and tell me to leave the investigating to trained law en-forcement officers. But lots of crimes are only solved because people are willing to step up and share infor-mation. They need all the help they can get."

"You trying to convince me or yourself?"

"Do you need convincing? Never mind, don't answer that. Finding a killer is maybe like a lot of things. It takes lots of people to figure it out, more than one, for sure, and . . ."

"And what?"

I blinked. Rafe was waving his hand in front of my eyes. "Stop that." I pushed his arm away. "I just had a thought. For the sake of this conversation, the assumption is that Whippy's murder and the attack on Carolyn are connected."

"Assumed."

"Thank you. Now, what if they're connected, but more than one person is involved? What if one person wrote the letters, one killed Whippy, and another went for Carolyn?"

"That's three," Rafe said. "Why would that many people get together on this?"

I threw up my hands. "Fine. Make it two. What if Dan wrote the letters, Rene was on the scooter, and together they killed Whippy?"

"Now you're just making stuff up," Rafe said.

I'd suddenly remembered something and was tapping on my phone, not listening to him. Part of me wondered if it was a bad sign for our marriage that I found it so easy to ignore things he was saying that I didn't want to hear. However, another part of me thought that was probably an excellent attribute for a marriage to have. Happily, the two parts had canceled each other out by the time I sent my text message to Kristen.

Minnie: *Do you know anyone who rides a scooter?*

Kristen (after a long pause): *Why?*

Minnie: *Will tell you later.*

Kristen: *Isabella Moncada has one. Adorable.*

Minnie: *What color?*

Kristen: *White. Gotta go. Kid feeding time.*

I stared at my phone for a long minute, reading and rereading but seeing the same words every time, no matter how hard I tried to see something different. I slid it over to Rafe. "Read that. The scooter that almost hit Carolyn was white. How many can there be in Chilson this time of year? It has to be Isabella's." And how Isabella could be mixed up with Carolyn or Whippy, I have absolutely no idea.

Slowly, he nodded. "Doesn't look good, but there are other possibilities."

"Name three."

"One, the scooter was stolen by the bad guy. Two, she always leaves the key in the scooter's ignition, because Chilson has almost no crime, and the bad guy—or bad gal—borrowed it. Three, Isabella sold it the other day and moved up to a Harley-Davidson."

Three reasonable explanations, which made me feel a lot better, because I didn't want to suspect Isabella of anything. "I can check," I said. "Ash will know if there was a theft, and I can—hey!"

Rafe, in the act of taste-testing the al-dente-ness of our future dinner, froze. "What did I do now?"

"Not you, him." I clapped my hands loudly, the signal I'd used for years to scold my cat. "Get down!"

Eddie, who must have briefly turned invisible, because he'd managed to get up on the kitchen counter without us noticing, ignored me. Someone hadn't quite turned off the faucet, and a thin stream was dripping down. Eddie's white paw was batting the water around, playing with it like a . . . like a cat with a mouse.

"I said down! Not a cat toy!"

"Mrr!" he said, giving me a look, but he jumped down and stalked off.

"Love you, too," I said to his tail end and turned back to Rafe. "Anyway, I can go to the sheriff's office tomorrow and talk to Ash and/or Hal, or we, meaning you, could ask Ash what he's doing tonight and see if he wants to stop by." I knew Chelsea had taken a long weekend to visit her parents downstate and wouldn't be back until late that night. "I'm okay with either. Up to you."

"I can ask." He took the pasta pot to the Eddie-free sink and dumped the contents through a colander. As it drained, he pulled his phone from his pocket and tapped away using the one-thumb method. Seconds later, we heard the *ting* of an incoming text.

"He'll be here in half an hour," Rafe said, reading.

"Thanks. Um, did you give him any reason for the invite?"

"Need him to settle our argument about where the gazebo should go."

"Are you going to tell me what, exactly, the argument is?" Because as far as I knew, we hadn't been fighting about that at all. More we just hadn't come to a final decision.

"Hard to do that when I don't know." He grinned, and even though I wanted to be annoyed with him, my heart went mushy and I felt nothing but love.

Half an hour later, the three of us—four if you counted Eddie's nose pasted against the kitchen window—were in the large backyard traipsing from one side to the other, considering tree heights, long and short views, and sun angles.

"Can't believe you're arguing about where to put it." Ash stood in the yard's far back corner and stomped his foot. "There's only one good spot, and this is it. Where else were you thinking?"

"Oh, here and there," I said vaguely.

"Well, it should be here. With a couple of steps up, you'll have a half-decent view of the lake, although most of it will be marina. And you should get morning sun, once it clears that back fence."

"Good point," Rafe said. "Hadn't thought about that."

I narrowed my eyes. Maybe he hadn't, but I had,

and I'd mentioned it more than once. Then he winked, and I remembered that we'd brought Ash here under false pretenses.

"Right," I said, turning to Ash. "Really good point. Thanks for helping us with this."

"Sure. No problem."

Rafe looked at his friend. "Beer? Owe you one for dragging you out here."

Since an off-duty Ash said no to beer about as often as Rafe did, which was basically never, Rafe went inside to fetch the adult beverages while Ash and I wandered up to the back deck.

"Thanks again for stopping by," I said as we dropped into the chairs. "And just for the record, we weren't really fighting. It was more we needed someone to push us to a final decision, especially if we want to get it done this summer."

Ash shrugged off my thanks, saying he hadn't been doing anything anyway.

"Still. It's appreciated." Then, before the conversation shifted to anything else, I said, "By the way, I did talk to my friend, the one who got the other letter. She said she'd put it in the mail . . . and you're nodding. You got it already?"

"Showed up this afternoon," he said.

"And?"

He shrugged. "Too early to tell. Hal is going to take both letters downstate to some expert, but she's backed up. It'll take weeks."

"What do you think?" Not that I'd seen the two letters side by side, but everything I could remember indicated the same person had written both of them.

"Minnie, you know I can't—"

Suddenly I'd had enough. "Don't go all Detective Inwood. If it wasn't for me, you wouldn't know about either one of those letters."

Ash sat back. We stared at each other for a minute, long enough for me to wonder what was taking Rafe so long. Of course, maybe he was at the back door, looking through the curtain, and waiting until the obvious tension subsided. I chose not to look to find out.

Finally, Ash said, "Here are the facts. Both are the same standard twenty-pound paper. Both were written with black marker that looks similar. Both were written in block handwriting. Any conclusions about them being written by the same person are going to have to come from the expert."

He came to a full stop, and I knew he wasn't going to give me anything else. "Okay. Thanks." I waited a beat, then said, "On the scooter thing. Did you happen to check if any had been reported stolen?"

"I did. And, no, there haven't been."

So much for that possibility. Now I had to drill down on numbers two and three, which wouldn't be nearly as easy. But that wasn't the main thing here.

"Aren't you bothered by that attack?" I asked. "Yes, in theory Toby could have done it, but it seems like a lot to set up in the few hours he was out of jail. And again, none of the other things he did were violent at all. Why would he change now?"

"Criminals do," Ash said. "Escalation. It's a thing."

I knew that. Anyone who watched cop shows—which had to be everyone more than one day old—did, too. "But there are other suspects," I insisted. "Why aren't you looking at them?"

"What makes you think we're not?" Ash asked.

"Are you?"

He paused. "Let's just say to shift the investigation away from its current track, we'd need some rock-solid evidence."

"Rock-solid," I repeated, and slouched in my chair.

At that moment the back door opened and Rafe came out, beverages in hand, which to me proved he'd been standing there, waiting for the *Minnie v. Ash* conversation to conclude.

He and Ash settled into a baseball discussion about losing a no-hitter, which made no sense to me, and I sipped my wine, thinking and planning.

If rock-solid evidence was what he needed, then that was what I'd find.

After work the next night, Rafe and I drove out to Kristen and Scruffy's house. Technically, it was the house owned by Scruffy's dad, star of the TV cooking show *Trock's Troubles*, but a few months ago Trock had insisted that the young and expanding family take it over, saying that he only spent a few weeks a summer in the place, so why should they spend their hard-earned money on something completely unnecessary?

That was the concise version anyway. From what Kristen told me, the discussion had been conducted during a marathon cooking session at Trock's New York City restaurant. The garrulous Trock had talked on and on, making extensive and expansive gestures with his huge hands as he worked on new recipes.

Kristen and Scruffy, so the story went, had decided early on that moving into the large renovated

farmhouse made sense but had let Trock talk.
"He'd spent a lot of time preparing his argument,"
Scruffy said now. "Didn't want him to think it was
time wasted."

"Besides," Kristen said, "if we'd stopped him, he
might never have finished his new flamiche recipe,
and that would have been a loss for humanity."

The starred restaurant world was not mine, but
Kristen thrived in it, and so I tried to take a sincere
interest. "You bet. A huge loss," I said, and ate my
last bite of cheesecake brownies, the eating of
which was the reason we'd been invited over.

Kristen gave me a look over the top of a sleeping
Eloise. "You have no idea what flamiche is, do you?"

"Not even a little." Clearly, I needed to work on
my cooking sincerity.

She smiled and kissed the top of her baby's head.
"Want to see how the nursery turned out? Rafe,
you saw it last week when you brought the presents
over, right?"

He had, and I did, so my best friend and I left the
men to cleanup duty and climbed the wide switch-
back stairs to the second floor. Years ago, Trock had
renovated the entire home, adding a massive kitchen,
opening up the living room with French doors, adding a main-floor master suite, and reworking the
second floor from five small bedrooms with no bathrooms to three with two full bathrooms. It must have
taken a mint of money, but the result was flat-out
gorgeous.

The large nursery had two of everything: cribs,
changing tables, and dressers. Furniture and wood-
work were white, walls painted in wide stripes of

off-white and a soft buttery yellow. There was also an antique rocking horse and a small wicker rocking chair, looking happy in their new homes next to the cribs.

"I hope you like them," I said quietly to Kristen, patting the horse's head as I tiptoed close to the already sleeping Cooper. Both chair and horse had been gifts from Rafe and me for the babies.

"They're perfect." Kristen gave Eloise another kiss.

I watched as she tucked her daughter into her crib, admiring the quick, deft movements that, just a few weeks ago, she'd never done in her life. She checked on Cooper-Lloyd and tapped the small wall screen that controlled the baby monitors.

"All set," she said, and she pulled the door not quite closed as we entered the hallway. "You know, I've been thinking about Eddie and the twins. Maybe it would be better if they met outside. Neutral territory."

I nodded. "Good idea." It was worth trying anyway. "There has to be a way to get him to adjust."

By now we were back in the massive kitchen. Scruffy was shutting the dishwasher and Rafe was supervising. "Adjust?" my beloved asked. "Which one are you talking about, me or him?" He pointed his chin at the Scruff. "Because if it's him, I'm good with it. If it's me, not so much."

"Eddie," I said. "He needs to be friends with the twins, and I'm not sure how to make that happen."

Scruffy shrugged. "It'll take time, that's all."

He was probably right, but that didn't mean I had to like it. I eyed him. "You think I'm crazy for caring so much about Eddie and the twins, don't you?"

"Do you really want me to answer that? You do. Okay, well, yes. A little. But I think I understand. Eddie is a big part of your life, so is Kristen, and now so are the twins. Having them get along makes a difference."

"Well said." Kristen hugged him from behind. "Leave it to you to figure out a way to tell Minnie she's nuts without making it sound like she's nuts."

"All in the delivery," Rafe said, doing a knuckle bump with Scruffy. "I should be taking notes."

I rolled my eyes, but it was funny, so I laughed along with the others, and after we got home, I sat down with Eddie and we had a long talk.

"Little humans are still human," I told him. "They grow. Soon they'll be walking and talking and will have enough hand-eye coordination to give you treats." His ears twitched. "Yes, exactly, more ways you can get what you want. And I know they're noisy, but you're noisy, too, sometimes. We all are, right? So it's only fair that we tolerate the noise from others."

He was purring now, and of course not understanding anything I said other than the word "treat," but I figured the discussion couldn't hurt.

"Are we set on this?" I asked. "You're going to try a little harder to be buddies with the tiny little humans? Be the adult and all that?"

No response, so I gave him a long pet and watched a few stray Eddie hairs waft off into space. "You know," I said, "Ash was right. If I want the sheriff's office and the prosecutor to seriously consider anyone other than Toby, I need to find some of that rock-solid evidence. The problem is, I have no clue how to do that."

Eddie gave a silent, sleepy "Mrr" and started purring a little louder.

This was my hint to keep petting him, so naturally I did.

"But how can I get evidence?" I mused. "I could find out more about the scooter, but since I'm the only one tying Carolyn's attack to the murder, that's not going to help much."

I ticked off the suspects. "Let's review. Other than Toby, there's Dan Calhoun, Kurt Wasson, and Rene Kinney."

Because of Kurt's height and Toby's disinclination to violence, Rene and Dan were at the top of my list. Dan because he had good reason to want Whippy dead and Rene because she had a bad history with both Whippy and Carolyn. But I didn't know of any connection between Dan and the hospital, or with Carolyn, and I had no good ideas on how to uncover one.

Maybe what I needed to do was eliminate a suspect or two. And I knew exactly how to get started.

My first task the next morning was to shoo Rafe out of the house so I could get to work on my suspect-elimination efforts. Since I was trying my best to be completely open and honest with my intended, I told him what I was planning to do on my way to the library.

Milk dripped from the edge of his cereal spoon as he tore his attention away from the sports updates on his phone. "You're going to do what?"

We were eating breakfast in the kitchen—cold cereal but with a healthy heap of blueberries—and

I'd just finished telling him that I planned to eliminate suspects, starting with Kurt Wasson.

"Pretty sure you heard me the first time," I said, "so I'm not going to waste time by repeating myself. And, yes, I have a plan." Possibly not a very good one, but a plan nonetheless.

"How good a plan?"

Rats. He was on to me. There was the occasional downside to a deeply loving relationship with someone who knew you inside and out, and this was one of them.

"Ideally," I said, "I'd keep it simple and just ask him what he was doing the night Whippy was killed."

"If he's the killer, you think he's going to tell you that he was in the candy store standing in the dark on a ladder, holding a piece of rope, waiting for Whippy to back into it by accident?"

I eyed him warily. "Are you feeling okay? That's a lot of snark for so early in the morning."

"Sorry." He leaned over and gave me a kiss. "I didn't sleep well last night. Didn't mean to take it out on you."

"Can we blame Eddie for your poor sleep?" I turned around, but the feline in question was not in his habitual morning spot on the windowsill, where he'd taken to perching in hopes of mostly empty cereal bowls put on the floor so he could suck up the last molecules of milk.

"Not this time." Rafe pushed his phone away and gave me his full attention. "Far as I know, he's still sound asleep on the bath mat next to the tub. Is it normal for cats to snore that loudly?"

"No clue." I'd long suspected that Eddie was a one-of-a-kind cat, a subspecies that, thanks to the handiwork of our veterinarian, would never reproduce. "Anyway, thanks to meeting with Kurt out at that new house, we know he was working in those big new condos on the other side of downtown. I can stop by there and ask some casual questions."

He narrowed his eyes. "Not sure I care for that, my little cotton candy."

"Your what?"

"I'm trying out new terms of endearment. What do you think?"

"Try harder. The condo is right next to the main road. There are a zillion people around all the time, and I promise I won't go into any basements with strangers."

"Or attics."

"Well . . ." I sighed heavily. "Okay. Attics too."

He seemed satisfied with that, although he also extracted a promise to text him when I got up to the library, something that would be easy enough to do; the trick was remembering to do so.

"Leave yourself a voice mail on your office phone," Rafe advised. "That blinking light will drive you bonkers until you listen to the messages."

"Genius," I said, pulling out my phone. "Simply genius. And as a reward, I'll do your breakfast dishes."

He looked at his bowl and spoon. "How will I ever thank you?"

"Don't worry. I'll think of something."

Rafe gave me a smacking kiss and headed out. I did indeed leave myself a voice mail reminder, then prepared my lunch by the simple means of opening the freezer and grabbing a bag of jambalaya from the big batch Rafe had made over the weekend.

"I am the luckiest person in the world," I said happily as I walked through downtown. I had no idea what I'd done to deserve my good fortune—nothing, almost certainly—and I wanted to make sure I demonstrated my gratitude to the universe.

I was also lucky that no one was out on the sidewalk to hear me talking to myself, but it was barely eight, two hours before most of the stores opened. Though it was too early for shopkeepers and shoppers to be about, it was the perfect time to check out an active construction site.

Pickup trucks, SUVs, and panel vans clogged the muddy parking lot of the future condominiums. I picked my way around the mud puddles, wondering who I'd find that would be willing to talk to me, then came to an abrupt halt.

Job trailer. A project this size would almost certainly have a general contractor and an on-site job trailer serving as the contractor's office.

I stood on my tiptoes to see over vehicles. I saw stockpiles of lumber, trusses, and concrete blocks. There were piles of dirt and gravel and—

I ducked down. Kurt Wasson was climbing out of a white truck just on the other side of the SUV I was hiding behind. He shut the driver's door, opened the crew cab door next to the driver's seat, and leaned inside. When he straightened, he had a toolbelt in one hand and . . . and what was in his other hand?

Frowning, I sidled around vehicles, following him, closing the gap, trying to see . . .

And then I figured out what he was carrying.

I backed up fast, suddenly not caring if my feet got wet, not caring if I splashed mud on my pant legs.

Kurt Wasson, the shortish man I'd almost eliminated as a suspect because of his height, was carrying a small collapsible step stool.

Chapter 17

My feet carried me to the library, where I let myself in through the back door and made my way through the dim hallways to the break room. I stood there for a moment, not quite sure where I was or what I was doing, because making sure you're in the here and now isn't easy when most of you is thinking about something else entirely.

I shook my head, trying to jostle my brains loose. "First things first," I said out loud, and surprisingly, the sound of my voice surprised me.

"Stop that," I muttered, then brewed a pot of coffee just the way I liked it, stashed my lunch in the freezer, and went to my office. I dropped my backpack in a desk drawer, picked up my mug, and stood there staring at the air in the middle of the room.

Since this was my investigation, not law enforcement's, I was crossing Toby off the suspect list. He was out.

Kurt was a different matter.

After I'd learned that Whippy had been killed by someone about six feet tall, I hadn't been taking him all that seriously as a suspect. The man was only a few inches taller than I was. Even standing on his tiptoes, he wouldn't come close to six feet. But if he routinely carried around a sturdy step stool, one that folded flat, was lightweight, and seemed as much a part of his everyday work life as a pipe wrench . . . well . . .

I meandered my way back to the kitchen, still thinking.

Owning a step stool didn't prove anything. But it did establish that Kurt had an easy way to get to six feet tall. A routine way.

I tried to picture the scene. Kurt, theoretically summoned to Whippy's for an emergency repair that night. Pipes probably ran between the drop ceiling of the downstairs retail area and the upstairs apartment he rented in the summer. Maybe there'd been a leak and Kurt was there to fix it. He'd moved some of the ceiling tiles and was up on the stool working on the leak. He'd looked down and seen Whippy, and . . . what?

Of course, I had no idea what a plumber might typically carry that could be used to strangle someone. Would a plumber have wire? Or maybe—

"Good morning."

I jumped. "Oh. Hey. Morning, Graydon. I started coffee. Should be ready by now."

"Great," he said. "And do you have a few minutes? We should catch up on a few things."

"Sure. Anything in particular?"

The answer to that was both yes and no. No, because he was an excellent boss and wanted to make sure I had everything I needed to do my job and didn't have any pressing concerns about anything he wasn't already aware of. But also yes, because he wanted to talk a little about progress on the strategic plan and to talk a lot about my nemesis, the book bike.

"Can't we do that the other way around?" I asked. "A little about the book bike and a lot about the strategic plan? Because that way makes more sense to me, as far as the overall health of the library goes."

"I don't disagree." Graydon smiled. "However, we serve at the behest of the library board, and the president of said board is very interested in the bike's success."

I kept my face quiet. Or at least as quiet as I could, which couldn't have been all that quiet, because Graydon's smile went a little smirky.

"Yes, I know. This is not an ideal way to start a new outreach program—probably the worst possible way—but this is what we have, and we're stuck with it. And keep in mind that Trent did this with the absolute best of intentions."

Which was true enough. Misguided though his intentions might be, they were good ones and were done with kindness and a sincere interest in the library.

I eyed my boss. "You're saying I should accept that decisions will be thrust upon me from time to time, aren't you? That change is inevitable and I should suck it up and get used to it. That I should work harder on setting a good example for everyone else. That I should grow up a little."

"Your words, not mine. But that's the subtext.

Well done," he said, grinning and toasting me with his coffee mug. "Now. What did Cody say about the repair timeline?"

I pulled out my phone and looked at Cody's latest text. "Late yesterday he said everything is done, except he's waiting for a new tire to show up, and that should be in today, no later than tomorrow."

"You'll figure this out," Graydon said. "I have faith in you. The Lakeview trip wasn't a failure, you know. It wasn't a complete success, that's all. Just keep trying, yes?"

I nodded. "I will. And thanks."

The sounds of heavy footsteps grew louder and louder, and Josh came in. "Any coffee ready yet?"

Graydon looked meaningfully at Josh, back at me, raised his eyebrows, and left.

"What was that all about? And who made this?" Josh asked, the coffeepot poised above his mug.

"I did. And Graydon was not-so-subtly hinting that I ask you about the book bike."

"What about it? Wait, let me guess." He filled his mug and put the pot back on the burner. "Trent is back in his basement, only this time he's making a drone to deliver books."

I reminded myself of the conversation I'd just had with Graydon and told myself to be the adult in the room. Or at least the adultier one of the two. "The bike will be repaired in another day or two. It'll be fine as long as we stay off the steepest hills. Do you think the place where your wife works would be interested in a visit from the book bike? You could ride it over there, she'd love that, you know she would, and—"

"Gee, look at the time!" Josh stared, wide-eyed,

at the wall clock. "I really need to get going, I have to patch in that setup for the SPRI before the TMP directory gets hardened. Can't risk leaving that open, you know."

And he was gone.

I spent the rest of the day working hard to grow my enthusiasm for Trent's pet project, reminding myself that my former boss had only very reluctantly agreed to support the bookmobile itself.

The only reason I'd succeeded was because a library patron, now sadly departed, had donated the money. No way would Stephen have supported diverting any regular library funds to something as out-of-date as a bookmobile. He hadn't been thrilled when I'd said I'd get grants and donations, and I was sure he'd tried to divert the money I had raised back to the general library budget.

Since I didn't want to become like Stephen, the second-worst boss I'd ever had, I sent an e-mail to the ABOS LISTSERV, asking how people felt about their book bikes. I also did some online hunting for photos, and up popped pictures of happy faces, young and old.

The e-mails soon came in. *People love our book bike*, wrote one fellow ABOS outreach librarian. *Just* love *it.*

By percentage, we have more borrows from our bike than from our bookmobile, wrote someone else. *Once last summer it was emptied out. I asked our board about buying another one, and they said go right ahead.*

Seeing it makes people happy, was another comment. *My mom says it reminds her of the ice cream cart that pedaled around her neighborhood when she was a kid. Of course, the kid that pedaled it around ended up being my dad, so be careful!*

Three happy face emojis followed the last comment. I smiled at them, and somewhere deep down inside of me, the pendulum that was my attitude swung the other way.

Trent was right. The book bike was a good idea. It was adorable. It was quirky. It was one of a kind. It was perfect for Chilson, and I would find a way to make it work.

I scribbled out some ideas on a pad of paper, crossed most of them off, scribbled some more, then left the pad on my computer keyboard when I went home. The ideas would percolate in my brain's background the next couple of days, and with some luck, the next time I sat down, a solution would spring fully formed out of my head.

Humming an upbeat tune, I walked home and, completely by myself, started dinner. After pulling cooked sausage and previously made balls of calzone dough out of the freezer, I patted myself on the back for a job well done.

Just then, my phone pinged.

Rafe: *talking a teacher off the quitting ledge . . . an hour out*

Minnie: *Thanks for the heads-up. See you whenever.*

Rafe: *Love ya*

"Well," I said out loud, "doesn't that just work out?"

Because now I had time to take my next investigative step—see what I could find out about Isabella's scooter. I really wanted to believe in one of

Rafe's explanation possibilities about how the scooter wasn't relevant, but I had to keep an open mind.

I walked over to the marina, but before I got even halfway there, I felt myself smiling at an unexpected sight. "Louisa!" I shouted, waving madly. "Louisa!"

The slim woman with long wonderfully white hair looked up from the boat window she was washing. "As I live and breathe, if it isn't Minnie Hamilton," she called. "Come on over and get a hug, you silly thing."

Louisa and Ted Axford had moored their boat at Uncle Chip's for years, and for years they'd been my other houseboat neighbor. In their early sixties and retired, they hadn't spent as much time Up North the last couple of years because of their first grandchild, who'd been born into the unfortunate circumstance of having parents who lived downstate.

I hurried up the Axfords' dock and onto their version of a houseboat, which was not that much bigger than mine but was far more luxurious. "How's your granddaughter doing?" I asked after Louisa had released me.

"Fit as the proverbial fiddle. I'll show you pictures when you have a couple of hours," she said, laughing. "And she's so fit that the kids are taking a month-long trip to see the other set of grandparents out in Montana."

"That's great. Well, not great that you're left without a grandchild to spoil but great that you're up here. We've missed you."

"Aren't you sweet." Louisa hugged me again.

"But it's all going to be different now, isn't it? Though I did appreciate the text messages that you're renting your boat. Who are they again?"

I told her what I knew about Isabella and Corey, that they both worked in the restaurant industry, Corey as a manager at Shomin's Deli, Isabella as a sous-chef at Kristen's restaurant.

"Is that how they met?" Louisa asked. "Working together in a restaurant somewhere? I love How We Met stories."

"Not sure. They're from downstate, the South-field area, and decided to try living Up North to get away from . . . well, everything."

Louisa nodded. "For years I've gone to a dentist in Southfield because it was closest to our old facility, but the traffic is just horrible. So glad I don't have to do that commute anymore."

A movement in the parking lot caught my eye. "Speaking of commuting, that's Corey."

The young man braked to a stop and hopped off his bicycle. "Hi, Minnie," he said, smiling up at us. "And you must be Louisa. Nice to meet you."

"Likewise," she said. "So your commute is, what, two minutes?"

He laughed. "Only if I take my bike. It's seven if I walk."

"And your wife?" Louisa asked. "The poor thing, her commute must be double yours."

"Just for now. We have this ancient scooter that Isabella rides, but it conked out on her more than a week ago. It's in the shop, waiting for some part, so now she's riding her own bike."

In the shop. Interesting that none of Rafe's three

theoretical scooter options had included what had actually happened. I hoped I'd remember to tell him so.

"Who's fixing it for you?" I asked, and was pleased to hear they'd been recommended to use the garage owned by Darren Bryant. Not only was Darren an excellent mechanic, but I was on excellent terms with him since he took care of the bookmobile. I could easily stop by to chat and could ask about the scooter, just to confirm.

Even though I'd never officially added Isabella to the suspect list, I mentally crossed her name off and left the marina in an excellent mood. Sure, I'd do my due diligence and check with Darren about the scooter, but my good mood was also due to the fact that Louisa was, once again, acting as the unofficial welcome wagon for marina newcomers, just like she'd done for me years ago. Which was wonderful, because I was pretty sure Eric Apney's efforts had fallen far short.

I mulled over the remaining suspects the rest of the night, running through everything I knew about them in case it kicked some ideas loose. It didn't, of course, and I wound up with a night of fitful sleep, waking with shreds of cobwebby dreams sticking to my thoughts.

"Dan Calhoun," I said to the mirror as I combed out my overly curly hair, post-shower, focusing on their names only. "Rene Kinney. Kurt Wasson."

"Mrr!"

My cat was now sitting in the middle of the still-wet bathtub, staring down at the drain for no reason I could fathom.

"What's the matter?" I asked. "Wait, let me guess. You're looking for that eensy-weensy spider, the one that tried so hard to climb the waterspout yet met such a sad end. Just so you know, waterspouts are outside things, not inside."

"Mrr!"

"Sorry to burst your bubble, but it's true. Look it up. Better yet, get Julia to look it up for you, which you can do soon because it's a bookmobile day, remember?"

He gave me a startled look, then jumped out of the tub.

"Dry your feet!" I called. He didn't, and I followed increasingly smaller paw prints all the way downstairs until they disappeared three feet in front of the cat carrier.

When I told Julia about it an hour later, once we were well underway to the morning's first bookmobile stop, she laughed hysterically. Wiping tears from her eyes, she eventually managed to say, "Tell me true. What would you have done if he'd stopped and wiped his feet on the bath mat?"

"Thanked him very much and given him a treat."

She laughed again. "I can just see you doing that."

I tipped my head, indicating the road in front of us. "Speaking of seeing, do you see that?"

Julia squinted through the windshield. "Ah, another sign that summer is nearly upon us, a car on the side of the road with its hood up. Wait, are you going to play Good Samaritan again?"

She said that because I'd taken my foot off the gas pedal and started braking. On this long straight back road, out in the eastern part of Tonedagana

County, there wasn't another car in sight and probably wouldn't be for half an hour, but as we slowed, I started the hazard lights. "Pretty sure that's Rene Kinney's car," I said, pulling over onto the road's grassy shoulder. Impaired though I was at car identification, I wasn't bad with colors, and Rene's silver sedan with its hood and trunk of basic beige was hard to mistake.

"Huh." Julia peered at the vehicle's back end. "Wonder what she's doing out here?"

Since I had no idea, I shrugged and said, "The cell service out here is spotty at best." I parked us and unbuckled my seat belt. "I'll be right back."

"What if it's not Rene?" Julia unbuckled her own belt. "Hang tight, Mr. Ed," she said to the cat carrier. "Your mom and I will be right back. If we're not, figure out a way to unlatch your door, run to the nearest house, and have them call nine-one-one."

"How is he going to open this?" I asked, nodding at the bookmobile door as we exited.

"Won't have to, because I'm leaving it open," Julia said, and did just that.

I shook my head—and people thought *I* was weird?—and called out, "Good morning! Do you need some help?"

Because even though I was ninety-nine percent sure this was Rene's car, maybe it wasn't. But it was a little weird that we hadn't seen anyone. You would have thought the noise of the bookmobile would have caused the driver to come around and see what was up. Of course, maybe the driver had already been picked up by someone.

Followed closely by Julia, I walked around the

street side of the car. I peered into the back seat and saw a coat I recognized. "Rene?" I asked, moving forward. "It's Minnie and Julia. From the bookmobile. We saw your car and—"

I came to a sudden and hard stop. "Julia," I said quietly, "it's okay. Go on back. I'll be a few minutes."

Julia, bless her, didn't ask any questions but simply turned around and left. I made a mental note to express my gratitude for her trust in me and sat next to the figure seated on the ground.

Rene was a tight ball. Her legs were pulled up to her body, her arms wrapped around them, her forehead on her knees. She was racked with sobs, and the keening noise she was making broke my heart.

I had no idea what to say, so I didn't say anything. Hitching myself up next to her, I put my hand out, laid it on her upper arm, and left it there.

For a long time, for forever, we sat there, her crying and me feeling as useless as I ever had in my life. Then, suddenly, Rene reached out and put her hand on top of mine, squeezing it hard. I turned so I could put my free hand on hers. A hand sandwich, with my hands as the bread, and Rene's hand as the peanut butter and jelly.

Eventually, even forever comes to an end. Rene pulled in a huge breath and slipped her hand out from between mine. "Sorry," she muttered, wiping her eyes with her fingers. "Didn't mean to . . . whatever."

"Seems like you've had more than your fair share of troubles." I kept my gaze on the road in front of us, not watching as she dried her face and finger-combed her hair.

She gave a very short laugh. "You could say so. I was headed to a friend's house, and my stupid car stopped working in the one spot of this road that doesn't have cell reception. The last straw, you know? I just lost it for a minute."

"If you want, I can call your friend," I offered.

She nodded and gave me the number. "Appreciate it," she said. "And just so you know, I didn't used to be like this. So mad and all. It's just . . . getting laid off from my payroll job at the hospital kind of tipped me over the edge for a while."

I murmured noises of understanding. "Could happen to anyone."

"Guess so." She sighed. "You know, my dad and I never really got along. He was a cranky old son of a gun. Always said not to let people run you over, that if you let people treat you like crap, crap is what you'll be. Back then, I didn't go along with that, but now?" Her voice went hard. "Now I think he was right all along."

We got to our feet, dusting our behinds as we went. "Thanks," Rene said. "For everything."

I smiled. "All in a day's work on the book-mobile."

Rene said the friend she'd been heading toward was an amateur mechanic and had a car-hauling trailer, adding that "if he can't come out right now, he'll know someone who can." I promised to give him a call as soon as we found a good cell signal and walked back, thinking.

Over the last few minutes, a couple of things had happened. First was that I'd evolved enough to now feel some empathy for Rene. But the second was that I'd heard enough to slide her up to the top of the suspect list.

It was toward the end of our noon swing back to Chilson, when we were driving into town to stop at the library and bring Hunter aboard, then drop me off at Cody's to pick up the book bike, that Julia asked the question of the day.

"Say, I drove past the boardinghouse this morning. What do you think of the new color?"

"Can we have a different question? How about, um, what's the word for 'a fear of long words'?"

"Hippopotomonstrosesquippedaliophobia," Julia said promptly. "Back to the paint color. What does Frances think?"

In a total of none of the text messages I'd sent to my aunt had I mentioned the boardinghouse. It was probably cowardly, but I just didn't feel up to that conversation at this particular moment in my life. I'd also taken to dodging Celeste. If she'd asked me the same question, I'd have to tell her because I was horrible at lying, her feelings would be hurt, I'd feel horrible for hurting her feelings, and the whole thing would spiral downward from there, creating a family rift that could last generations.

At least that was the scenario that was keeping me from texting photos to Aunt Frances. Celeste wasn't big on the whole technology thing, so I was pretty sure she wasn't in contact with my aunt and Otto. My new moral conundrum was whether to let them know ahead of time about the new color or to let nature take its course.

"Um," I said.

Julia laughed. "Never mind. That it took half an hour for you to get to 'um' tells me a lot."

"I'm okay with the color," I said. "Honest. There was some adjustment time, sure, but I got there in the end."

"How much time did it take?" Julia asked, clearly amused.

"Does it matter? It does not. Anyone who asks, I'll tell them it's a nice, happy color, and Celeste did a great job picking it."

"Of course, since she owns the place, she could paint it royal blue if she wanted. Or fluorescent yellow. Or a bright turquoise. Or black. You know," she mused, "I've seen some black houses that look fantastic. And just think of all the heat it would soak in come winter when the sun comes out."

"All five days of it?" I asked, because I'd heard that was the total amount of sun we typically got in December and January. Though it might not be exactly correct, it certainly felt true. "Besides, Celeste isn't here in the winter, remember?"

Julia ignored my comment. "I'm sure she's pleased you came around to liking the color." When I didn't say anything, I felt her give me a look. "Minnie Hamilton, you haven't told her. Shame on you. She's probably on pins and needles waiting to hear."

"I've been . . . busy."

"Oh, snarf. That's no excuse."

I squirmed. "I feel funny going over there and talking about it without Aunt Frances seeing it first."

Julia snorted. She and my aunt had been friends for decades. "For someone so smart, you can be pretty dumb sometimes. Your aunt is a big girl. It's just paint, for crying out loud."

She was right. I knew she was. But if so, why did I feel so conflicted about the whole thing?

I was still wondering about that as I waved good-bye to the bookmobile, its two humans, and its one cat, and kept wondering as I walked downtown to pick up a to-go sandwich from Shomin's.

Since I had no response and couldn't come up with any theories that didn't make me feel like a petulant two-year-old, I switched to thinking about my suspects. Dan Calhoun, Kurt Wasson, and Rene Kinney. The murder motive for Rene and Kurt would be revenge, the end result of the "Someone had to pay for this" attitude. Rene had reason to hate Carolyn, but I didn't know of one for Kurt or for Dan. Dan's motive was that Whippy's death might let him get his hands on the candy store property.

But there were problems with that. Even with Whippy dead, there was no guarantee that Colleen would sell the store to Dan. And why, if Dan had been working with Bianca for years to buy the property, would he suddenly up and kill Whippy for it?

"Not sure that makes sense," I said to myself. Of course, sensibility wasn't a shining hallmark of murder, so I should probably stop using that as a criterion. What I should do was find out what I could about Dan. Find out where he lived and what he drove. Check if he had a scooter. Learn his pattern of movements. See if I could get him to volunteer an alibi.

If he owned a house, figuring out where he lived would be easy enough through the county's parcel information website. And all it would take to find out what he drove would be a walk down the alley that ran behind the downtown stores.

Since there was every reason to do that right then and there, I took a right turn at the next street, went down the half block, and eased into the narrow alley. As I walked, I realized that most people never saw this piece of Chilson. Alleys weren't something you typically walked down unless you had a reason, and what reason would most people have?

To my left were the back entrances of downtown stores, under my feet was crumbling asphalt, and to my right were the backs of an odd assortment of buildings. Concrete block storage buildings. A barber shop I hadn't known was there. A long carport full of motorhomes and boats.

It was a vastly different world than I'd been in a hundred feet ago. Utilitarian, definitely a space the beautification people hadn't yet taken up as a cause, and not creepy, exactly, but . . . maybe a little.

I shook off the feeling that someone was watching and crossed into the next block, the block of interest.

Dan's place was on the corner, so if his store had left enough room for parking at the back, I should see his vehicle right away. And there it was. A big black pickup. I walked behind it on tiptoes, looking over the tailgate.

"Minnie. What are you doing?"

I jumped. The man himself was standing in his store's back door. "Hi, Dan," I said, smiling. "How are you doing? I was just wondering about your truck. Rafe is thinking about getting one like this."

Dan came down the steps and put his hand on

the hood. "Haven't had any problems with it. You know, I've been wanting to talk to you. What's with you and that Carolyn Mathews? You seem to be getting all cozy with her."

"Cozy?" This was unexpected. And odd. "She's a new library board member."

"That woman is a menace. A nice girl like you shouldn't have anything to do with her. You know what they say about reputations. Once they're gone, they're gone forever."

I took a breath, and another one, as I tried to decide what to say next. If I spoke up for my own self and for any adult who'd been called a "nice girl" by someone who barely knew her, I'd be doing something to combat the eons of oppression. If I kept quiet about that and sent the conversation in a different direction, I could learn something pertinent to the murder. My internal war raged and the concern of the immediate won. For now.

"Menace?" I asked. "What do you mean? If there are problems with Carolyn, the library board should know."

Dan scoffed. "They all know. Maybe that Trent doesn't, but the rest of them do. That woman killed my wife and everyone knows it."

"Killed?" My eyes went wide. "You mean, murdered?"

"Might as well have." Dan's face was a hard mask. "Carolyn Mathews was my wife's doctor. If she'd caught the cancer earlier, my wife would still be alive. What do you call that if not murder?"

I murmured vague agreement, but I doubt he heard me.

"Now look at her," he said. "Soon after my wife

passed, Mathews left her practice to take up that administrator job. If that's not a sign of a guilty conscience, I don't know what is. It's wrong that she's walking around, not a care in the world, when my wife is—"

Abruptly, he stopped talking. He squinted at the sky for a moment, then shoved his hands in his pockets and gave me a hard glare. "That woman is a menace. She has to go."

I watched as he went back inside.

And moved him past Rene up to the very top of the suspect list.

Chapter 18

Without hesitation, I abandoned my lunch plans for Shomin's and, instead, made my way over to Cookie Tom's. He had some hearty muffins that could serve as lunch. Better yet, maybe it was close enough to summer that he'd have some of those way yummy croissant sandwiches. Sure, one was about twenty thousand calories, but I'd need lots of energy for the afternoon.

The bells on the door jingled happily as I came inside, into the full sensory experience that was the bakery. Scents of warm sugary dough, sounds of happy people sitting at the tiny tables, the wood floor under my feet, the glorious sight of fresh baked goods in the long glass case, and the future taste of it all in my salivating mouth.

"If it isn't our friendly neighborhood bookmobile librarian," Tom said, hurrying in from the back. "Run out of cookies, did you? Back for more?"

"I was hoping for a lunch thing. You have anything savory-like for me?"

Tom held up one finger in the classic "Hang on just one second" gesture, and whisked himself into the back. I used my time alone wisely by inspecting the contents of the glass case and deciding that I'd have to have a cream cheese Danish next time I stopped in to make sure they were as good as I remembered.

Just when I'd chosen the fourth next thing I'd have, Tom returned, holding a small white bag and smiling. "Here you go. The last steak with rutabaga pastie of the day, all warmed up and ready to eat."

"Sounds fantastic." I pulled my wallet out of my coat pocket. "And now I have a nonfood question. You're friends with Dan Calhoun, right?"

Tom tapped at the register and nodded for me to run my debit card through the reader. "Have been, but things have been . . . different the past couple of years."

"After his wife died, you mean?"

"It started when she got sick." Tom handed me the receipt. "My wife and I did what we could, but he pulled away from everyone and everything. Focused totally on her."

Understandable. I could see myself doing the same thing. However, it probably wasn't the best way to deal with traumatic issues.

Tom looked across the street. "After she died, we all expected he'd come back to life, if you know what I mean. But he hasn't. He's stayed inside himself. He's said no to coming over for dinner so many times, I've stopped asking."

It was horribly sad. I murmured something to that effect, and Tom nodded.

"Sure is. At least he has the store, I suppose. It's the only thing he cares about now."

I thanked him for my lunch and walked slowly up to the library, thinking about what I'd learned, and vowing to hug Rafe tight the next time I saw him. My pace quickened. The sooner I got back to the library, the sooner I'd be able to see him, because it was time for the next adventure of the book bike, and this time we were both involved.

It was a small group of children, but what they lacked in numbers, they more than made up in volume.

"Hi, Ms. Minnie!"

"Are you the bookmobile lady?"

"When are you and Mr. Niswander getting married? Can we come?"

"I thought the bookmobile cat was going to be here. Is he in there?" A medium-size hand reached out to lift the box's lid.

I wanted to stop the kid from doing so—not only was the lid locked, but it wasn't good policy to let anyone other than library staff handle the equipment—but I was too winded to say anything. To do anything other than hang over the handlebars, sucking in as much air as I could into my lungs.

"Back back back, youngsters. Down down down." Rafe plowed his way through the group. "Minnie, you okay? Kids, give the book bike lady some room to breathe. Everyone will get a turn."

"Thanks," I said. Or tried to say. It came out more a whisper than a word because of that lack-of-air thing. I knew I wasn't in the best shape of my life, but I wasn't a complete couch potato. I'd figured riding the book bike from the library to the middle school wouldn't tax me too much. After all, the road from there to here was basically flat, and the school was only a couple of miles away. Easy.

What I'd failed to take into account was the rise in elevation from the roadway to the school's entrance. In a car, you'd hardly realize there was a hill at all. On a book-laden bike with one gear, however, it became a small mountain, one that sucked away your breath and your will to do anything other than abandon the bike forever.

"Sorry I missed your entrance," Rafe said. "Had to take a phone call. Union issues."

I nodded, using as little energy as possible. "It's okay." This time my voice sounded almost like my voice and not like the wheezing of an elderly woman who'd spent her adult life smoking cigarettes and drinking whiskey. "Glad the kids seem excited."

"The trick is to keep it under control." He grinned and I reached out to squeeze his arm. The big hug would have to wait until we were alone.

One more lung-filling breath, and I had the energy to dismount and face my audience. "Hi. I'm Ms. Minnie Hamilton, the bookmobile lady, and this afternoon I'm the book bike lady. I've brought lots of books you can have for your very own."

I'd asked the Friends of the Library about letting me take books from their sale shelves for this trip. It had taken some painful groveling, but in the end I'd managed to extract a nice selection.

"Is Eddie in there?"

The question came from the front, from a girl

with long blond hair who was now pointing at the big yellow box. "Eddie is a bookmobile cat," I said firmly. "Not a book bike cat."

"Oh," she said, and drifted to the back of the group.

I exchanged glances with Rafe. This wasn't how I'd hoped the trip would begin. "Okay," I said cheerfully as I unlocked the box. "Who's first? Tell me what you like to read, and I'll find something for you."

A slim boy with what even I could tell was an expensive haircut spoke up. "I haven't read the latest Theodore Boone book. You know, by John Grisham. Do you have that?"

I blinked. "No, I don't." What I mostly had were books at least ten years old.

"Oh. Well, you can go back and get me one, right? I'll wait."

"Sorry," I said. "I can't. But why don't you try this?" I reached into the box and handed him a copy of *The Haymeadow* by Gary Paulsen. "Read the first couple of chapters, and let me know if you like it or not."

The boy stared at the book. Up at me. Back at the book. Rafe cleared his throat. The kid sighed and took it from me. "Thanks," he muttered, and slunk away.

"I like graphic novels," said the next kid in line. "Which ones do you have?"

Absolutely none.

"Where are the Harry Potter books?"

"I like Rick Riordan."

"Maggie Stiefvater's books are the only thing I read."

The sinking feeling that had started with the first request became a plummet. The second official voyage of the book bike was going to be another epic fail. How was I going to tell Graydon? Worse, how was I going to tell Trent?

"It wasn't that bad," Rafe said.

My eyebrows went up. "Okay. You're right. It wasn't that bad. It was way worse."

Four of us were sitting at the preferred table in Hoppe's Brewing. Preferred for Rafe anyway, since it was the only table that had the same distance to the dart board, pool table, bar, and restrooms. I was surprised that he cared about table location so much and was just as surprised that he'd bothered to measure, but since he cared so much, I went along. I probably had preferences he considered equally wacky that he went along with, although I couldn't come up with any.

"It was fine," Rafe said. "You didn't hear them talk afterward."

"What did they say?" his dad asked. Rick was doing that half-smile thing that Rafe had inherited through either nature or nurture, and for the thousandth time, I got a glimpse of what Rafe would look like in twenty-five years.

Lois, his mom, laughed. "Bet they said how cool it was that Ms. Minnie, the bookmobile lady, rode the book bike. How great it was they were the first school it had visited ever, and that they couldn't wait until the fall when it came back again."

Rafe bumped knuckles with his mom. "Knew I got my smarts from you."

"They said all that?" I asked.

The love of my life patted me on the head, something I didn't tolerate from anyone else. "And more. Like I told you, it went fine. You did good."

Though I wasn't so sure he was telling the whole truth and nothing but the truth, I nodded. "Okay. Thanks. Still, I'm not sure one trip to the school is enough to make the program a success."

"Not unless you have school year-round," Lois said, then laughed at the expression on her son's face. "Do you see that look of panic?"

His dad nodded. "Deer in the headlights, for sure."

"Thought he might faint dead away," I said. "Not sure I've ever seen him look so scared."

Rafe took a long swig from his pint glass, then put it down, saying, "Not going to happen. Not in my lifetime." He grinned. "Well, maybe. But as long as it doesn't happen before I retire, I'm good."

"So your opinion is based on pure selfishness?"

"You bet," he said.

His mom rolled her eyes, his dad shook his head, and I laughed. The four of us were having a pre–Memorial Day dinner. The upcoming weekend marked the unofficial opening of the summer season, and the surge of summer visitors would soon make restaurant-going less attractive to us locals.

We'd still go out to eat, of course, because "less attractive" meant we might have to actually wait for a table instead of being able to walk in the door of any restaurant in town and sit right down. We got accustomed to doing that since we could from October through May, and having to stand in line, or having to remember to make a reservation, created a seasonal mental barrier that wasn't always easy to overcome.

It was life Up North, and I looked around at our fellow restaurant patrons. Rafe and his dad were lifelong Tonedagana County residents, and his mom wasn't far behind, having moved north with her parents as a small child. Between the four of us, we knew ninety percent of the other diners, and the remaining ten percent looked familiar. Summer people, probably, who'd been coming north for decades.

Half of the servers at Hoppe's were former students of Rafe's. The other half had been lured north by the promise of blue water, sun, and big tips, and I hoped they'd all found decent housing. Hiring seasonal staff was hard for everyone, even Hoppe's, the most popular brewery and eatery in town. A big piece of the employment puzzle was finding a place to live and—

My slightly depressing thoughts were interrupted by a bump from Rafe's elbow. "Yo. Min. What are you having?"

I turned my attention to the waiter standing table-side. "Sorry," I said, looking up. "I was just—" I stopped, because I'd suddenly noticed who'd come in the door.

"No worries," the waiter said. "Did you hear the special?"

"Um." With an effort, I yanked my gaze away from the woman at the front desk. I gave the waiter my order and returned my focus up front.

Yes, it was Rene Kinney. Even in the brewpub's dim light, her height and uneven haircut were unmistakable. But she didn't seem to be picking up a to-go order, and she wasn't being escorted to a table. So what was she doing here?

The host handed a paper to Rene, who nodded and left.

Hmm.

"Be right back," I said, and made my way up front. "Hi," I said to the host, a solid twenty-something with shortish dark hair. "Was that Rene?"

A shrug. "Sorry, she didn't say her name."

"Pretty sure it was her," I said. "She's a friend of mine, but I haven't seen her in a while." Sort of. "Does she come here often?"

"Didn't look familiar." Another shrug. "She wasn't picking up a menu, though. She took a job application."

I murmured my thanks and drifted back to the table.

If Rene was applying for other jobs, maybe that meant she was accepting what had happened to her, was dealing with it in an adult fashion, and was moving on with her life.

Then again, maybe she was now able to move on because she'd killed Whippy, the first person who'd fired her, and had come close to seriously hurting Carolyn, the second person who'd fired her.

A frightening possibility occurred to me, and I stopped stock-still in the middle of the room.

Or . . . maybe Rene was finally able to move on because she'd come up with a way not just to hurt Carolyn but to kill her.

Holding hands, Rafe and I walked home along the waterfront. I kept a sharp eye out for scooters, and it worked well as a preventative measure, because I didn't see hide nor hair of a single one.

"Something wrong with your neck?" Rafe asked.

I stopped swiveling my head around. "No. Just . . . you know."

"That's what I like most about you," he said. "Precise and definitive answers every time there's a question."

"Might as well start as we mean to go on, right?" I smiled.

"Speaking of goings-on." He nodded in the direction of the marina. By now we'd come close enough to hear scraps of conversations floating about, and could match words to people. "Sounds like your campaign to indoctrinate the Moncadas into marina life is working out."

I was hopeful, because from what we were hearing, Louisa was taking the recommendation I'd thrust upon her to heart. Corey was on one side of her, Isabella was on the other, and they were progressing from dock to dock, Louisa calling out to boat owners as they went.

"Ahoy! Bobby! Come meet your new neighbors. Yeah, I don't care if you're watching a baseball game. These kids need to know who to avoid. Once you hear how they can cook, you'll be after them to run the Friday-night cookout."

Bobby immediately popped his head out of his boat's cabin. So did the owners of the adjacent boat. "You mean you're real cooks, not hacks like us?" Bobby asked. "Why didn't you say so? Come on up, we have things to discuss."

And just like that, the Moncadas were in.

Smiling, Rafe and I swung our hands back and

forth. "Don't forget I'm getting up early tomorrow," I said.

"This is your trip to Cadillac, right?"

"Yup. I'm meeting Lillie for an early lunch, so I'll have plenty of time to drive down, but there's construction and traffic, and there's always a chance of me getting lost."

"You sure you're okay going alone?" he asked, squeezing my hand tight. "My mom might go. Or how about Tabitha Inwood? Is she back in town?"

My friend Tabitha was married to Detective Hal Inwood. She was cheery and pleasant, and her white curls always seemed to be quivering with internal laughter. I hadn't seen her in some time because she'd been taking care of her sister. The older sister, who, late last winter, had taken a bad snowboarding spill and hurt her wrist so badly that she'd needed surgery.

"Not yet," I said. "I got a text the other day. Her sister felt so much better, she said she'd pay for a week in Hawaii, so they're flying out tomorrow. But I'm fine. We'll be in a public restaurant; it'll be perfectly safe."

Rafe extracted promises that I'd text when I got there, when I left, and when I got back home. I was happy to agree, because that meant I'd be able to extract the same type of commitment from him in the future.

After Rafe was ensconced in front of the television watching the hockey playoffs, I pulled a library book out of my backpack—*A Morbid Taste for Bones* by Ellis Peters—and headed upstairs, where after some searching, I found Eddie sitting inside the bathtub.

"Some would say you look like a sphinx," I said. "And I almost see the resemblance. But I think the resemblance is more like a meatloaf."

Eddie continued to stare at the nothing that was in front of him.

I leaned against the doorframe. "Did I tell you we've cut down the suspect list? Since I'm not counting Toby, we have three. Rene, Kurt, and Dan."

Still nothing from the feline peanut gallery.

"I know I should wait until I find out more about Leah's birth mother, but after learning that Rene had been fired by both Whippy and Carolyn, I figured she had to be the top suspect. But now that I know Dan wanted Whippy's property and that he has this huge grievance against Carolyn . . ." I sighed. "Sure seems like solid motives to me."

"Mrr!"

"What's that?" I asked. "You agree with my reasoning? Good to hear. I appreciate your input. I really do. You're the best cat ever, and—"

Eddie jumped out of the tub, landed on the bath mat, and tried to run. For a few strides, he looked like a cartoon cat running and going nowhere. Finally he got some traction. The bath mat hit the side of the tub, and he bolted out of the bathroom, down the hallway, and down the stairs, where I heard a shout from Rafe that meant a spilled beverage of some sort.

Mom had always said my tendency to exaggerate would get me in trouble one day. I'm just not sure she realized that it would be cat trouble.

The drive from Chilson to Cadillac, the vast majority of which was southbound on US 131, was uneventful. Keeping an eye out for deer, raccoons, turkeys, and anything else that might run across the road took part of my attention, and the rest of it was filled with thinking about what I was going to say to Lillie Siler, or Lillie Davis as she'd been for decades.

Half an hour later, I didn't feel any closer to a persuasive speech than I had before I started, so I gave up, trusting that my brain would rise to the occasion—or that fate would step in and intervene.

I thought about listening to an audiobook. Thought about listening to one of the many podcasts waiting for me on my phone. Then I decided I could do that on the two-hour ride home and turned on the radio. After finding a station playing songs I both recognized and could sing along to, I happily sat back and warbled along with Billy Joel, No Doubt, Maroon 5, Nickelback, and Juice Newton.

Exit 180 directed me straight toward downtown and Lake Cadillac, with Lake Mitchell beyond. These lakes were much smaller and way more shallow than Janay Lake, which I was told made them excellent for fishing, and they warmed up faster in the spring. Janay Lake hadn't yet reached sixty degrees; out in front of me on this Friday before Memorial Day, I counted at least three people on Jet Skis tossing up rooster tails of water.

After 26 was the name of the restaurant Lillie had texted to me. "An old train station," she'd added. I found it between a set of active railroad tracks and a gorgeous pavilion filled with farmers and their wares.

I parked, got out, stretched, and entered through the tall double wooden doors. The tin ceiling reached high above, and the brick walls were broken up by massive windows with light streaming in, a view of Lake Cadillac beyond. A small sign posted by the door caught my attention, and I read that the restaurant was a nonprofit corporation whose mission was to employ adults with developmental disabilities. The name came from the age when adults aged out of the school system.

After a pause to absorb the sheer rightness of it all, I looked around for Lillie. She'd said she had short and very blond hair and would be watching out for me. What she hadn't said was that she'd be waving madly and calling my name out across the nearly empty space. "Minnie! Over here!"

"Hi," I said, weaving through the tables and chairs. Lillie had taken a back corner seat, and it was a long room. "Thanks for meeting me. Hope you weren't waiting long." I sat down and surreptitiously peered at her for signs of resemblance to Leah. Didn't see any, but then Leah's resemblance to her paternal grandmother was so strong, maybe there wasn't room for another family likeness.

"Just long enough to order coffee. How about you?" Lillie looked up and caught the attention of the tall dark-haired young man who was coming our way. "Joel, can you please get my friend here some coffee? Thanks so much, kiddo. You're the best."

Lillie looked back at me. "Anyway, I'll do anything I can to help Will's family. Although I'm not sure what that could be. I haven't seen him in years. Not since our twentieth high school reunion."

My new friend bustled over with a mugful of

the life-giving liquid. "Thanks, Joel," I said. "This looks great."

He beamed. "You're welcome," he said. "I'll get more whenever you want."

Lillie smiled after him. "He's a great kid. Anyway," she said, picking up her mug. "Let's wait to order until we get our business done, if that's all right. Now. How can I help you?"

This was the tricky part. A smarter person would have taken the time on the drive down to think through this conversation. Then again, it wasn't good to rehearse too much. No point in being all scripted and stilted.

"The police are focused on Toby Guinn," I said. "They think he was in the store, stealing whatever wasn't nailed down, when Whippy came in. They think Toby panicked and killed him."

Lillie looked at me over the top of her white mug. "And you don't?"

"No. And a lot of people agree with me. Yes, Toby broke into a number of places, but he's never hurt anyone. There's a first time for everything, sure, but . . . it just doesn't seem to fit."

She nodded. "And now?"

"Now I'm checking out other people who might have killed him." And there it was, the burst of inspiration I'd been hoping for. Ta-dah! "Here's how I'm hoping you can help," I said quietly. "I'm wondering if there's anything from Whippy's past that could have any impact on his murder. A high school rivalry. A fight over a girl. A competition that got out of hand. Anything you can think of, anything at all."

But she was shaking her head. "Will was one of those guys everyone liked. I just don't see how it could be something like that."

"Could he . . ." I swallowed and said it straight. "Could he have gotten a girl pregnant?"

Lillie stared at me, then burst out laughing. "You think it was . . . ? Minnie, I was such a Goody Two-shoes back then, you wouldn't believe it. Did what I was told from sunup to sundown. Didn't talk back, didn't question anyone or anything." She gave me a smiling look. "I got better, of course, but it took years."

"So, no on that?" I asked, laughing along with her and thinking that the two of us had a lot in common.

"A hard no. But . . ." She suddenly got a faraway look in her eyes. "But I heard there was this girl. Will and I broke up right after graduation. I went downstate to work in a hardware store my great-aunt and great-uncle ran, and I was going to college in the fall. I didn't plan to come back, and never really did. Will wasn't ever going to leave Chilson—he was always going to run the candy store—so there was no reason for us to keep on going."

"He was seeing someone that summer?" I inched closer.

"My sister called to tell me about it. This was long before cell phones, so she couldn't take pictures and text them, but she said Will and this girl were hot and heavy during the Fourth of July fireworks."

"A local?"

"No, it had to be a summer girl. It wasn't anyone from school."

"Do you know her name?"

She pursed her lips. "It was such a long time ago, Minnie, I'm not sure." She hummed a few bars of what sounded like "Happy Birthday," then snapped her fingers. "Carrie. Caitlyn. Cara. Something like that." Her eyes went wide. "I remember! Her name was Carolyn."

Chapter 19

My mouth gaped wide. "Carolyn Mathews?"

Lillie squinted at me. "Out of the depths of my memory, I manage to dredge up the name of someone I've never met, and you want a last name, too?"

I laughed. "Sorry. I thought maybe there was a chance the sudden question would jog a few brain cells loose."

"Always a chance," she said, nodding. "Just not a very good one. But how on earth could an out-of-wedlock child have any bearing on a murder umpteen years later? Back a few decades, maybe it made a difference to lots of folks, but now?" She shook her head. "Not sure you're on the right track, Minnie."

It wasn't anything I was sure about, either. Then again, maybe, just maybe, some of the puzzle pieces were starting to fall into place.

The drive home didn't take nearly as long,

thanks to the happy circumstance of the Department of Transportation shutting down construction projects early on the Friday of a holiday weekend, and I zipped home so fast I barely had time to finish the audio version of *Anxious People* by Fredrik Backman that I wanted to return to the library early. Yesterday, my phone app told me there was one person waiting, and I hated knowing I was the one keeping someone from a book they wanted.

I pulled into the garage just as the book was winding up, and I sat there listening all the way to The End. "Nice," I said, giving the absent author a nod, and got out of the car.

Since our garage had, in its long-ago past, housed a horse and carriage—and maybe cows for all we knew—it was detached from the main house. I punched the button to close the garage door and shut the side people door behind me.

I was halfway up the steps that led to the back deck when I heard a horrendous howling noise. There was only one creature on earth that could make a racket like that. I looked and saw my cat, his nose against the windowpane, mouth open, eyes shut.

"Mrrr!!!"

For a fraction of a second, coward that I was, I seriously considered flight. Eddie was in a mood, and in a mood like that, it was possible, even likely, that he'd spilled his water dish, tipped something over, broken something, gotten sick on something, or all of the above. I was tired after the drive and really didn't want to deal with whatever it was that he'd done.

"Mrr," he said. And winked.

I smiled, of course. "Did you do that on purpose?" I asked as I unlocked and opened the door. "So I wouldn't punish you for whatever it is you did inside?"

My cat jumped down from the windowsill and started winding himself around my ankles. "A snuggle, is that what you're after?"

I off-loaded my backpack and picked him up. "Ready?" I gave him a big smacking kiss on the top of his head and hugged him not-quite-tight. "Too much? Nope, I hear a purr. I must be doing something at least a little okay."

His purrs were so comforting that I kept holding on. "So, today I met Lillie, who used to date Whippy in high school. She said she's not the birth mother, and since she has no reason to lie, I don't see any reason not to believe her about that and about Whippy seeing a summer girl named Carolyn."

Eddie rotated and bumped my upper arm with his head.

"Sorry," I said, although I wasn't sure what I'd done wrong. With Eddie, it could have been basically anything. "What I'm thinking about is how to find out if Carolyn Mathews is the Carolyn of long ago. I know that she's from downstate and that she met her husband at a conference there. I never thought to ask if she'd spent any time up here as a kid."

Eddie's purrs rumbled deep into my bones. It was all very nice, but he was getting heavy. I sat on a kitchen stool and put him on my lap.

"So the question of the day is how do I find out for sure if Carolyn Mathews is Leah's birth mother? I mean, what am I going to do, just up and ask her?"

My fuzzy friend swiveled his head around and bumped my cheek with his nose.

"You are so weird," I said, wiping the dampness away. "But seriously. How am I going to find out?" If Leah had looked like Carolyn, that would have helped a lot.

I sat there, with Eddie getting hair all over my pants and shirt, and tried to come up with other ways of determining the biological relationship between Leah and Carolyn. Even one way would be good.

But there wasn't. Not even one.

After Rafe got home, I discussed the problem with him.

"Let me see if I have this right," he said. "You think there's a strong possibility that Carolyn Mathews is Leah's birth mother."

I nodded.

"And you think that fact might tie into Whippy's murder due to the fact that Whippy was Leah's birth father."

I nodded again.

Rafe rubbed his chin. By this time of day, it was getting a bit bristly with whiskers, and I could hear that *scritch scritch* noise that summoned two feelings in me: mild annoyance and extreme fondness. How I could hold two completely opposite opinions simultaneously and not explode from sheer hypocrisy, I wasn't sure, but it happened on a regular basis. Though I wondered if the same kind of thing ever happened to anyone else, I wasn't sure I was brave enough to ask. Because if I was the only one, what did that mean?

"If I were Ash," he said, "I'd see two big problems with that. One, why would anyone kill Whippy and threaten Carolyn over something that happened so long ago? Two, if Carolyn has been keeping this secret for years, what makes you think she's going to tell you?"

"No idea. But I have to try."

He gave me that slightly crooked smile that turned my heart all mushy. "If anyone can do it, you can."

"Oh, great." I crossed my arms. "Now you've raised the bar up high. Increased expectations far beyond the land of contented mediocrity. Nice. What's going to happen to my self-esteem, my confidence, my sense of self, if I fail?"

Hugging me, he said, "You'll figure out another way."

I snuggled into the front of his shirt, taking in his warmth, his strength. He was right. I would. But doing so would take time, and I wasn't sure there was much. I'd pried a few text messages about the investigation out of Ash the last few days, and it sure sounded like they were getting closer to charging Toby with Whippy's murder. And once that was done, the wheels of justice would gather a grinding speed that would do nothing but gather momentum.

"What's the matter?" Rafe asked. "You're shivering."

"Just a chill." I gave him a hard hug. "I need a minute to go think. Are you okay starting dinner by yourself?"

He was, and I went into the backyard, Eddie at my heels. I'd hoped for some feline conversation, but my cat trotted straight for the back corner, deep into our mass of hosta plants, and disappeared from sight.

"You're no help," I called, and the only response I got was a slight quiver in the leaves of the most distant plant.

Without Eddie's help, I ended up talking out loud to myself, but quietly, so no one in a neighboring house or at the marina could hear. Not only would they think I was a freak, but I was about to say confidential things. Still, talking out loud helped me to sort things out in my head.

"Leah needs to be told," I said. There was no question about that. But how much of it did she want to know? My suspicions and hunches? Or did she want to wait until I could say for sure, one way or another?

I took out my phone and started texting.

Minnie: *Turns out that while looking for Whippy's killer, I might have found your birth mother.*

Leah (after a long pause): *Might?*

Minnie: *Not sure yet. Could learn soon. How much do you want to know?*

Leah: *Not sure yet* [half smile emoji]. *Let me know if/when you know something for sure.*

Minnie: *Okay. Will do.*

"So, how do I do this without being a jerk?" I murmured, wandering over to the stakes we'd hammered into the ground. I mimed walking up the few steps to the gazebo's floor and sat in the folding chair I'd put in place the other night. "Is there a way?"

After thinking it through forty-two times, I decided there wasn't; I was going to have to initiate a conversation with Carolyn under false pretenses.

"Hope she forgives me." I sighed, then pulled out my phone and started texting.

The next morning, the Saturday of Memorial weekend, was not the chamber of commerce weather we'd all hoped to have. Instead of summerlike temperatures, endless blue skies, and a light breeze, we had low gray clouds and a breeze chilly enough to make me zip up my light jacket and pull on the thin gloves that were always in all my coat pockets.

"Life in the Up North," I commented to Carolyn as I peered up at the sky. No rain for now, and with any luck, that would last through the weekend.

She gestured at the long expanse of sandy beach, devoid of any human presence other than ours. "On the positive side, this means our conversation will be completely private."

Last night, I'd texted Carolyn that I had a personal question to ask her, one of some urgency, and could she meet me sometime soon for a short meeting? She'd said yes and suggested an early morning walk at a nearby Lake Michigan park. Now, she said, "I often come here on weekend mornings, so no worries that you're inconveniencing me."

We walked for a bit, and the sights and sounds of the big lake soothed me. Waves rolled in from an unseen Wisconsin and crashed onto the beach, seagulls squawked overhead, the sand squeaked underneath our shoes.

"Here's the thing," I finally said. "The question I have isn't personal for me. It's about you."

"Oh?"

Very consciously, I didn't look at her. If I did, I'd see whatever expression was on her face, and I wasn't sure I could keep going if I saw her current surprise, and next her . . . what? Shock? Anger?

I pulled in a deep, calming breath, took out my cell phone, and opened it to Leah's baby photo. "This is a picture of Leah Wasson."

"Leah . . . Wasson?"

I suddenly realized I didn't know Leah's maiden name. "That's her married name. Although now that she's divorced, I imagine she'll be changing it back." I heard myself starting to babble, shook my head to get it out, and plunged onward.

"Leah was born in late April, almost exactly forty years ago. She was adopted by a local couple. Whippy Henika was her birth father. This photo was found at his murder scene, and I think it's directly related to his murder."

Carolyn didn't say anything, and I still didn't dare look at her.

"I don't like interfering in someone's private business," I said, "but the police need to have all the pertinent facts; otherwise, they might arrest the wrong person for Whippy's murder."

Waves from the lake continued to roll in, seagulls continued to squawk, and the sand keeping on doing its squeaking thing.

Still nothing from Carolyn.

"Yesterday, I talked to Whippy's high school girlfriend. Right after graduation, she broke up with Whippy and moved downstate. She's not Leah's birth mother. But she remembered something. That summer, right after high school, Whippy dated a summer girl named Carolyn."

Waves. Seagulls. Sand. Nothing else.

"So," I said, sounding strained even to my own ears, "here's the question I really don't want to ask."

More waves. More seagulls. More sand.

"Carolyn?" I asked gently. "I'm so sorry, but this could be critical to finding Whippy's killer. Are you Leah's birth mother?"

I heard a soft sigh and wasn't quite sure if it was a trick of the wind and waves or if it was from Carolyn.

Finally, the answer came.

"Yes."

Chapter 20

A dark line of clouds came rushing across the lake. Carolyn and I hurried back to the parking lot and clambered into her vehicle just as the rain started hurling itself down.

"That was close," I said, or that was what I tried to say, because it came out mostly as a wheeze, thanks to our near run.

Carolyn didn't respond. She turned the engine on and set the interior thermostat to a comfortable seventy degrees. Then she sat back and stared through the windshield. She put her hands on the leather steering wheel, ten and two, tapping her fingers.

I spent the next eternity vowing to keep quiet, knowing that anything I said at this point would be the wrong thing. I needed to wait for her to talk, I knew that, but there had to be a limit, right? I'd just settled on the outside limit of an hour when Carolyn put her hands in her lap.

"Yes, Leah is my biological daughter. Will and I . . . well, it was a long time ago. I won't make the excuse that we were young, because we were old enough to know better. But I was young and ambitious and driven. Medical school was my only goal. Nothing was going to get in my way, so I hid the pregnancy from everyone. Including my parents."

My breath caught. "How . . ." But then I had the sense to go back to being a bump on a log. My interruptions wouldn't help anything.

Carolyn went on as if she hadn't heard me, and maybe she hadn't. "It was August when I realized I was pregnant. I started college in September, but convinced my parents I'd exhausted myself getting those straight A's and needed the next semester off. I came back north, and Will found a place for me to stay."

She slid me a glance and her mouth quirked up. "You might ask your aunt about that. Tell her I said to tell you the soap-in-the-bathtub story."

I silently nodded.

"Anyway, your aunt and Will helped me through my pregnancy. I gave birth in late April, a very nice couple adopted her, and I went back to my life." Her words sounded matter of fact, but there was a tight timbre to Carolyn's voice I hadn't heard before, even after she'd been attacked.

She sighed. "Fast-forward roughly ten years. When the relationship with my future husband, a Chilson native, turned serious, I had some trepidations, knowing that I'd be in Chilson at some point. That I'd see Will. That I might see the daughter I'd never even held."

A sudden squall moved across the water, tossing the waves even higher. Rain hurled itself against the windshield. Carolyn and I both flinched, and she turned the thermostat up two degrees.

"The first time I came up to meet the Mathews clan, I made an excuse to go downtown. I managed to get Will alone in his store, and we had a long talk. He was married by then, with two small children. He told me that the couple we'd given our daughter to had named her Leah and that she was doing fine. It was a quiet, confidential adoption." Finally, she turned toward me, her face set in deep lines. "And I want to keep it that way."

"I understand," I said. "But you are almost certainly in danger."

"The ache in my shoulder is a constant reminder to be careful." She rubbed at it ruefully. "No one in my husband's family can know about Leah. They're . . . they're good people, but they have very little tolerance for mistakes of this caliber. I would be ostracized. My children would suffer. And my husband might lose the upcoming election. Judges are supposed to be above reproach, and if word got out to the voters that the judge's wife was a teen mom who abandoned her baby the second it was born?"

Her voice cracked and she coughed it away. "Please, Minnie. Please keep this quiet. What good would come of telling anyone? Who would benefit?"

To me, the answer was obvious: She would. So would Leah. But even more important was making sure Whippy's killer was put behind bars. "The police need to know," I said. "This information is critical."

After a long moment, Carolyn nodded. "Yes." Her voice sounded resigned. "I can see that you're right. I'll call after the holiday."

"What about Leah?" I asked. "She knows Whippy is her birth father."

"Yes. Well. I need to think about this."

And that was the way we left things. I slid out of her vehicle and into my car, not succeeding in my attempt to dodge between the raindrops. I hurried home to pick up Eddie for the short Saturday bookmobile run but didn't have time to change out of my wet clothes.

Hunter, kind and thoughtful man that he was, pushed open the bookmobile door as I approached, cat carrier in both hands.

"Nice raincoat," he said, nodding at the ancient vinyl tablecloth I'd used to cover the carrier. Somehow I'd ended up with the red-and-white-checked family relic, which I was pretty sure my mom had inherited from her mother. It had seen many a family picnic, and Rafe and I used it often for excursions.

"Eddie doesn't like wet," I said, whipping off the tablecloth like a stage trick. I wasn't pulling it out from underneath dishes, but the reveal was a cat with his face pressed up against the wire door, whiskers poking through.

Hunter laughed. "And some people think cats don't have personalities. If that expression doesn't say, 'This weather has got to stop,' I don't know what does."

"You should see him in January."

Hunter picked up the carrier. "Who's driving?"

I gestured at his damp pant legs. "I'm assuming you did the precheck? As a reward, you get to pick."

He grinned, and soon we were on the road with Hunter behind the wheel, me with my toes tapping on Eddie's carrier. Just outside of town, a battered silver car with a beige hood came toward us, heading into Chilson. Even though it was doubtful Rene would see it through the rain, I waved.

"Can't believe she's still driving that hunk of junk," Hunter said.

I blinked at him. "You've known Rene for a while?"

"For years. In high school, I worked at Fat Boys. She was shift manager."

Interesting. How did I not know that fun fact? "She's a little prickly," I said, testing the waters.

"A little?" Hunter laughed. "You must see her on her good days. She's more bark than bite, though. She'll flare up at the drop of hat, and she rubs some people the wrong way—that's why she has trouble sometimes—but she calms down fast, and she works harder than anyone I've ever known. Not too proud to do any job, no matter what it is. We got along fine."

I listened to what was both a concise personality summary and a character testimonial, and came away with two thoughts about Rene Kinney.

That Rene, in spite of all the tough breaks she'd had, was making her way through the world.

And I could cross her off the suspect list. Anyone who could adapt like that wasn't a killer.

It was late in the afternoon when Eddie and I got home. The rain had stopped, the clouds were blowing away, and it just might turn into a fine evening, if you didn't mind temperatures ten degrees below what you really wanted them to be.

When we got inside the house, I set the carrier on the kitchen floor and unlatched its door. Eddie bolted out like he'd been stuck in there for days, not half an hour. I watched him run from kitchen to dining room to living room and back again, then he sat by my feet and looked up at me as if he deserved a treat for his efforts.

"Just this once," I said, reaching for the canister. "And don't tell your dad, okay? I'm not sure he's up for casual treat dispensing." A total and complete lie. Rafe was a softer touch than I was. "Besides, too many treats might give you tooth decay and—"

The *bong* of the doorbell interrupted me. "Expecting someone?" I asked.

Eddie, of course, didn't say, but he did follow me to the front door. "Isabella, Corey. Hi, how are you? Don't tell me the houseboat has a leak. Or that it's sinking."

"Do you have a minute?" Isabella asked. "Corey just got off work, and I have to be at the restaurant in half an hour, but we really want to talk to you."

"Sure." I pushed the door wide open. "Come on into the kitchen. I was about to brew a pot of half caf if you want some."

They did, and while the coffee dribbled down, Corey and Isabella kept exchanging glances that communicated much between them but told me nothing at all.

"Okay," I said, pushing full mugs, cream, and sugar across the kitchen island. "You two have something to ask, but you don't know how to, so whatever it is, it's awkward. Is it about the houseboat?"

They shook their heads.

"Good. Is it about your jobs? Hang on. Don't tell me you've had offers from some place in Petoskey or Traverse City and you need to break the lease on the houseboat."

More head shaking.

"Is it the marina? The marina management? Chris made one crass joke too many?"

"No, nothing like that," Corey said.

"Okay," I said again and took a sip of coffee. "I can go on like this all day, my imagination is deep and wide, but Isabella doesn't have that kind of time."

"It's the candy store," Isabella blurted out in a rush.

That was unexpected. "What about it?"

"Do you know what's going to happen? Is the family going to sell it? Or close it down?"

I studied the bright young faces. "As far as I know, no decision has been made. They're considering options, but it's going to be hard to run it with Whippy gone. He did most of the day-to-day work himself, and his wife isn't interested in that."

The two exchanged another glance, and she gave him a nod. "This is going to sound bad," Corey said, "but when we heard he was killed, we started wondering about the business."

Isabella leaned in. "We would love to help keep it going. I don't go into work until late at the restaurant, and Corey gets done early. The timing would work out great."

"We don't have the money to buy it, or anything," Corey said. "But . . . we love that place and we hate to see it like this, sitting empty."

"It looks lonely," Isabella said, which sounded like something I'd think to myself but not have the courage to say out loud to someone who wasn't much more than a stranger.

Corey touched his wife's arm and looked at me. "You know everyone in town and what's going on. Do you think there's any chance of this happening?

If we can run Henika's, we could stay here year-round."

"Not on the houseboat," I said absently. "The marina closes in late October."

"We'd find something," Isabella said. "But . . . what do you think? Should we stop dreaming about this?"

My decision had already been made. "I'll talk to Colleen, that's Whippy's wife." They started smiling, and I held up a hand. "No promises, of course. It hasn't been that long since Whippy was killed. She might not be ready for a decision. But I'll pitch the idea in the next few days and will let you know."

They thanked me way too many times and were still thanking me when they were walking out, across the front porch, and down the front steps.

I shut the door on a distant "Thanks, Minnie!" and looked at Eddie. "Sounds like an excellent idea, other than the sheer volume of work involved, but they're young and full of energy, and I'm sure they'd do a great job." Though Dan Calhoun wouldn't be happy, of course. "What do you think?" I asked my cat.

"Mrr," he managed to say through a wide yawn. He was now on the back of the couch putting a big dent in the cushion.

"Exactly. And even though I'd wondered a little bit about those two because of the scooter, I'd already crossed them off the suspect list, not that they were ever really on it, and now they're double-crossed." I frowned. "That didn't come out right, but you know what I mean, right?"

"Mrr."

"Cool. Rene is also off the list, so we're left with two."

Kurt Wasson, who had learned from Leah that Whippy was her birth father. Could he have found out about Carolyn? Maybe. I wasn't sure how, but maybe.

And there was Dan Calhoun, who wanted Whippy's store and who blamed Carolyn for his wife's death. I'd considered asking her about that this morning but had left it alone. The emotional turmoil had already been too high.

"What's next?" I asked.

There was, naturally, no answer from my cat. It was up to me to figure out what to do.

Chapter 21

My newest piece of information, that in the past Rene had worked at Fat Boys, gave a whole new twist to that part of the investigation. Sure, I'd already eliminated her as a suspect, but there was no reason not to make sure, and there was every reason to double- and triple-check to see if I could establish an alibi.

And because sometimes that's the way these things work, maybe doing all that would jog something out of my brain. Or at least that was my hope, because right that second, I didn't have any ideas on how to determine the guilt or non-guilt of Kurt Wasson or Dan Calhoun.

"No ideas at all," I said to Eddie, who was now sitting in the middle of the kitchen floor, meatloaf-style, looking at me with unblinking yellow eyes. "No good ones. Not even any bad ones."

Eddie continued to stare at me.

"When you look like that, it feels like you have all the answers to every question ever asked but also that you don't feel like sharing, so we're out of luck with that cold fusion thing."

More of the yellow stare.

I stared back, but my eyeballs began drying up, and I was forced to blink or lose my sight forever. "Fine," I muttered. "You win. But I'm not giving you a medal. Being a cat, you started out with a huge advantage. Not that I'm calling you a cheater, but still."

Eddie, with the contest won and me put in my place as a lowly human, closed his eyes and went to sleep.

"You could do that somewhere else, you know," I said, because he was still in the middle of the kitchen floor. But he was a cat, and cats sleep wherever and whenever they choose. I sent Rafe a text that I was headed out on a few errands downtown and would be back soon. Rafe himself was at a buddy's house helping rip shingles off the roof and wouldn't have his phone on, but at least he'd know where I was.

"Well, sort of," I said to myself as I walked up to Fat Boys. I'd decided to start there, then stop at the other downtown restaurants to ask about Rene. If she'd been working for Fat Boys with Hunter years ago, there was a good chance she'd worked at other restaurants, too. Finding staff was a huge problem for everyone, so maybe someone had called her in to fill a shift the night Whippy was killed.

That was my idea, at least, when I walked into Fat Boys. The shift manager looked at me blankly, though, when I mentioned Rene's name.

"Never heard of her," he said, shaking his head.

"You don't work every night, do you?" Maybe there was another shift manger I could contact and—

"This last month I have." He grinned. "Love that overtime pay."

I thanked him and moved on to the Round Table, where they also disavowed any knowledge of Rene. Same at Shomin's Deli and Angelique's, the high-end restaurant with a wine list twice as long as the menu. I knocked on the back door of Three Seasons and poked my head inside. It was a Saturday on a holiday weekend, and dinner preparations were in full swing.

"Minnie!" Harvey, the forever sous-chef, waved a knife at me. "You can come on in, but Her Highness isn't here."

I laughed. Harvey was the most devoted employee Kristen had ever had, and also the most irreverent. The mix made for an entertaining—and mentally healthy—work environment. "I know. I'm headed over there in a few minutes." It was going to be another try at introducing the twins to Eddie, this time on their turf.

Harvey swept the carrot he'd cut to smithereens to one side and started slicing up another. "What can I do for you?"

"I'm trying to track someone down. Has Rene Kinney ever worked here?"

"Not yet."

"Yet?" I echoed. "You mean she will be?"

"If she's still interested when we get a little busier, sure. Misty and I talked to her one day a few weeks ago. Everyone knows what Rene's like, but I think she'll fit in fine here. We're not busy enough yet. Soon though." He pushed aside the completed carrot parts and reached for a whole one.

"Do you happen to remember what day you interviewed her?"

"Not a chance," he said promptly. "Why? Is it important?"

I bit back my impatience. "Maybe. Could you try to remember?"

"Oh, geez." He shut his eyes, making me fear for his fingers, as he was still cutting, then he opened them. "Beginning of May. Had to be, because we didn't do any local interviews in April. Sorry, but I have no idea about the exact date."

I made one last try. "Did you put the interview time in your phone?"

Harvey brightened. "You know, I think I did." He put down the big scary knife, pulled his phone out of his pocket, tapped a few keys, and slid it over to me. "There you go."

On the day Whippy was killed, Harvey's calendar included an appointment titled "Interview Rene K," but it was an all-day appointment, which couldn't have been accurate. "Do you remember what time you talked to her?"

"She came in around eleven in the morning, but she ended up staying until we closed." He looked up sheepishly. "We had her helping with the new barbecue. It's out back, and none of us have used one like that. Rene has, and she was really helpful."

I thanked Harvey, and, just like that, Rene had a solid alibi. Done and dusted, as they said on the BBC, and I was back to two suspects: Dan and Kurt.

But which one? I'd need a law enforcement badge to get any direct information out of either one of them. So now what did I do? Get information indirectly, I suppose. But how?

I glanced at my phone to check the time. And something clicked.

Timing. That's what it was all about.

I needed to get Eddie over to Kristen's, so I went home, started the hunt, and found him in the small downstairs bathroom. "What are you doing in here? Never mind, I can see what you're doing. Sitting in the middle of the floor doing nothing. Come on. We have a stop to make before going over to meet the twins."

He heaved a small kitty sigh as I picked him up.

"I know they're loud," I said, carrying him through to the kitchen. "And they're smelly and a lot of work. But they get bigger. Big enough to someday give you treats, remember? Ah, that got your ears twitching, didn't it?"

I didn't know if Rafe would remember that I was going over to Kristen's, so I sent him a quick text, then sent him another, telling him I was making a stop at Lake Street Gifts.

"Because," I told Eddie as I buckled his carrier into my car's passenger seat, "if I want him to tell me where he is, I should do the same thing. Only fair, right?"

Eddie yawned and rotated himself around one and a half times before settling onto the pink blanket in the back corner.

"Glad you agree with me." I started the car and drove downtown. What I'd managed to forget was that it was a holiday weekend. And though the rain had stopped, the weather was still not ideal for outdoor pursuits. I'd learned that the downtown folks called this Retail Weather and I saw why. The streets were filled with cars and the sidewalks were packed with people.

"Timing," I muttered, reminding myself why I was doing this. I needed the answer to one more question. Just one more and I might know who had sent the letters, who had killed Whippy, and who had attacked Carolyn. It had to be the same person, nothing else made sense, and it had to be either Kurt or Dan.

A block and a half away from downtown I slid into a just vacated parking spot. The temperature was still cool and the cloud cover thick; Eddie would be fine for the few minutes I'd be gone. "Back soon, pal, okay?"

His mouth opened to say something, but I shut the door and hurried to Lake Street Gifts.

In addition to the fortyish proprietor, half a dozen people were milling about inside the store, exclaiming over the Petoskey stone jewelry, the moccasins, greeting cards, coffee mugs, water bottles, clever T-shirts and sweatshirts, and the framed photos of historic Chilson.

But none of that interested me, not today. What I wanted to see was the clock on the wall behind the cash register.

I zigged and zagged my way around people and product, and finally arrived at the counter. In front of me, a tall man was having his gifts bagged, and I leaned around him, standing on my tiptoes. He left, and the clock stared at me.

"Minnie, right?" The store owner smiled. "How's your plumbing project coming along?"

I gestured at the clock. "It's fifteen minutes fast." Just like I'd remembered from when I'd been in there earlier. I realized my tone had been almost accusatory, so I quickly added, "Was it slow and you just replaced the batteries? Or is it always that way?"

She laughed. "Always. For years, I managed a bar downstate. I got so used to it that now I set all my clocks that way."

"When you say the time to someone, do you use real time or your clock's time?"

"Clock time. Why?"

I murmured some sort of thanks and left her to her customers.

The clock was fifteen minutes fast. Which meant that Kurt was not in the basement of Lake Street Gifts working on fixing a burst pipe when Whippy was killed.

Did this point directly to Kurt as the killer, or was it just coincidence?

I walked back to the car and slipped inside. "What do you think?" I asked Eddie. "Evidence or coincidence? Is Kurt the killer?"

"Mrr!"

"You're right," I said, sighing. "It's time to talk to the sheriff's office."

After thinking for a moment, I decided that the conversation I needed to have with Ash should be face-to-face. I wanted to be able to gauge his reaction to this new, and potentially game-changing, information. Plus, if I was right there in front of him, it would set me up better to push him to do something. It was far easier to say no to someone over the phone than it was to say the same thing to someone sitting across the interview table from you, her eyes pleading with you to do this one small thing for her.

"What do you think?" I asked Eddie. "Are you okay with sitting in the car while I talk to Ash before we go to Kristen and Scruffy's?"

"Mrr!" he said, and I took that as him saying he was fine with the wait, because making sure a killer was caught before he did any more harm was more important than his own short-term comfort level. Or far more likely, he'd said he was absolutely fine with whatever I did so long as he got treats at the end of it.

Either way he approved, so I started the car. Then, just before I pulled out into traffic, I remembered it was a holiday weekend. I sat there and drummed my fingers on the wheel.

The other day, when Ash had stopped by the house, had he said anything about working this weekend? He'd be working the Monday morning parade, but what about today? I couldn't remember one way or another. Texting Rafe wasn't an option because he was still roofing.

A few more finger drums later, I nodded to myself and started driving. One point about living in a small town is that even if you were vehicularly challenged, like myself, recognition of people's vehicles eventually seeped into your brain. And you learned not only vehicles, but also where people parked in big parking lots, because basically everyone tended to home in on the same location day after day.

I figured it was a remnant of our distant ancestors, a harkening back to the days when our time was spent making sure we lived through to the next day, now manifesting itself in parking habits. If we survived the day we'd parked in the spot next to the third light pole, it only made sense to park there again.

The one time I'd vocalized that theory in the library's staff kitchen, the response had been eye rolls, smirks, and outright laughter, but I stood by my theory, and someday I'd find a peer-reviewed journal article that backed me up.

Now, as I drove past the sheriff's office parking lot, I noted that the undersheriff was in the building, but the sheriff was not. Detective Hal Inwood was not there; neither was Ash. Or Chelsea. None of that was very surprising, as it was a Saturday.

More finger drumming. At the stop sign, I looked at Eddie. He was curled up into a tight cat ball, and I thought I heard a light snoring.

Okay then.

I drove up the hill to Ash's house and found an empty driveway and a house that had the look of emptiness. Still, I got out of the car and pushed the front doorbell. Nothing.

"One more stop," I said to Eddie as I got back in the car. "Then we'll head over to Kristen's."

The last stop was outside of town a couple miles, at Chelsea's duplex. Her car was there, but not Ash's. I hopped up to the front door and knocked, and wasn't surprised when no one answered. Almost certainly, they were out somewhere together, having fun in spite of the marginal weather.

"Not what I'd hoped for," I said, getting back into the car. Now I had to resort to either text messages or a phone call or both, and it was entirely possible that Ash wouldn't be paying any attention to his personal phone. I knew he had a separate phone for sheriff's office work, but he reserved that number for internal use, and I didn't blame him. Well, not much anyway, because right then it would have been very handy to have.

I thought about the places Ash and Chelsea could be, about all the things they could be doing this weekend. When I ran out of mental fingers and toes, I abandoned the effort. Even if they'd stayed local, there were far too many possibilities.

"All right," I said. "What can I write that would get Ash to stop whatever he's doing and call me?" Eddie didn't give me any ideas, so I was on my own.

I opened my phone and tapped on Ash's contact info to start a text message. I'd just finished typing SO and was about to type a second S when the phone began ringing.

Leah's name and photo popped up. I abandoned the text message and put the phone to my ear. "Hi, Leah. How are you?"

"Not so good," she said. "Something . . . happened. I need to talk to someone."

My breath went still. "Are you okay? Are you hurt?"

"Hurt? Oh. No. It's just . . . I got this letter. Yesterday, I guess, but I didn't see it until today."

A letter. My mouth went dry as a desert. "What does it say?"

"Not much." She laughed. At least that's how I interpreted her stilted choking sound. "Only a few words. Six. Guess that's several, not a few."

"What does it say?" I asked again.

A deep sigh gusted into the phone. "It's silly, but

part of me thinks that if I say them out loud, it'll be true. But it's a joke, right? Some sort of sick joke?"

At this point, it was hard for me to know. "Let me guess," I said. "It's a single sheet of white paper. The words are written in thick black ink, all in capital letters, right in the middle of the page."

"How did you know that?" she whispered.

"Leah, what does it say?" And this time, the third time I asked, it was more demand than question.

"It says . . ." She paused, and the rustle of paper came through the phone. "'Now it's your turn to die.' This has to be a prank, right? What else could it be?"

Everything clicked into place, suddenly as sharp as that final whir of options at the optometrist. Kurt. It was Kurt.

"Leah, where are you? Are you somewhere safe? Around people?"

"No, I'm—" She gasped. "Oh, no. He's here. Minnie, what am I going to do?"

There were only three options: hide, fight, or flight. Fighting didn't make sense if you were a woman who hadn't been trained in hand-to-hand combat, so it was hide or run. "Get to your car," I said urgently. "If you can't, hide somewhere. I'll call nine-one-one and get there as soon as I can."

"Minnie, I—"

She screamed.

And the phone went dead.

Chapter 22

I stabbed at my phone, calling Leah back, but it went to voice mail. "Leah," I said, "call me. But I'm coming, okay? And getting help."

I tossed the phone onto the car's seat.

"Hold on," I told Eddie. I wasn't sure what, exactly, he could hold on to, but I figured some warning was better than none. Leah had said she didn't live far from the elementary school where she worked. She'd moved in late last winter, and from the bookmobile had pointed out its green shingles through the then bare tops of the maple trees. "Just a hop, skip, and a jump," she'd said, smiling. "I love that it's so close. My commute is barely five minutes."

Now I pushed down hard on my car's gas pedal. Even though I'd never driven down the road where she lived, I knew where it was, and I knew how to get there.

We roared north to the next section line road, then turned east. It was a clear run for a few miles, and no traffic to be seen. I poked at my car's steering wheel buttons, sending a telepathic thank-you to Rafe for bugging me to take the time to figure out the hands-free cell phone dialing function.

"Central dispatch," said the calm voice. "Where is your emergency?"

Not knowing the name of Leah's road was suddenly a huge problem. "At my friend's house. Leah Wasson. She's a teacher at Dooley Elementary, and she lives just north of the school. Sorry, I don't know its name, but it's an east-west road."

"Yes, ma'am," the calm voice said. "I know the road. Do you have Leah's house number?"

"No, sorry." My voice was pitched high and tight and was spiraling even higher. "I don't. All I know is it has green shingles and—"

"I have the address, ma'am."

"Okay." I blew out a breath, blessing modern technology. "Great. She called me just a minute ago. She'd just opened a threatening letter. It said it was her turn to die. Then she said, 'He's here,' screamed, and the phone went dead." I heard the horrifying sound again, and any calm created by the dispatcher magically knowing the address vanished.

"Yes, ma'am. Do you know who she was referring to?"

"She didn't say, she didn't have time, but I'm pretty sure it was her ex-husband. I'm headed there now, and—"

"Ma'am, can you tell me your name? Minnie? Oh, you're the bookmobile lady, aren't you? Minnie, do not approach the house. It could be a very volatile situation, and you should not put yourself at risk."

"Okay, I hear you." How could I not? The voice

was filling the whole inside of the car. "Do you know how long it will be before anyone can get there?"

"A call has been sent out for the first available officer"—keyboard keys clicked—"but out on the highway, a loaded semi just overturned. Any officer anywhere nearby is working on that, along with EMTs and fire trucks."

I was easily able to picture the frightening scene and hoped no one was hurt, or at least not badly. "But what about Leah?" I asked. "She's a fifth-grade teacher. Hardly anything rattles her. It would take a lot to get her to . . . to scream like that."

"Minnie, an officer will be there as soon as possible," the dispatcher said. "Tell you what. I can stay on the line. You drive by the house and describe what you see, and I'll relay that to law enforcement."

"Okay. Yeah. Okay." The words came out jittery and uneven. I shook my head, trying to shake away my fear and anxiety for Leah. Didn't work, of course. "I'll do that."

"How close are you?" the dispatcher asked, still calm and cool and collected.

Sadly, the calm didn't leak over to me. I was leaning forward in the seat, as if that would make the car go faster, clutching the steering wheel, and practically vibrating all over. "Just a couple of miles . . . no, wait. Here's Winkle Road."

"Good. Turn right, then in a quarter mile you'll see the road where your friend lives. She's on Boettcher Road. The second house."

I followed the quiet directions, part of me thinking I should be taking deep calming breaths, but the vast majority of me wanted to smash the gas pedal down to the floor and rocket to Leah's rescue.

"Okay," the dispatcher said. "You should be almost there. A green roof, right? What do you see?"

My foot came off the gas, and the car slowed as I peered at the ranch house. And its empty driveway. "I . . . don't see anything." It came out almost as a question. "But that doesn't make any sense. Leah said he was here. There should be a truck in the driveway. Unless . . ."

Unless Kurt had broken in and forced her into his truck.

I pulled to the side of the road. "I'm taking a look," I said.

"Minnie, please don't—"

"It'll be fine," I said. "I'll keep my distance. If there's no one here, there's no reason to send a deputy here, right?"

Fear bit at me hard. Because if Leah wasn't here, where was she?

I parked in the shade of a tall maple tree, gave Eddie's carrier a quick pat, and jumped out of the car.

"Minnie?" my phone said.

"Here," I panted quietly, trotting down a line of pine trees, most of me hidden from the house's front windows. "I don't see any lights on inside. The front door is closed." I kept trotting and scooted around into the backyard. "So is the slider to the back deck. The back door to the garage is shut, but it has a window."

"Minnie, don't go any closer. A deputy will be on-site in less than ten minutes."

If Kurt had Leah, would she still be alive in ten minutes?

I started toward the back door. "I'll just go up

and see. It'll be fine." At least I hoped it would. And I truly hoped that my heart was in better condition than the rest of me, because it was going a million miles an hour.

"Minnie—"

I turned my phone's volume way down and inched forward, keeping an eye on the windows, keeping an ear out for anything, trying not to think about what might be happening to Leah, hoping to hear the sound of an approaching siren.

The closer I came to the back of the garage, the harder I listened. Surely if Kurt was inside with Leah, there would be . . . noises. Of some sort. But the only thing I heard was the twittering of songbirds and the sigh of the wind.

Closer and closer to the house I crept, crushing grass with every footstep. No noises, no thuds, no nothing. I flattened myself against the wall of the garage and craned my neck around, trying to see through the back door's window.

Inside was a tool bench, a rack of wooden shelving full of boxes, and a sedan as old as mine.

I put my face closer to the glass and peered inside. On the far wall I saw a bicycle, a set of downhill skis, and a kayak, but other than that, Leah's car sat alone in the garage. Kurt hadn't fit his vehicle into the garage, and neither had anyone else.

Huh.

I watched my hand move to the doorknob and hoped Leah was one of those laid-back Up North people who hardly ever locked their doors. The brass knob turned and I pushed the door open.

Screech!

I took none of the hide, fight, or flight options

and, instead, froze in place. Well, my outside froze. My inside was ramped up and operating past peak efficiency.

But I heard nothing. And saw nothing.

"I'm fine." I whispered into the phone, assuming the poor dispatcher was still on the other end, and slid the thick electronic rectangle into my pocket. I eased inside the garage, leaving the door slightly open for a speedy exit, and soft-footed over to the door that led inside the house proper.

No lights, no noise. No nothing.

My mouth was so dry, I wasn't sure I'd ever be able to talk again. Step by quiet step, I went up the three stairs. Put my hand on the doorknob and leaned my ear against the door.

Still nothing.

Softly, softly, softly, I turned the knob and, inch by slow inch, opened the door.

More nothing. Lots and lots of nothing. The house's very air had the feel of vacancy.

I edged inside, this door also open for a potential speedy exit, and looked around.

Everything looked normal. Kitchen counter clear, chairs in place, mail stacked tidily on the kitchen table. Silently, I moved deeper into the house and still heard nothing. Saw no one in the living room, bathrooms, bedrooms, or closets, saw nothing out of the ordinary.

I pulled on my mental big girl panties, took a deep breath, and carefully opened the door to the basement. Not being completely stupid, I didn't rush downstairs but turned on the light, leaned way down, and looked into the depths. Concrete floor, concrete block walls, and a few big red and green plastic tubs. Nothing else.

Huh.

I stood, shut the basement door, and looked around the kitchen, thinking.

If Kurt had broken in, grabbed Leah, tossed her in his truck, and roared off, there'd be signs of a fight, wouldn't there? Only there was absolutely no evidence of that. No overturned furniture or broken glass anywhere. No curtains or blinds pulled awry. No untidy pile of papers or books. Not only was Leah a far better housekeeper than Rafe and I were, but she was far more organized.

I pulled my phone from my pocket. "Leah's not in her house," I said to the now-frantic dispatcher. "But her car's here. I'm going to check with the neighbors."

"Minnie—"

Phone went back into pocket and I slipped into the garage and outside. The house to the right looked empty, with longish grass and pulled-down shades. But on the other side, a fortyish woman in shorts, flip-flops, and a thick fleece sweatshirt was pulling dandelions on the far side of her yard. She looked familiar, but I couldn't quite place her. The bookmobile, the library, a parent of a middle school student— all were possible, but right now I didn't care.

I called out a hello and approached slowly, trying to remember her name and failing miserably.

"Oh, hey, Minnie," she said, smiling and pushing her hair back. "What are you doing here?"

"Looking for Leah. Do you know where she is?"

"Well, about an hour ago, she was headed over

to the school." She gestured at the large one-story building just barely visible through the trees.

"But her car's still in the garage."

"That's because she walks." The woman pointed. At the very back of Leah's backyard, there was a narrow but very visible path. "Leah's renting the house from a retired teacher, so the trail was there already. I used it myself, back when my kids were—"

"Thanks!" I called over my shoulder. "Appreciate the help!"

I ran flat out to my car and jumped in. "Did you hear that?" I asked Eddie as I buckled my seat belt. "She's at the school."

Suddenly, I understood Leah's phone call. She'd said she'd received the letter the day before but hadn't seen it until now. That made complete sense if the letter had arrived at the school, if she'd left for home before it had been distributed, and if she'd gone over today to get some work done and found the letter in her school mailbox.

I made the car do a quick turnaround and sped toward the school.

"Mrr!"

"Right." I nodded and slid my phone from my pocket. "Did you hear any of that?" I asked the dispatcher. "Leah's at the elementary school. Can you reroute whoever is on their way? Thanks!"

I shut my ears to everything the poor dispatcher was trying to say and put the phone away. Someone in law enforcement would show up soon. "All I have to do is make sure Leah is okay," I said. All I had to do was to keep Kurt away from her. "Assuming that I'm not wrong about all of this and that Kurt is the one scaring her."

"Mrr!!"

"How nice that you're so sure. Are you ever *not* convinced of your own infallibility?" I assumed his answer would be no, and no answer was what I got. But I didn't follow up on that because I was focusing on the parking lot next to the elementary school.

It was empty.

I pounded the steering wheel. I'd been so sure Kurt's white truck would be there. So sure it would sitting there solo for all the world to see, and—

"Duh," I said out loud. Any bad guy with half a grain of sense wouldn't park out front for all the world to see. No, any bad guy who hoped to get away with a crime would hide his vehicle in the back, out of sight.

I zoomed in through the school's entrance and whirled around the south side of the building. More parking lot, but no cars. I went on zooming around to the back, where the building jutted out in what must have been multiple additions over the years. One wing to the south, another to the north, with a paved courtyard between.

A courtyard that was empty.

My heart was pounding, my breaths coming fast. Had Kurt made his way inside, grabbed Leah, and already left? If he'd taken her, there was practically zero chance I'd find them in time to . . . to . . .

No.

I shook my head and kept driving. Toward the back side of the north wing, around the wing's corner, and—

And there it was. Not the white North Lake Plumbing truck I'd expected to see but a black pickup. It was the truck I'd seen the day Carolyn had been attacked, unless there was another black pickup around with that same crack in the rear window.

"Okay," I said to the dispatcher, who amazingly was still on the line. "I'm at the school now, and the truck Leah's ex-husband drives is outside the building."

"Minnie, do not—"

"Back side of the north wing," I said over whatever was going to come next. "Thanks so much."

The phone went back into my pocket, and for the second time my mouth went dry. This was suddenly real. I had a decision to make and I had to make it right then. Stay put and stay safe? Sensible people would. But what if a sensible person heard a friend give out a scream of terror? Would that person try and help her friend?

"Mrr!"

"Not helpful," I muttered, and looked at my cat. Then I looked at the parking lot, which was completely absent of any shade. At the car's thermometer, which said the outside temperature was just past the comfortable range. No way could I leave Eddie in the car.

"I have to bring you inside," I said. "But you have to promise to be good."

"Mrr."

"Okay, then." Carrier in hand, I approached the nearest door. Not long ago, it had probably been securely locked. Now most of the knob was on the ground, and what was left dangled loosely.

I started to pull out my phone to talk to my dispatcher, paused, and slid it back into my pocket. Any arriving law enforcement officer would see the same thing I did. Better now to run silent and learn what I could as quietly and as invisibly as possible. I could always retreat and then pass on the information.

At the door, I leaned down, turning my ear toward the gaping hole that had once been a doorknob.

Nothing.

I sucked in a deep breath and pulled the door open. Eddie and I slipped inside, and the first thing I did was look around for a safe place to stow the cat carrier.

We were in a small room that doubled as the employee entrance and janitor's closet. Mops, brooms, buckets on one side, employee bulletin board and stock supplies of yellow sticky notes and paper reams on the other. "Be good," I whispered, and tucked the carrier out of sight behind a huge mop bucket. "I love you."

Eddie blinked and opened his mouth in a soundless "Mrr."

I blew him a kiss and poked my head into the hallway. This, too, was silent and empty. When I'd entered the school before, I'd come in the front, so now I felt backward and upside down. Where was Leah's classroom? Fighting off the panic that was threatening to swallow me whole, I closed my eyes to reorient myself and almost instantly opened them.

Got it. She was halfway up this wing on the right side.

Ears and eyes wide open, I walked up the hallway, keeping close to the right, as out of sight as I could get in a hallway that contained nothing but empty coat hooks. Although Rafe worked in a school every day, I hadn't spent much time inside a school building since I'd been a student myself, and certainly I'd never been in a school that was almost fully vacant. I'd never quite realized how stark and open the space was. Wide halls with walls unbroken only by doors, brightly colored posters about a carnival, and those weirdly low coat hooks.

Then again, if there was nowhere for me to hide, there was nowhere for Kurt to hide.

Though the thought was horrifying, it was also comforting, and it gave me the courage to keep putting one foot in front of the other, step after silent step, all the way up the hard floor to Leah's classroom door.

Barely breathing, I flattened myself against the wall and sidled close, trying to catch a glimpse of . . . of whatever was inside. I saw the back wall of the classroom, saw the small desks. Nothing out of the ordinary.

I moved closer, my ears straining to hear anything except the sounds of my thudding heart and the air gasping in and out of me.

Closer, closer . . . and there was Leah's desk, all alone at the front of the room.

Completely alone.

The room was empty.

I looked left and right, up and down the hallway, then opened the door and slipped inside. And found no signs of a struggle, not even an overturned wastebasket.

Huh.

I hurried over to Leah's desk. Papers were piled in untidy stacks, and a red pen was laid across a half-graded paper. A laptop was flipped open, its mouse in the ready position.

There was no way someone with a house as neat

as Leah's would leave her workspace like this. She was here. Kurt was here. Only . . . where?

Okay. Clearly, it was time to retreat and wait for the police to show up. That's what any reasonable person would do. That's what a smart person would do. That's what I should do.

I turned to leave, and the toe of my shoe nudged something. I looked down, saw nothing, then crouched and peered under the desk.

Leah's phone. I'd managed to kick it farther under the desk.

Reaching long, I pulled it toward me, but even before I had it completely in hand, my head played a short video of what had happened.

Leah's classroom windows looked out on the drive that circled around the north side of the building. She'd been on the phone with me when she'd seen Kurt drive in. She'd been so scared, so agitated, that she'd dropped her phone, which had made her scream. The fall had shattered its screen, making it useless. Leah had abandoned the phone and fled from her classroom, looking for . . . what? Another phone? A place to hide?

Frantically, I riffled through her desk drawers, looking for something, anything that would give me a clue, anything that would help. I shoved a set of keys, a letter opener, and a handful of paper clips into my pockets and hurried to the door.

The hallway was still quiet.

If I'd been in a horror movie, I would have called it eerily quiet, but I wasn't going to think about that. I was going to think about finding Leah, about getting her out of the building, about getting her into my car and away safe.

Positive thoughts. Nothing negative, no siree. Not going there.

I slid up to the next classroom and tried the door. Locked. I peered in the tall narrow window and saw nothing that shouldn't be there. Moved up to the next classroom—same thing, and same thing in the other two classrooms. If Leah had managed to hide in one of them, she was safe and sound.

But if she was safe and sound, why was Kurt's truck still here? Why hadn't he given up and tootled off?

I felt my face set into grim lines. No. Kurt was here in this building, and I was going to do everything I could to help Leah. I was not going to abandon her.

The end of the hallway opened up into the main corridor. I held my breath as I peeked around the corner, looking, listening . . . and saw nothing. My exhale seemed to echo off all the hard surfaces, and I froze. Had Kurt heard that? Had he heard me?

But there was no sound, no movement.

I pulled in a long breath and tried to think. How long had it been since Leah had called? An hour? Forty-five minutes?

My brain, which had been nonfunctional for some time, yelled at me to look at my phone. *About time you started working*, I told it. I pulled out my phone and discovered that at some point in the last few minutes I'd hung up on my friend the dispatcher. I apologized silently, tapped open the calls list, and stared at it.

The recent events—my drive to Leah's house, my search inside, my rush to the school, and this tiptoe-y hunt—had all started barely twenty minutes ago.

It didn't seem possible, yet it had to be true. But if the past twenty minutes had seemed like forever to me, how long would they have felt to Leah? Did she think help was on its way, or did she think she was on her own against an ex-husband bent on murder?

Without any conscious command from my head, my feet started moving again. Leah was here, and I had to find her.

But how? Where? *Think, Minnie, think!*

So I did, making assumptions left and right.

If Kurt didn't think Leah was in the building, his truck would be gone, so Leah was here. Somewhere.

The keys in my pocket opened other rooms in the school. I had no idea which ones, but if I could find Leah, maybe we could escape to a room that we could secure until the police arrived.

Every classroom door I'd tried had been locked. Same with every storage door. The administration offices up ahead were bound to be shut up tight, but . . .

Restrooms.

Listening with every part of my body—ears, fingers, toes, even my skin felt like it was trying to hear—I moved forward. Restrooms were . . . there. On the right.

I eased open the door marked GIRLS and slid inside, then crouched down and looked for feet. Saw none. I stood and squinted through the gaps of each stall door, just in case Leah—or Kurt—was hiding by standing on a toilet's edge.

Nothing. Same thing in the other restroom.

I took a quick look at my phone. The bathroom

search had taken two minutes. There was surely another set of bathrooms at the other end of the
school. Gripping the letter opener in my fist, I went
back into the hall.

Still empty. Still silent.

I pushed away the part of my brain that was freaking out about how long it was taking law enforcement
to arrive and moved along the wall, wishing I'd had
the foresight to be born with the superpower of ultra-
hearing.

The administration offices were dark and quiet.
The door was locked and I didn't bother going in.
The second set of bathrooms was empty.

I pulled in a deep breath and kept going. The
only place left to search was the other wing, where
there were more classrooms and—

The gym.

Ten thousand thoughts simultaneously flashed
through my head, all thinking essentially the same
thing: *How could I be so stupid?*

I'd seen posters all over the place about the end-
of-school-year carnival. To be held in the gym. For a
school-wide event like that, there'd surely have been
days of preparation and a ton of materials brought
in. It made all sorts of sense for Leah to hide there,
waiting for help to arrive. Help in the form of Minnie
Hamilton, because no one else had heard her
scream.

I rushed to the metal double doors, put my ear to
the narrow gap between them, and heard . . . something.

Slowly, so slowly it was hardly movement at all, I
pushed a door open.

The last time I'd been in the gym was for Julia's

story hour. Then, the space had been empty except for us and the chairs Julia had used, sometimes as actual chairs, more often as props. Now, the room was filled with carnival booths. I could see a ring toss game, a cornhole game, a fabric panel set up for a fishing game, a wall of balloons, huge tomato cans set up into a pyramid, a wading pool with yellow rubber ducks, and off in the corner, a dunking booth.

The room also had a stalker.

Up above the balloon wall, I saw the top of Kurt's head moving slowly forward, looking left and right.

"Leah," he said in a singsong voice. "I know you're here. You have to be here because you're not anywhere else. Come on out, baby, okay? I just want to talk to you."

I snaked inside, keeping the door from making any noise as it slowly shut, and I sank down as far out of sight as I could. In my crouch, I caught sight of Kurt walking between the booths. Steadily and calmly, he was looking under each table, behind each box. Hunting. And even if I hadn't already pegged him as a killer, the huge pipe wrench he held in one hand, slapping it into his open palm with a sickly *splat*, was proof to me that talking wasn't what he had in mind.

A shiver coiled up the back of my neck as my stupid imagination pictured what that wrench could do to Leah.

No. That would not happen. I wouldn't let it.

Only . . . how?

I touched my pockets. A cell phone that was essentially useless because I didn't dare use it within Kurt's hearing, even to text. A truly useless set of keys. A letter opener. A cluster of paper clips. Not even MacGyver could have fashioned a weapon out of that assortment.

Still, a kernel of an idea started sprouting, an idea that only had to work long enough for law enforcement to arrive. But first, I had to find Leah.

So where was she? Was she skittering around ahead of Kurt, just out of his sight? I didn't think so. By now he would have seen or heard her. I thought back to the day when Julia had performed a story hour in this very same space. She'd brought her own props, except for the chairs, and—

The chairs.

Of course.

When Julia and I had arrived, the janitor had pulled the folding chairs out from underneath the left side of the small stage, out of cabinets designed to be unobtrusive and nearly invisible.

If Kurt didn't know the cabinets existed, that's where she'd be hiding.

"Lee-aahh!" he called. "Come out, come out wherever you are!"

I watched him weave his way through the booths. When he was on the far side of the room, I crab-walked forward, keeping low, keeping quiet. I rounded the booth of pyramided tomato cans and peered at the low, wide cabinet doors.

One of the doors was open the tiniest sliver.

No way could I call out to get her attention. Was she watching, or had she slid herself behind the chairs, way in the very claustrophobic back of the cabinet?

With one eye on Kurt, I watched the cabinet door. And waited.

"Leee-aahhhh, I'm starting to get mad. You don't like it when I get mad, remember? So come on out!"

The door opened oh so slowly, and I caught a glimpse of light brown hair and one wide blue eye.

I blew out a silent sigh of relief and made frantic "Stay there" motions with my hands, wishing not for the first time that a working knowledge of American Sign Language was part of every school's curriculum.

Leah nodded. The cabinet door started to shut slowly, then stopped. Her eye went even wider.

Kurt was still on the other side of the room, so—

I felt a soft bump against the small of my back. I came within a millisecond of shrieking out loud but then recognized the bump as a furry one. A familiar furry one.

Eddie.

I whipped my head around and gave him a glare that should have reduced him to an apologetic puddle but in reality didn't do a thing.

Now what was I going to do?

"Leeee-aaahhhhh!"

Kurt had come around the end of the far line of carnival booths and was headed back this way.

It was time to implement my tiny little plan.

Shooo! I mouthed, giving my cat a push. I pulled the pile of paper clips from my pocket and hurled them across the room as hard as I could.

They dropped down in a tinkling clatter, rattling into the plastic wading pool and onto the floor.

"There you are." Kurt's heavy footsteps crossed the room. "About time."

I let him go past and jumped up, pulling the

letter opener out of my pocket. I gripped it tight and ran forward.

He must have heard me, because he started to turn.

No. That couldn't happen. I flung myself forward the last few feet. "Hold it right there," I said in a low, guttural voice that, weirdly, came out in a cowboy kind of accent. I jabbed the point of the letter opener into the small of his back. "Drop that wrench. Put up your hands."

He paused. "Who are—"

"Now!"

But he didn't drop the wrench. Didn't raise his hands, either.

The abject fear that had been lying in the bottom of my stomach started to rise into the rest of me. I shoved it down and pushed the letter opener deeper into his back. "Drop it!" I shouted. "Now!"

He didn't move.

Panic flared from a small ember to an engulfing flame. I had no other plan. This was it. There was no plan B, other than rapid flight. All I could think to do was continue to prod Kurt with the letter opener.

Suddenly, two things happened, one right after the other.

Crash!!

The pyramid of tomato cans fell to the floor, rolling in every possible direction, and Eddie rolled along with them, howling every inch of the way.

Kurt and I, of course, both turned to see what was going on, and Leah jumped up from behind the wall of balloons and hurled a bean bag directly at her ex-husband's face. A direct hit.

He gave a surprised grunt and staggered back, dropping the huge wrench. He reached up to cover his face, but before he could, two more bean bags *thwacked* him square in the stomach.

"Uhh," he groaned, and dropped to his knees.

I kicked the wrench away and put the point of the letter opener into the side of his neck.

"Don't. Move," I said quietly.

And this time, that's what he did.

Chapter 23

Detective Hal Inwood looked down at me, hands on hips. His face was as blank as I'd ever seen it, which was saying something. "There's a lot of this I don't understand."

I put on a helpful smile. "Which part? I'd be happy to explain it to you."

A group of us were gathered together in Leah's classroom. Soon after what had already been dubbed the Bean Bag Beaning, two sheriff's deputies had burst into the gym. Leah at that point had been tying Kurt's wrists and ankles with lengths of ribbon she'd found near the balloons. She'd calmly handed the ribbons to a surprised deputy, walked to the nearest chair, and huddled there, shivering.

"Shock," said deputy number one.

I'd nodded, and as Kurt was handcuffed and marched out the front door, I helped Leah to her classroom and found a blanket and water. Eddie had trotted along at our heels and quickly discovered that his new favorite place to sleep and snore was Leah's blanketed lap.

As the minutes wore into the hour mark and past, more people joined us in the classroom. At almost two hours in, the group had become myself, Leah, Sheriff Kit Richardson, Detective Hal Inwood, Ash, Rafe, and Deputy Nowlin, also known as deputy number one.

Plus Eddie, of course.

By now, Leah was starting to look more like her former perky self and hardly anything like the shivering shell she'd been. She was moving her gaze back and forth between Hal and me, tennis match–style, and I was almost sure she was smiling the teeniest bit.

"Of course you can explain it," Hal said, straight-faced. "Of that I have no doubt. The possibility of hearing a Minnie Hamilton explanation is why I get up in the mornings."

It occurred to me that the man might actually have a sense of humor.

"So tell me, Ms. Hamilton. Why did you enter the building after the dispatcher clearly told you to stay outside and wait for law enforcement to arrive?"

Then again, humor was a very subjective thing. I gave him a hard look. "No one knew when any deputies would show up. What I did know was that Kurt's truck was in the parking lot and that Leah was almost certainly inside. What was I supposed to do, just sit there and wonder what he was doing to her? If he was hurting her?"

"He would have," Leah said quietly. "If he'd found me, he would have killed me."

The only noise in the room was the ticking of the wall clock, black-and-white above the whiteboard.

I glared at the detective. He glared back.

Finally, the sheriff, who was leaning against the wall, murmured something to Hal. He sighed, took his small notebook from his shirt pocket, and flipped pages.

"Ms. Wasson," he said. "Your ex-husband is stating that you incited the death of Mr. William Henika and the attack on Ms. Carolyn Mathews. Would you please respond?"

Leah laughed. "That's what he's saying? You seriously want me to respond to that?"

"Yes, ma'am," Hal said. "As best you can."

She shook her head. Gave Eddie a few pets. Shook her head again. "My best response is that my ex-husband is a control freak. After the divorce was final, he took some time to figure out how best to hurt me. He probably decided that the worst thing he could do was kill my parents, but they've moved downstate, and he had no idea where. He knew Whippy was my birth father, though, so he went that route instead. My guess is he threatened Whippy until he gave up the identity of my birth mother, then he killed him. Then he tried to kill my birth mother. And now he tried to kill me."

The matter-of-fact way she went through the horror was chilling. I rubbed my suddenly cold arms.

Detective Inwood finally stopped writing. "All of this happened roughly the time that you discovered you were adopted."

"That's right," she said. "Learning that I was adopted? It made me reevaluate everything in my life. My marriage wasn't working. It hadn't in years. Any more time spent in it would be a waste."

"Your ex-husband was punishing you," Hal said.

Leah gave Eddie another pet, sending stray cat hairs up into the air. "That's my best guess."

"Thank you, Ms. Wasson. I have just one more question. How did you learn to throw bean bags like that?"

This time her smile was broad and very real. "Softball, Detective. Years and years of pitching softball."

We found out later that Kurt had, in fact, learned the identity of Leah's birth mother from Whippy before he'd killed him. We also eventually found out that, unbeknownst to anyone at North Lakes Plumbing, he'd borrowed a white scooter from his employer's office manager, who often used it to run errands in Chilson during the summer.

Much later, at Toby's circuit court trial for the jewelry store theft, we discovered what Dan Calhoun and Toby Guinn had been talking about the day of the Trout Lily Festival. Dan was called as a witness for the prosecution and testified that he'd interviewed Toby for a retail clerk position and that Toby had asked odd questions about the jewelry store's hours, interior layout, and security measures. At the festival, Dan had told Toby he wouldn't be hiring him, in part because he'd seemed more interested in the jewelry store than in Dan's.

Sheriff Richardson pushed herself off the wall. "Thanks, Leah," she said. "We'll be contacting you."

I knew that Leah would be enduring a multitude of phone calls, interviews, and court appearances stretching months ahead, every one of which would almost certainly test her emotional strength. The sheriff knew it, the detective knew it, Ash knew it, and probably the young deputy and Rafe knew it, too. The only human who didn't was Leah, but there was no reason to burden her with that knowledge now. It could wait.

The sheriff herself took Leah home. Rafe carried a sleepy Eddie the Escape Artist back to his carrier and into the back of his truck. "Hal Inwood," he said. "You know he acts like that because he cares about you, right?"

I snorted. "That's one interpretation. Another is that he wants me to leave law enforcement business to law enforcement officers. Which do you think is more realistic?"

Rafe, who'd just shut his back door after he'd snapped a seat belt around Eddie's carrier, folded me into his arms and kissed the top of my head. "I'm glad you're safe," he said into my hair.

I snuggled into him. I was glad, too. And I was very glad that Leah was safe and that Kurt was in jail and wasn't likely to get out on bail or to see the outside of the jail—except from the inside of a transport van on his way to court or to prison—for a long, long time.

The next morning Rafe and I walked up to the Round Table for breakfast. We slid into our favorite booth and were barely in place when Sabrina, the diner's forever waitress, came over with two mugs of coffee.

"Long time no see, either one of you. Thought maybe you'd moved or something."

"Never thought that maybe we found another breakfast place?" Rafe asked.

Sabrina gestured, palms up, at the room around us. Tables and chairs circa 1960 in the middle, the walls lined with vinyl booths that had last been re-covered when high technology meant having a push-button phone. "And what, leave all this?"

She snorted and pulled a pencil out of her bun of graying hair. "Now. You could order what you nor-mally order, or you could order the new pancakes Cookie came up with. Blueberry, with a hint of malted milk, cooked to a golden brown, served with a pat of fresh butter, and drizzled with grade A am-ber maple syrup made from trees so close you can almost see them from where you're sitting."

Rafe and I blinked. Who was this person and what had she done with Sabrina? The real version would never have sounded like one of Kristen's waiters, not in a million years.

"Stop looking like that." Sabrina rolled her eyes. "Cookie bet me that I'd never trot out that little spiel he'd prepared, not in a million years. Showed him, didn't I?" She smirked, and the world shifted back into its proper place.

Our pancake orders were given, Sabrina went on to terrorize the people at the next table, and as I added creamer to my coffee, I asked Rafe about his plans for the day. "And I'm going to be here for a while after you leave, remember?"

He nodded. "But if the twins and their parents are coming over for dinner tonight, we need to have something to feed them."

Kristen and I had texted about this the previous night. "She'll bring the food, we'll supply every-thing else."

Rafe squinted at me. "Is it wrong to let The Blonde cook for us all the time?"

"Absolutely."

"Glad we agree." He grinned.

My heart went all mushy around the edges, and the final fragments of yesterday's anxiety, frustration, and fear, which had whispered around the edges of my dreams the previous night, dissolved away.

Our blueberry pancakes were as good as Sabrina had made them sound, and Rafe polished his off quickly, saying that he was headed over to a buddy's house to help pour concrete pilings for a pole barn.

He stood, leaned down for a kiss, and I watched him go, a goofy smile on my face, because I loved the man so very much. Although I was also wondering if I'd ever actually meet all of his friends, as he seemed to have a never-ending supply of them.

"Good morning." Carolyn Mathews slid into Rafe's spot.

"Thanks for meeting me. Coffee?" I caught Sabrina's attention and made a mug-drinking gesture. "If you're interested in breakfast, I highly recommend the blueberry pancakes."

"Coffee is enough. Thank you," Carolyn said to Sabrina, who'd approached and was peering at her.

Sabrina narrowed her eyes. "You look pale. You need to eat something. I'll bring you one of those egg muffins. Don't worry, it'll be a small one."

"Is there any reason for me to expend my energy arguing?" Carolyn asked.

Sabrina made a *hmph*-ing noise. "You should be grateful I'm not bringing you a full Irish breakfast," she said, and walked off, muttering.

The exchange amused me to no end. "Thought I was the only one Sabrina bullied."

Carolyn laughed. "She's been telling me what to eat for twenty-five years. Now," she said, lowering her voice. "Tell me everything."

I did, starting with Leah's faint on the bookmobile, moving on to Leah's plea for help, adding in a few details about some of the suspects, and ending with the classroom meeting. It took time to tell, and when I'd finished, the egg muffin was long gone, and we were deep into our third cup of coffee.

Carolyn's face looked calm, but her tight grip on her mug was telling a different story.

I sat. Waited. Waited some more.

Finally, she looked up. "One of the reasons I moved out of private practice was because of the death of Dan Calhoun's wife. There was nothing I could have done differently, her cancer was too deep and too aggressive, but it weighed on me. I want to provide resources that will help doctors detect cancer earlier, and effective hospital administration is one way to achieve that goal."

And that explained that.

"Thank you," I said. "I did wonder."

"And now you're wondering whether or not I told my husband about Leah. If I told our children."

Of course I was. "It's none of my business."

"Perhaps not, but you have a vested interest in the whole muddle." She gave a half smile. "Yes, I did tell him. And then we told the kids. It was . . . difficult for me," she said. "But oddly, he was very understanding. So were the kids. They all want to meet her."

"Do you want to?" I asked softly.

Carolyn looked at me, and the longing on her face was so naked that I had to look away.

"Yes," she said. "I do. As soon as possible."

That afternoon, I was sweeping the front porch and feeling pleased with myself. Earlier, once I'd left the restaurant, I'd texted Leah, then called her and talked for a long time. After that, I'd started a long round of texting, first Leah, then Carolyn, then Leah, then Carolyn, culminating in a three-party text group that had ended with an agreed-upon date and time for the two of them to meet.

"Remember why Leah was trying to keep it a secret that she knew Whippy was her birth father?" I asked Eddie.

My cat was lying on the porch railing, front feet stretched out ahead, back feet behind, tail dangling lazily and flicking occasionally from one side to the other. How he didn't fall off, I did not know, because the railing was decidedly narrower than he was.

In response to my question, Eddie opened one eye, then closed it again.

"Sure, I can refresh. Leah was concerned about her dad's health. She was worried that talking about Whippy would be a stress that could . . . well, that could have made things worse."

The eye of Eddie opened again and this time stayed open.

"Thought that might get your attention. So yesterday, after everything, Leah drove straight to her parents' house. She wanted to talk to them before they heard anything about it from anyone else."

Eddie lifted his head and gave me a long look.

"Anyway," I said, sweeping at the dust, dirt, and flowery bits that had wafted off the trees in the front yard, "it turned out her parents were relieved she finally knew the whole story."

In fact, Leah had told me that having the knowledge out in the open seemed to have lifted a weight from both her parents.

"Her mom and dad," I told Eddie, "hadn't felt free to share Whippy and Carolyn's names because the adoption had been so unusual." They'd been in a continuous state of anxiety, worrying about Leah's reaction if she ever found out, worrying about what Whippy might do, worrying about what Carolyn might do.

Eddie heaved a huge sigh and, exhausted from the effort of holding his head up for so long, dropped it to the railing, making a small thunking noise with his chin.

"And it's all set. Next week, Leah and her parents and Carolyn are having a virtual meeting."

Via text, we'd decided that plans for Leah to meet Carolyn's husband and children were on hold for now, but I thought there'd been more of a "when" than "if" mood when the question had been posed. The truth about Leah's birth parentage wasn't hurting anyone, and the overall feel to our conversation had been one of a happy family expansion.

There was one detail left: Should Colleen Henika be told about her husband's first child? That conversation, however, was none of my business. It was also a decision that didn't have to be made today.

"Some things shouldn't be rushed," I said. "Right?"

"My sentiments exactly."

I looked up and smiled. Leese Lacombe, my larger-than-life attorney friend, was waving at me from the sidewalk. After a few lean years, her private practice was starting to take off, and from the big briefcase in her hand, it looked as though she was working on the Sunday afternoon of a holiday weekend.

"Haven't seen you in forever." I leaned the broom against the house and leaned myself against the porch railing. I wanted to finish sweeping before Rafe got home and Kristen, Scruffy, and the twins arrived, but there was plenty of time. "What brings you down here?"

"Your tenants." She gestured at the houseboat, just visible through the trees. "This is the only time all three of us could sit down together."

I blinked at the idea of the tall Corey, tallish Isabella, and the tall and big Leese jammed together at the tiny houseboat table. "Um, do you want to meet here?" I nodded at the house. "We have lots of room."

Leese's laughter boomed across the front yard. "You're the best. No, we're good. Setting up outside, see?"

And sure enough, I saw Isabella and Corey sitting themselves at a picnic table.

Leese was still laughing. "I can see from your face that you want to know what we're meeting about, but you're too polite to ask."

It was nice to know someone thought I was polite. I'd have to tell my mother. "I'm that transparent?"

She smiled. "It's not a horrible thing. But this

deal isn't a secret; Colleen and Corey and Isabella have said to spread the word."

"Colleen?" My heart started thumping.

"Yep. She's handing over the store management to the Moncadas. If everything works out, they'll end up part owners."

I watched her go, pleased as punch in so many ways. That the candy store would keep on going. That Isabella and Corey were getting warped into the weave of Chilson life. That Leese was doing well. That—

"Hey, boss!"

"Hi, Minnie!"

Hunter and his wife, Abigail, were braking their bicycles to a stop in front of the house.

"Hey and hi back," I said, smiling. "Ready for tomorrow?"

Hunter nodded. "That's what we're doing, checking the route. I think it will work out great."

I did, too. It was remembering a chance comment about scooters from Mitchell Koyne that had eventually made something go *click* in my head. During the Trout Lily Festival, Mitchell had said scooters were different from cars and from bicycles, that it was hard to find a place for them to belong.

The book bike was like that, too. It was a fun thing, a cool thing, but it was too big and too heavy for daily use in Chilson, so where did it belong?

In the Memorial Day parade, for starters, leading the Friends of the Library, who carried banners with the names of Chilson's fallen. In the Fourth of July parade, pedaling along in front of the bookmobile. At the farmer's market. At all the town's festivals.

It was an obvious solution, but I'd been too stuck

on trying to find a way to fit it into our regular operations. The book bike was different, though, and that was okay. More than okay. So much more than okay that I was actually looking forward to presenting my report to the board.

"Well, hello there, stranger!"

Hunter and Abigail had pedaled off, and Cousin Celeste was now standing on the sidewalk, hands on her hips.

I was reminded of the saying about Times Square, that if you stood there long enough, you'd meet everyone. Was our porch the Chilson version of that?

"Hey, Celeste." My voice sounded weak, so I took a breath and tried again. "Um, how are things going up at the boardinghouse?"

"Peachy," she said.

I couldn't help it; I started laughing. "That's so not funny."

"Not a bit. Still, it got you going." She grinned. "You finally get over it? The change in color, I mean?"

"Sorry," I said. "I really am. It's just . . ." There wasn't anything to say that didn't make me sound like a whiny three-year-old, so I shrugged. "I'm sorry."

"No, I get it." Her voice was warm and sympathetic. "The boardinghouse was your childhood refuge. The place that never changed. Now here I come along and turn everything upside down. It was my fault for not making sure you knew about the change. I thought Frances told you, she thought I did."

"Wait." I blinked. "Aunt Frances has known all along?"

"Child." Celeste laughed. "The woman lives across

the street from me. You think I'd do that without talking to her? She helped me pick the colors before she and Otto left."

I dug deep into my personal dictionary and could only come up with one intelligent response. "Oh," I said.

Celeste, thankfully, ignored me. "Say, I've had an idea I want to talk to you about. I keep hearing about how hard it is for young people to find housing in Chilson. I'm considering changing over to year-round rentals. Won't make quite as much money doing that, but it'll be enough."

"That is," I said slowly, "a fantastic idea."

"Really? Oh, good. Now, I still don't want to spend my winters in Chilson"—she shuddered—"but if I can find someone to manage the place October through April, this might work out just dandy."

"You know what?" I said, looking over at the marina picnic table where Corey and Isabella were still talking to Leese. "I might have the perfect solution."

Celeste and I made plans to talk to the Moncadas the following week, she continued on her walk, and I turned to reach for the broom.

"Minnie, how are you doing?"

It was possible that the porch would never be fully swept. Ever. Ash and Chelsea were standing on the sidewalk, hand in hand, looking up at me.

"Doing fine," I said. "How about you two?"

Chelsea ignored my question and pressed for a more complete answer to the one she'd asked. "Ash told me about yesterday. It sounded horrible. You sure you're all right?"

"Far as I can tell." I smiled. "In the end, no one got hurt, and the bad guy went to jail. I talked to Leah this morning"—at length, more than once—"and she said she'll call the trauma counselor the sheriff recommended."

"But what about you?" Chelsea persisted.

There was one loose end I wanted to tie up. "That dispatcher. The one I talked to and then left hanging. Is it okay if I contact him? Tell him thank you?"

Ash and Chelsea glanced at each other. "How about this," Ash said. "I'll talk to Travis, see what he says. Some of the dispatchers want to detach from calls, others want to know the end of the story."

That made sense, and I said so. "If he doesn't want to talk to me, please let him know how grateful I am for his help." My next words came out in a rush. "And that I'm sorry for hanging up on him."

Ash grinned. "Will do."

They headed down to the waterfront, and I reached for the broom.

"We're back!"

I gave the broom a quick toss into the far corner of the porch and ran down the front steps to meet Aunt Frances and Otto.

"When did you get home?" I asked after a round of quick hugs. "How was the trip? You must have been out of cell phone range most of the time, seems like we hardly heard from you. I bet it was spectacular. Pictures, show me pictures!"

"Goodness, so many questions!" my aunt said, laughing.

"We got back to town around noon." Otto pulled out his phone, opened the photo app, and handed it to me. "Slept in Sault Ste. Marie last night."

"So pretty," I murmured, flicking through the pictures.

"Minnie, I need to talk to you." My aunt tugged me up to the porch and sat me down at the small table.

"Uh-huh," I said vaguely, still looking at photos of spectacular coastlines and big blue water.

"Last week," Aunt Frances said, "I decided something. I know you and Rafe came up with that scatterbrained idea of a reveal party for the wedding and reception venues, but I am going to tell you the locations here and now. There are some things that should be told privately, and this is one of them."

"Okay. Ooo, that's a gorgeous sunset!"

She gave an exasperated sigh and yanked the phone away from me. "Sit down and listen to me," she commanded.

And so I did.

I was still sitting on the porch when Rafe got home. He came up the front steps, gave Eddie—still on the railing—a pat on the head, and dropped into the chair Aunt Frances had vacated a few minutes earlier.

"My aunt is a genius," I said.

"Never doubted it." Rafe leaned back and put his legs on the railing, crossing his ankles. "Any particular reason? I take it they're home."

"This noon. She and Otto just left."

"What's the genius part?" Rafe reached over with the toe of one shoe, lightly trapping the tip of Eddie's tail.

"She said our reveal party idea was stupid and sat me down and told me where our wedding and reception are going to be."

He squinted, then shrugged. "Okay. Not sure that's very genius-y, though."

"Coming soon." I beamed. "Our wedding will be at the library in the big community room. Our reception will be right over there on the marina grounds. She's reserved a big fancy tent. Are you ready for the genius part?"

Rafe eyed me. "It has to be good. You're practically vibrating."

"Kristen is doing the catering, that's been a given from the start. But . . ." My grin stretched even wider and I started to bounce a little. "We're going to have the bookmobile as a temporary food truck. The bookmobile is coming to our wedding!"

"Huh." The love of my life nodded slowly. "That's pretty cool."

"Can't think of anything better."

As we sat there trying to think of something that might possibly be cooler, Scruffy and Kristen's SUV pulled up to the front curb.

The adults got out. Scruffy popped the rear hatch and hauled out the stroller as Kristen leaned into the car's interior and started unlatching the baby seats.

Rafe and I walked down the porch steps. "They've got the routine down, don't they?" I commented.

"Almost don't want to offer to help," Rafe said.

"We'd probably mess up the sequence, and they'd have to start all over again."

"As if," Kristen said. "Minnie, get over here." With a free elbow, she pointed at the sidewalk just in front of the stroller. "Keep it from rolling away. The brake's not working right." She made a complicated series of moves with the baby carrier and stroller. "Okay, Cooper's in. Scruffy, did you get Eloise? Okay, good, and . . . she's in. Rafe, grab those two bags out of the back. No, not those, that's the food. Scruffy, can you get those and put them in the kitchen? Rafe, those are the diaper bags, put those in—"

"Mrr!!!"

I sighed. So much for Eddie and the twins getting along. I turned to scold him, then stopped.

Because what Eddie had noticed, and the rest of us in the flurry of arrival logistics hadn't, was that an unleashed dog was galloping straight toward the twins. A huge creature whose growl was more terrifying than anything I'd ever heard.

Scruffy shouted and ran straight toward the dog. It dodged him easily and kept on running.

Rafe threw the bags he was holding, one after the other.

Kristen yelled. Shouted. Screamed.

Still the dog kept on coming.

I planted myself in front of the stroller. No way was I going to let this monstrosity hurt the twins. No way whatsoever.

A black-and-white blur caught at the edge of my vision. It was Eddie, leaping off the porch, going straight for the dog, howling at the top of his lungs as he went.

"Mrr!!! *MRR!!!*"

The dog's headlong rush slowed, then stopped.

Eddie ran at it, growling and hissing and spitting. His fur stood out all over him, and his tail was puffed out to ten times its normal size. He looked huge, a wild thing with sharp teeth and lethal claws.

"MRRRR!!!"

He lashed out with one paw, not quite reaching the dog's nose.

The dog gave a short yip and took himself off in the opposite direction, back the way he'd come.

"Well," Kristen said shakily. "What do you know?"

"Eddie is the hero of the day." Scruffy's smile was weak but visible.

"Mrr," the hero said as he trotted past us, casual as ever, his fur already down to normal. He jumped up onto the porch and settled himself back down on the railing. Nothing to see here folks, just move along.

Rafe put his arm around me and murmured a few words into my hair.

I put my head on his shoulder and smiled, because I could feel deep in my bones that what he'd said was absolutely right.

Everything was going to be just fine.

Ready to find
your next great read?

Let us help.

Visit prh.com/nextread

Penguin
Random
House